BY THE SAME AUTHOR

Night in Tunisia
The Past
The Dream of a Beast
Sunrise with Sea Monster
Shade
Mistaken
The Drowned Detective

Carnivalesque

NEIL JORDAN

BLOOMSBURY PUBLISHING
LONDON • OXFORD • NEW YORK • NEW DELHI • SYDNEY

BLOOMSBURY PUBLISHING
Bloomsbury Publishing Plc
50 Bedford Square, London, WC1B 3DP, UK

BLOOMSBURY, BLOOMSBURY PUBLISHING and the
Diana logo are trademarks of Bloomsbury Publishing Plc

First published in Great Britain 2017
This edition published 2018

A catalogue record for this book is available from the British Library

ISBN: HB: 978-1-4088-8139-2
TPB: 978-1-4088-8138-5
eBook: 978-1-4088-8136-1
PB: 978-1-4088-8135-4

2 4 6 8 10 9 7 5 3 1

Typeset by Integra Software Services Pvt. Ltd.
Printed and bound in Great Britain by CPI Group (UK) Ltd, Croydon CR0 4YY

‘Come away, O human child!’

W. B. Yeats

mother told him, she was beyond the age for little sisters, or even little brothers, now.

Anyway they were happy enough to stop, to wait by the level crossing for the mechanical arm to rise and to drive on to the waste ground where the carnival had parked itself.

And the first thing he noticed was how large it was, but at the same time how contained. He knew that spot of waste ground; he had played on it when they first moved here and could measure the extent of the field by his running feet. But the carnival that filled it now seemed endless, somehow. It had its own little backstreets, its alleyways of hanging bulbs and ghost trains and Punch and Judy stands and caravans with painted carnival folk sitting on the steps smoking and laughing with each other like his family once used to laugh, he seemed to remember. It had its bumper rides and its old-fashioned carousel and even a small circus tent where he could glimpse athletic girls in tutus twirling on ropes that seemed to vanish into the gloom above them. But there was a queue outside that so he gave it a miss. He played the dodgems with his father while his mother bought candy-floss and it was sometime after the ride on the old-fashioned carousel with his mother, his face buried in that same candy-floss, that he noticed the Hall of Mirrors. His mother couldn't take gravitational pulls and centrifugal forces and the crashing of bumper cars so the gentle up and down movement of the painted horses suited her fine. So when he tired of it his father took his place behind her, with his arms around her waist, and the boy left them both to it and hoped for the return of happier times and went wandering down the bulb-lit alleyways that had filled what was once waste ground.

And at the end of one of them he saw the Hall of Mirrors. There were looping strings of carnival lights leading towards it on either side, and a large sign written in mirrored glass reading 'Burleigh's Amazing Hall of Mirrors' and the sign reflected the lights in all sorts of magically distorted ways. There was a mirrored entrance beneath the sign and it looked lonely, somehow, with no one queuing up to get in. A Hall of Mirrors didn't seem like the most exciting prospect, after all, given the distant screams of delighted horror he could hear from the ghost train and the helter-skelter. But he was drawn towards it, like a fly towards a light bulb. Maybe it was the emptiness that drew him. Maybe it was that weird name, Burleigh. Burleigh who, he wondered, Burleigh what, and what could be so amazing about this Burleigh's Hall of Mirrors?

So he went through the mirrored entrance and sometime later, it could have been minutes, it could have been hours – his parents would later punish themselves with worrying over that fact – quite a different boy walked out.

This boy looked the same, wore the same clothes, the same jacket, frayed at the elbows, the same scuffed trainers; he had the same curl of browny-blond hair falling over his freckled forehead. He even spoke the same, with that slight girlish lisp when he said his S's, but everything inside of him was different. And perhaps it was a measure of how things had changed between his mother and his father that it took them so long to realise that everything inside of the new boy was different. But by that time the carnival had long moved on.

What happened was this. Roughly, although there was nothing rough about the happening. It was smooth and soft-edged and mysterious and had a gliding quality to it but it was an immense happening so to describe it in rough detail would be to save many pages of description. It had a strange temporal quality to it as well, meaning time was stretched and bent and turned in on itself, so to delineate the beginning and the end of the happening would be difficult, if well-nigh impossible. It would be like describing a butterfly's wings in measurements used for a milk bottle, which wouldn't make any sense at all, really. So, roughly what happened was this:

He walked through the entrance to Burleigh's Amazing Hall of Mirrors and could see a small, squat version of himself coming towards him. It frightened him at first. It looked like a small fat brother he had lost along the way there. But he had no brother, small or fat, so he knew it must have been him. It moved a fat arm to scratch its fat head when he moved his arm to scratch his own, quite normal one. Then he realised of course it was a particular quality of the mirror he was facing and began to laugh. He saw the fat one laugh in time with him. And the strange thing was – the first of many strange things on that long afternoon – that he heard a fat, booming laugh coming back towards him. He knew his own voice, his own laugh, and he was a good laugher, he had to admit, he had a loud guffaw that erupted when anyone told a joke that he found funny, which somehow managed to make the joke funnier. But the laugh that came back at him was nothing like that laugh. It was a fat and round laugh that seemed more appropriate to a policeman. And then he remembered that he had passed a laughing policeman on the journey there and he wondered was this policeman somehow laughing back at him. But no, it was the fat version of him laughing back at the real version of him and both laughs echoed around that strange interior. He stopped laughing then, placing a hand over his mouth, and saw the fat version of himself do the same. And he heard both laughs echoing as if they were running away from him, down the different mirrored halls. He turned then, following the echoing laughter, and saw a long, thin version of himself turning too. This thin version didn't seem to suit laughter at all. Again it moved when he moved, it paced forwards with his gradual footsteps into the strange interior. I am in Burleigh's Amazing

Hall of Mirrors, he thought to himself, and of course there will be many different versions of myself in the differently distorted mirrors. But this thin version of himself seemed to demand something other than laughter. It was pale and somehow sad and had a kind of a lantern jaw that when he opened his mouth seemed to reach down to the belt that held his trousers up. His mouth became an elongated circle that seemed to droop downwards, as if it was made of dripping water. And when he stretched his hands up above his head, they stretched like rubber bands and vanished into the ceiling. He followed those elongated hands with his eyes and saw that the ceiling itself was a mirror, as was the floor beneath his feet, and he saw an oddly stretched head staring back at him, with the rest of his body yawning away from it as if it wanted desperately to vanish into the mirrored floor below. There was a weeping quality to his thin self and he wanted it to go away, fast.

So he closed his eyes and walked.

When he opened them again he found himself in a mirror-maze. There were multiple versions of himself wherever he looked. He found this mildly amusing and smiled, but was careful not to laugh because he didn't want to hear that fat-policeman laugh echoing his own. He smiled, raised his hands above his head and twirled, like a ballet dancer. Now he hoped this twirling wasn't observed, by anybody, least of all anybody his own age. But all he saw was the multiple versions of himself twirling in turn so he tried a small airborne leap, and clicked his heels together before they hit the glass floor again. He saw an infinity of versions of himself twirl and click their heels and twirl and click as he tried it again. And it was then that the music began.

It was a waltz, if you can imagine a waltz being played by a rushed waterfall with the buzzing of bees to accompany the swirling melodies the water made. It soared and looped and repeated its melody though the melody always seemed fresh, as if repetition was a new kind of invention. It seemed to bear his weight as he leapt once more and found that his landing was as light as a feather, or as if a hive of invisible bees had somehow borne his weight and taken the curse of gravity from his feet. So he leapt again and again and clicked his heels like a crazed version of Michael Jackson and each leap took him higher and the frothy surging of the melody enveloped him and took him upwards, or was it sideways, he couldn't be sure since the mirror-maze seemed to be revolving with him now, he had lost all sense of where the ground was or the ceiling, there was no north or south or up or down, he was in an anti-gravitational dance and the only bearing he had was the melody like a waterfall that took him in its wake.

And then the music stopped. Not suddenly, since there was nothing sudden, where he was now. It rippled and it echoed and grew more distant with each echo until it was gone entirely, and there was just silence and it began to dawn on him what had happened. He was inside the mirror now, and there was somebody else outside that looked like him but that couldn't have been him since he was just this one's reflection, inside the mottled glass.

Yes, he realised for the first time, the glass was mottled. Those little silvery bits, those mirrored cracks were all over his hands, his shirt, his face, everything that was him. And the thing that wasn't him was there, outside the mirror, staring back, turning, at the sound of his mother's plaintive voice.

'Andy,' she was calling. 'Andy, where are you?'

And the thing that was not Andy turned and said, 'I'm here, Mum,' and his multiple reflections turned too, and he was one of them.

And the thing that was not Andy walked outside to be swept up in his mother's arms, and he was in the mirror now.

2

THE THING THAT WAS not Andy – or the Andy that was not him, for it was a him more than it was a thing, it had a definite himness to it – didn't seem that interested in Burleigh's Amazing Hall of Mirrors or in the carnival in general. When his mother asked him what he was doing in there, he said simply, 'walking', 'looking'.

'We thought we'd lost you,' she said, not realising the truth behind her words. Because she had lost him, for ever. Or for ever and a day, as they say in fairy tales, of which this could well be one.

'We searched for hours, we almost called the police.'

'I'm sorry,' he said, 'but it takes time to get your head around that mirror-maze. It goes on for ever.'

And his mother clutched his hand and walked him through the muddy ground of the carnival stalls to the small circus tent where his father was waiting.

The queue had diminished outside the canvas entrance for the one last performance. A clown stood there with a painted smiling face in the fading light with a plastic money bucket in his hand. 'Thank God,' said his father and the boy that was not Andy could tell that for a moment he had believed in God, had said a confused prayer after his son had gone missing. The boy that was not Andy had a way of knowing things like that, the private thoughts of others that he kept very much to himself.

'He got lost,' his mother said, 'in the mirror-maze. Because he—' And here she turned to him once more, 'How did you put it, Andy?'

'I said that mirror-maze goes on for ever.'

'Yes, that's what he said,' she said.

And his father smiled at him, puzzled, and relieved. The reason for his relief was obvious, since the boy that was not his son looked like his son in every possible detail. But his puzzlement came from the strange lack of colour in his returned son's speech. From the phrase 'goes on for ever'. But he was growing up, he imagined, and would be well able to look after himself soon.

He bent down to his returned son and tousled his head and asked him had he had enough of the carnival by now.

The boy that was not Andy nodded and said, 'Yes, I have.'

And again the father noted the strange colourless inflection of his speech. As if his words were water that had been fed through a filter of some kind. And the filter had drained out all of the minerals.

He said there was time for one last visit to the circus.

And the father saw a sudden flash of panic in the boy's eyes.

He remembered how he himself, as a child, had been terrified of clowns.

He saw the clown raise a battery-powered megaphone to his painted lips and appeal to the departing crowds.

'Your very last chance – to see Lydia on the high wire—'

The crackling tones of the amplified voice echoed round the darkening stalls.

But the boy didn't seem to want to see Lydia, whoever she may have been, on the high wire.

'To see Paganina play the violin with her feet—'

Nor did he want to see Paganina playing the violin with her feet.

'Enough of the carnival?' his father asked.

And the boy that was not Andy nodded. He had had his fill of carnivals and circuses, for a long, long time.

He was a reflection. And the thing that reflected him had walked out with his mother some time ago now. He could see the light was darkening outside and noticed for the first time the strip lights that were hidden in the upper corners of the mirror-maze. This new light gave his reflected face an unreal, pasty quality; like a ghost, actually. And he wondered had he actually become that, a ghost. And for the first time, he felt real terror.

He could see the looped bulbs of the carnival outside reflected in the distant corners of the mirror-maze and realised it would soon be night. There were fewer and fewer people wandering through the carnival ways now. He wanted to cry out, long and hard, but he knew now that he couldn't, that if he did, nobody would hear. He wanted to smash his fingers through the mirrored glass, but he couldn't, since his hands were themselves part of this strange mirror thing. He could punch outwards, and saw the multiple reflections of himself punching outwards too, but it was as if the thing he reflected was punching towards him and he was reflecting it, confined to the mirror, but the thing that had reflected him was gone.

He tried crying then. He squished his face up like a lemon and thought of the bitter taste of the lemon and felt a tear gather in his left eyelid. And he opened his eyes then, to see the tear fall, and he was amazed at the result.

The tear was dripping down the outside of the glass. It hung there, like a small pear-shaped piece of reflective silver, and itself reflected all of its multiple reflections. He reached out to touch it and realised he couldn't. It was on the outside of the mirror, and he had somehow put it there. He tried to work out how, and wondered was it something to do with the emotion he had felt when he closed his eyes. He began to hope then that if he could do that with a tear, he could do it with the rest of himself;

his hands, his feet, his face, even his eyes could lose those tiny silvery cracks and get outside the mirror and could become what he was when he first walked in there – the thing that reflected instead of the reflected thing.

And he saw the tear then begin a slow slide down the glass and saw something reflected in it, other than himself.

It was a girl.

She had come through the entrance and her multiple reflections followed her as she walked. She was a carnival girl, he knew that without knowing how. Something to do with her clothes: the smock she wore, the spangled tights beneath the smock, the shoes like ballet pumps, the braid that held back her brown hair, which was tied into a pony-tail behind the crown of her head.

She walked through the mirror-maze without a glance at him and he grew really terrified now.

If there was anything worse than being nothing but a reflection, he realised, it would be a reflection that couldn't be seen. By others, by anyone, in particular by this carnival girl who had a quality to her that he desperately needed to be seen by. He waved his arms as she passed right by him, but she didn't look sideways or stop. She had a large bunch of keys in her hand and vanished then, through the other end of the mirror-maze. He heard the sound of a shutter being pulled down and saw some of the reflected carnival lights vanish as the sound of the shutter hitting the floor echoed around him. She walked back in then and pulled a switch and the lights went off and the maze was plunged into darkness. The darkness was absolute and the boy wondered for a moment had she vanished with the light. But he could hear breathing then, and could feel a face close to his, and when his eyes accustomed themselves to the darkness they began to distinguish something – a soft, warm oval with dangling hair framing each side of it.

And he realised she was looking at him.

'Goodness,' she said.

It was an old-fashioned word for so young a person. She was about his age, he surmised, or maybe just a little bit older.

'Help,' he said, 'I'm stuck.'

'Kcuts mi pleh,' she said and he wondered what language she was speaking, until he realised she was repeating what he said, backwards. But he felt a strange relief, knowing that she could hear him, at least.

'In the mirror,' he said.

'Rorrim,' she said.

She vanished from his sight then and he could hear her footsteps traversing the glass floor and he heard a switch being pulled and the lights came on again.

He saw her reflections moving back towards him before he saw her herself, her pert smiling face and her brown hair with the ponytail and the smock thing she was wearing.

'What's your name?'

'Andy,' the boy said. But his name didn't come out as Andy. Because he was in a mirror now. It came out as Ydna, which he realised, with a growing sense of unease, was Andy, only backwards.

'Ydna,' the girl said. 'That's an odd name.'

And the boy tried again. He spoke carefully this time, enunciated what he knew were the vowels and syllables.

'Nyad.'

'That's even less of a name. That's a girl thing, a kind of nymph.'

And it was, the boy realised. He remembered illustrations in his Greek and Roman mythology books, of the water creatures who didn't look too unlike the girl herself. And the brown eyes that faced him were reflected endlessly in the multiple mirrors, an infinity of nymphs or naiads.

So he took a breath and bravely tried again. But he could feel the letters already rearranging themselves, between his intention and his voice, as if they had a will of their own. Or as if he had suddenly been afflicted with some form of dyslexia.

'Dany.'

'Dany. At least that sounds like a name. Nice to meet you, Dany.'

And it was useless for him to try again, to rearrange the letters back to the name his mother had given him. He would be Dany, for a while at least, if it helped the strange rearrangement of things that seemed to be happening.

'I can get you out of there,' she said, 'but you have to realise that once I do, it will be nose to the grindstone, all the way.'

And the boy repeated what she said, knowing it came out backwards, but he was beyond caring. Nose to the grindstone. He had heard of the phrase, but never bothered to think about it before.

'Shoulder to the wheel,' she said. 'The carnies need all of the help they can get. And you do look like a capable lad.'

'Dalelbapaca?'

She had that old-fashioned way of phrasing things again. And he felt vaguely stupid, repeating what she had said to him. Backwards. Like an echo. It sounded like some kind of spell, from a magician's handbook. But he was only a reflection after all, and maybe it was silly to want things to make proper sense.

'We always need a pair of strong hands,' she said.

And she reached her hands out towards the glass. To his utter amazement and relief, her hands moved through the glass as if it was rippling water and he saw her hands, with the tiny mirrored cracks all over them, reaching for his.

He grasped those hands and felt a living surge go through him, like a wave of electricity.

'You're coming in,' she said.

It was a statement, not a question. And again it had that old-fashioned thing about it.

'Ningimoc reyou,' he echoed. And it wasn't even backwards now, it was jumbled up as if the syllables had been tossed into some kind of a blender. A sound blender.

'From outside?'

This one was a question. Or it sounded like a question, to him.

'Suditoe?' he echoed again. Or kind of echoed, since the blender was doing its thing.

'Don't want to get caught there again.'

'On.' That was easy. Even she seemed to get it. No.

'You have to say yes, now.'

He tried to say yes but it came out garbled.

'Or nod your head.'

So he nodded, furiously. Yes yes yes.

And her small, strong hands pulled.

4

HER HANDS WERE SMALL and strong and indescribably ancient. They had criss-crossing lines, not so much lines as indentations that had once been circles and were trying, somehow, to be circles again. Dany spent days, in later years, thinking about those hands. How a series of concentric waves went through him when they first touched his. How before they pulled him he was one thing and afterwards, quite another. But that thinking would take place in a much different time when all of these events have become part of memory or myth or the space that is occupied between them, where one gets lost in the other. Because this is a story of losing and finding, amongst other things. How one child gets lost, and quite another one finds himself; how memory gets lost, how a whole race managed to lose itself, then found itself again in the great dreamy corridors of the mythical lost and found.

Anyway, her hands. They were a young girl's hands, his age, but stronger than any young girl he had ever met. Their strength seemed to come from old practices, like kneading dough and pulling the udders of cows and goats, or rummaging in the earth for hidden tubers, tearing away the roots of certain trees. There was something either very old, that should have died a long time ago, or something very new, that had not yet been born, about those hands. The nails were scuffed and bitten and looked like they had never known nail varnish. There was a decidedly unwashed quality to them and the lines on the palms as she reached through the glass were like maps to an unknown ocean. This he could see, despite the distortion of the glass, and the tiny mirrored cracks all over. And when he touched her hands, he felt the full force of their strength. He would find out later that it came from quite another dimension, and its immediate heft came from grasping the down-hanging circus rope and the wood of the trapeze bar. Because she was an aerial artiste, among other things.

Anyway, he was pulled by those hands and came in from the outside, or outside from the in, back through the glass and found himself standing in the mirror-maze with the girl who had just pulled him. The shutters were down and the lights were still on and the multiple reflections shimmered around them both, but to his immense relief he was the reflected one now, as was she.

'What on earth—' he began to say, and then stopped himself. What he would have said normally was 'what the hell' or something like that but the 'what on earth' just came out of him.

'I know,' she said. 'It must be strange for you.'

'I was stuck in a mirror.'

'Not stuck. You were confined. It's a different thing.'

'How did I get—' And he tried the word she had used, 'Confined?'

'The other one walked off, am I right or am I wrong?'

'You're right.'

'Well, there must be a reason. We'll find out about it later.'

'Can I go home now?'

'Oh,' she murmured and he saw a half-smile on her face. 'We'll have to see about that.'

'I kind of have to.'

'Why?'

The question came out of her beautiful, rich mouth. And he couldn't immediately think of an answer.

'My mum and my dad. They'll be missing me—'

'Are you sure about that?'

And when he thought about it, he wasn't sure. The one that wasn't him had walked towards his mother, embraced her as if he was him, and could still remember the relief on her face.

'Anyway,' she said, and took his hand again in hers, 'there'll be time enough to think about all that. All the time in the world.'

The feel of her hand again in his seemed to still all of his questions. For the moment, at least. It was a different clasp this time, a sideways one, as if she didn't need to pull him anywhere now, through any glass or reflections, as if all she needed to do was keep him calm, by her side.

And an immediate calm did come over him. It was like falling into a warm bath that he never knew he needed, pulling a familiar blanket round himself that he never knew he had missed. 'What's your name?' he asked her. It seemed odd, asking ordinary questions like that in these extraordinary circumstances, but he needed to fill the silence. And the silence in there was huge and immeasurable; it seemed to reach, like the multiple reflections, into some kind of infinity.

She told him her name was Mona. He had never met anyone called Mona before – the only Mona he knew was the one in the painting, *Mona Lisa* – and when she repeated the name she had somehow pulled from him, he felt the need to correct her.

'Dany,' she said. 'And you're called Dany.'

'Not Dany,' he said. 'I'm sorry, that came out wrong when I said it. And I was inside the mirror. My name is Andy.'

'You said Dany,' she replied, and gave his hand a comforting squeeze, 'so Dany it is.'

'Is there a rule here?'

'There are many rules here.'

'So you're called the first name that comes out of your mouth?'

'Don't worry about rules, for the moment. You said Dany, so that's who you are. Dany Dan Dandy.'

'And what happened to Andy?'

'Andy is,' she whispered, 'where Andy is. But Dany is here now, with his new friend Mona. And we have to hurry.'

'What's the hurry?'

'The hurry is,' she whispered again, 'that they're packing up.'

5

He could hear a jumble of sounds from outside as she led him back through the maze of infinite reflections. A clatter, a wallop, a litany of instruction: 'grab a hold would you', 'throw her down here'. And outside of Burleigh's Amazing Hall of Mirrors, sure enough, he saw that they were packing the whole carnival for the business of moving on.

And it was a very strange business.

Small, squat men walked between the carnival fixtures, wrapping the coils of light bulbs around their arms, their necks, their chests until they looked like bulbmen. Lithe, agile boys not many years older than himself crawled up the skeletons of the rides and unpicked them, girder by girder, tossing them like matchsticks down to a strongman below. They were tall and impossibly thin, these boys, and could twist themselves into all sorts of improbable shapes and squeeze their limbs into all sorts of inaccessible places. They wore dungarees, like the short and squat ones, but where the dungarees of the short squat ones bubbled round their ankles as if they were for a much bigger human, the dungarees of the tall thin ones barely reached below their knees, as if they were for a much smaller boy. The bits of the dungarees that went over the shoulder, which Andy searched for a name for and couldn't find – he thought of the word 'braces' but it didn't seem quite right – always seemed to pull much too tight, so the tall ones walked stooped, while the small ones walked with exaggerated steps that dragged, as they were afraid to trip up over the useless yards of denim around their ankles. Someone should get them to switch dungarees, so at least they had a chance of fitting, Dany remembered thinking, at the same time as he thought he had to at least pretend to be Dany now. But things in this carnival, like his name, didn't make absolute sense, as he would gradually discover. A bunch of clowns pulled up the guy-ropes of the circus tent and it billowed downwards, like a deflating mushroom, leaving the centre pole like a skewer in the earth, with a half-moon above it. And by the light of this half-moon a trapeze artist twirled like a spinning top, wrapping the various ropes around the pole before it was gently lowered to the ground on to the giant soft petticoat of the canvas tent.

And Andy, or Dany, as his new friend introduced him, turned out indeed to be a capable pair of hands. He dragged metal hawsers across the crushed grass, packed dodgem cars into crates that seemed impossibly small to hold them; he rolled the circus tent with numerous other and stronger hands into a long white tube that slid magically into a longer canvas bag. In fact everything, he found, every facet of the seemingly endless carnival, fitted into something smaller than itself, as if its instinct was to shrink and almost vanish.

And vanish it gradually did, in to a series of crates that were roped on to a line of waiting vehicles, old tractor trailers with exhaust pipes that pointed upwards and billowed dark smoke into the moonlit night.

The last thing to be packed was the Hall of Mirrors. The Burleigh sign first, into a deep wooden crate that was filled with wood shavings, then on top of that the fat and thin mirrors, then the multiple panels of the mirror-maze, more than a thousand of them, it seemed to him, into a separate wooden container that was stamped, in industrial lettering, with the legend 'Mirror-Maze, Handle With Care'. He felt sad for a moment, as all of the reflections vanished into the container of sawdust, for those mirrors that had nothing to reflect, but then he felt relieved that he himself wasn't being packed in with them. He was no longer a reflection, he was a carnie now, and he felt, irrationally, that he had been a carnie all of his life, that the life of Andy, with his mother and father and the thing that had started with his father sleeping downstairs and his mother weeping as she chopped the vegetables and blamed it on the onions, was part of another, imagined life that he was glad to escape from. He felt giddily released from all of those only-child duties and hoped the one who had walked home with them would do a better job than he did at being the perfect son.

And the moon was sitting in the sky over the flattened glass and the pale disc of the sun was shining, threatening to obliterate it, when Mona thanked him for his services and his capable hands and lifted the canvas flap of a lorry and told him to creep inside and get his fill of sleep.

He climbed up gratefully, for he was as tired as he had ever been, and curled himself up on a bed of straw that smelt of some kind of animal, not unpleasantly at all, and she let the flap fall and as the carnival convoy began to move he allowed the rocking of the lorry to lull him into a deep, deep sleep.

6

ANDY, WHICH SEEMS THE best name for him now, since having appropriated the shape, the sound, the smell of the reflected one he would appropriate the name too, travelled back mostly in silence with his new-found parents. The windows of the Cortina kept misting up, since the defogger wasn't working so the outside world became a kind of blur except for the small wedge of clarity that his father kept wiping clean on the front windscreen.

'Too late now,' his father muttered.

'I suppose,' his mother replied.

'What do you think?' his father asked.

'What do I think of what?' asked Andy, with an odd kind of directness.

'The Roebuck Centre. The film. Too late for all of it.'

'I suppose.' Andy echoed his mother's tone.

'But the carnival was better than any old cinema.'

'Maybe.'

'So home again home again jiggety jig.'

'Why jiggety jig?'

'Oh, you know. The market. To buy a fat pig.'

The old Andy would have smiled at the recognition of a childhood rhyme. But the new Andy just blinked as if to say, silently, whatever. With that neutral, clear-water kind of feeling. He was definitely growing up, his father thought. Get ready for it. The silences. The locked bedroom door. The teenage face lit by the iPhone screen, the thumbs clicking.

He glanced at Andy's mother. She was lost in thought, staring out at the streetlights and the strange halations they made in the fogged-up windscreen. Well, he thought. At least she isn't— And he didn't want to finish that thought, about all the things she wasn't.

They were home within a half-hour. The small house, overlooking the dark park. The railings, the razor wire around the football field and the gleam of empty Coke and beer cans on the grass. He had walked that grass with Andy many times, before it was a football field, when it was a forest of small saplings, before the mechanical diggers came to raze them. They had hoped the football field would work its magic on the neighbourhood, but the grass grew quickly overgrown and became mostly a home for late-night cider parties.

There was the glint of a sputtering fire behind the razor wire, the sound of tinny music and laughing, adolescent voices. Andy was always a good boy, his father thought, as he swung the car between the gateposts, into the garden with the overflowing privet hedge, had kept himself to himself and had let those cider parties keep their distance. And he hoped that that at least wouldn't change, what with this new thing between them both and this strange tension in the air.

What was it?

He couldn't put his finger on it, as he turned off the ignition and listened to the car whirr itself into silence.

'Shall we go in, love?' he asked her.

He used the word more in hope than in expectation. And she smiled briefly, as if grateful for the gesture.

The house was dark when they entered it. All houses are dark, of course, before the lights are turned on, but this house, this sweet little bungalow with the single stairs up to the dormer bedroom, had grown a particular kind of darkness around it that was accentuated – or thickened, in a way – by the new Andy's entrance. It hung around the walls like an invisible cloak and wasn't at all dispelled by the lights coming on.

Eileen – for that was the mother's name, and Jim was the father's – recognised this darkness with the immediacy of caught breath. And she knew it had grown, in their absence, had thickened with Andy's entrance. And she didn't want to explore why. So her breath grew softer, her slight asthmatic sough became more prominent, as if there was a small bird dying inside her.

'Tea,' she said, as if the small household chores would put everything back to right. 'I can make a Welsh rarebit with some coleslaw.'

She moved through the hallway towards the small, dim kitchen.

'Would we all like that?'

'Yes, Mother,' Andy replied. And Jim nodded, as he divested himself of his coat.

'Dear me,' she said, 'how we're growing up. It's Mammy no longer?'

'I suppose that makes me Father,' Jim said. 'Not Dad?'

And the boy repeated the word softly to himself, as if it was the first time he had heard it.

Father.

They had tried hard for a child, she remembered, as she placed the bread inside the yellow toaster, too hard maybe. And when Andy had finally arrived it had seemed like the end of one thing, and the beginning of something else. The end of early-morning thermometers, visits to the clinic on the other side of town, all of that ovarian-stimulation business, egg retrieval, test tubes, et cetera et cetera. She had always wondered how she had become surrounded by Latin terms, *in vitro*, *in utero*, et cetera et cetera, and so Jim greeted the news of her pregnancy as if it was a miracle, a miraculous delivery from an arduous clinical process, and what she had never shared with him was the fact that it actually was. A miracle. An intrusion of something else on the here and now.

The miracle had been foretold, though, somehow prophesied, by some odd, eccentric John the Baptist, who seemed to be preparing the way. A man with a shabby suit and a shapeless beret had knocked on the door one bleak afternoon, a travelling salesman, not too unlike her husband, though she hoped Jim would never have to stoop so low as to go house to house. This man was selling what she would have called geegaws, which was as good a word as any for the useless object he presented to her on her doorstep, just as the fumes of the number 30 were seeping through the privet hedge. The bus shuddered, out of sight, its engine still ticking despite the fact that it would be parked there for ten minutes at least, and she resolved one more time to write a letter to the bus company, about the waste of fuel, the pollution of diesel fumes, and most annoying, the noise; the noise of the Bombardier engine, which almost drowned out the salesman's patter, as he pulled a succession of scarves and mirrors from his sad cardboard case. Why he imagined she wanted mirrors, she had no idea – hand mirrors, small heart- and wing-shaped ones that could have hung on a bathroom wall – and she realised, with an odd sense of revulsion, that the scarves were decorated with mirrors too, tiny ones, like perfectly broken bits of mirrored glass. And she felt guilt, then, because of the strength of her feeling of revulsion, and told him softly that she had no need of them, gently, as the bus began to move down towards the seaside road.

But he was saying something now that she couldn't quite hear. The bus ground its gears as it rounded the corner, redoubled its acceleration into an enormous bellow or whine. There was disappointment in his voice, she knew that, although she couldn't hear what he was saying, and a rather furtive, pleading quality to his eyes, and she distinguished one word, above the departing bus's whine: the word 'futures'.

'Futures?' she asked. 'Of course. You don't only sell useless knick-knacks and geegaws, you tell—'

'Fortunes. Only in certain, and very specific, cases.'

'And I am, no doubt, one of those?'

'Each of us is specific, Madame. You, however, are more specific than most.'

And I would bet you say that to all the ladies, she thought. But what she said was different.

'There's a housewife in every bungalow behind me. And I'm sure you'll find one more . . . specific . . . than me.'

It was an odd word, that 'specific'. But it seemed at one with his face, which was neither pale nor dark, but had a decided foreign quality to it. 'I most seriously doubt it, Madame.'

And yet there was an English tint to his words, something that said 'pool' to her: Liverpool, Hartlepool, Blackpool. And she began thinking about the word 'pool', then, and it rippled backwards and forwards uselessly in her mind, like a pool itself, and before she knew it, and she would never quite know why, she was inviting him inside.

She led him towards a seat by the empty fireplace, since she never bothered lighting it until her husband was half an hour away from home. And the salesman placed his cardboard case upon the floor, opened it and from underneath the plethora of mirrored scarves took a perfectly round glass ball, like ones she used to find as a young girl, on a sandy or a stony beach, next to the drying frames on which fishing nets hung.

'Madame,' he said, 'is missing something.'

Indeed Madame was, she thought, as she watched his short, stubby fingers ripple over the glass ball, with a deftness and agility that surprised her. Madame was missing many things.

'But if I can be more specific, Madame is missing something specific.'

That word again.

She could sense his eyes flitting over the walls, registering the decorations hung there, and thought to herself, indeed, he is perceptive, would there be a madame in this small cul-de-sac who wasn't missing something? And when the next statement came, although she could have anticipated it, nevertheless it struck her like a hammer from an invisible hanging cloud above.

'Madame is missing, and has a longing for, a child.'

Now, anyone could have told, she remembered thinking, from the absence of childhood things in this room, that a child had been discussed, considered, imagined, if not quite longed for. 'A child,' she repeated uselessly.

'And Madame will be blessed, soon and quite unexpectedly,' Burleigh said. For it was Burleigh, into whose Hall of Mirrors her child would one day wander; Burleigh, who had been expelled from his carnie heaven for infractions too numerous to enumerate or count. Burleigh, whose shoulders were bowed with a sense of impending doom that kept him wandering; Burleigh, whose beret concealed a balding pate and a fringe of uncut hair beneath it. Burleigh, who could see far more in his orb of glass than he would ever reveal to her. For luck had finally returned to Burleigh's luckless days; he had happened, in the strange small bungalow surrounded by privet hedges, on the unexpected surrogate, the vessel that would churn the past into a future that he had feared would never arrive.

'There is a wood,' he said, 'that you knew in your childhood days. And you will see that wood again, before you are blessed with child.'

And the term 'blessed with child' somehow unnerved her. It had biblical connotation, it was old and gnarly, it was itself a tangled wood.

She stood, suddenly and spikily. She reached for her purse.

'You're a charlatan,' she said. 'And you want money, am I right?'

'Money is beside the point,' Burleigh said, although he was perilously low in funds.

'So I shall have a child, then?'

'And soon,' said Burleigh, 'in a way most unexpected.'

'I'm attending a clinic,' she said, and at that moment took the brochure from the Auberge Fertility Clinic from the mantelpiece, 'as I have no doubt you've already noticed.'

'Whether I noticed or not, Madame, is irrelevant,' Burleigh continued. 'The fact is that your efforts will be blessed with fruition, all of the chickens will come home to roost, you will hit the bull's-eye, the oranges and lemons will fall into line, you will hit the jackpot.'

'As in a slot machine?'

'Or a carnival. The great slot machine that governs your future is all gearing up to—'

'Thank you,' she said then, standing, burrowing in her purse for whatever coins she could find. This talk of carnivals and conception was suddenly distasteful to her. She shivered, and had the odd, foreboding sense that this man knew more than he was admitting to. She wanted him gone, suddenly, and wanted to pay him to be under no obligation. She found a pound coin, and placed it on his cardboard case, beside the glass ball, which enlarged it and bent it, in reflection.

'Don't insult me, Madame—' Burleigh began, although he knew her name, Eileen, and could have used it. He had seen many things about her, in his small orb of bubbled glass.

'You want more?' she asked, and tried to find incredulity in her tone. She didn't know what he wanted, but would have paid him twice as much to get rid of him now.

'I want thanks, maybe,' Burleigh said, sadly. But his hands closed around the coin. Because he could make use of it, his needs were many and his purse was almost empty, always.

'Thank you,' she said, and made sure she walked behind him towards the door. This man could steal things, things she hardly knew were there.

'The bus?' he asked, with a kind of dignified forlornness. And another great hulk was belching there, she saw, behind the privet hedge.

'It leaves every fifteen minutes,' she said, 'for town.'

'For town,' he repeated, and walked directly towards it, his gabardine coat billowing and his cardboard case swinging by his side.

He didn't once look back.

7

THE AUBERGE FERTILITY CLINIC was some forty minutes to the far north of the ever-expanding city.

She had grown exhausted by the thought of eggs and ovaries and had lately discontinued her visits there. But the odd travelling salesman with his ludicrously transparent predictions somehow renewed her interest. She was between jobs then, with too much time on her hands. So she called once more to make one more appointment and was told they could fit her in on 22 June. And on the way there she had grown once more exhausted by the thought of eggs and ovaries and *in vitro* and all of those Latinate terms and had fallen asleep on the train. She woke in a panic then, seeing clear bright sea outside where there should have been the manicured gardens of the new industrial estate. She saw the old fencing of an approaching station against the blue-green sea, neglected and bleached of all of its paint, sagging in places. Then she saw the small wooden house above the platform coming towards her, with its quaint, storybook simplicity, and her feelings of panic subsided. Because she recognised it, from her childhood. The blue and white eaves of the station roof, each with its tiny droplet of water. It must have rained, she realised, while she slept. There were pools of water along the old-fashioned platform. They would holiday here, each summer, in a time that seemed part of another century now. In fact, she realised, stepping from the train, it was part of another century. They would descend with their cases, bags and boxes to be met by a charabanc, which would transport them to the small wooden bungalow – more of a hut, really – with the corrugated-iron roof amongst the sand dunes, which probably no longer existed.

She stepped from the train now, as she had done then, full of excitement and mystery and a queasy sense of expectation in her stomach. She saw from the digital display that the next train back was due in an hour, so she decided to take a walk.

By the sandy path along the tracks at first, which ran along a slight rise above the metal-green sea. It had been trodden into hard sand by generations of feet, some of them bare, some of them sandalled, like hers. The path departed from the tracks then and she descended gradually into a lowland landscape, towards a small glistening river threading its gentle curves through unkempt fields. The sandy path gave way to wooden girders that were once railway sleepers, which led her towards a handrailed walkway beneath a bridge, which carried the tracks above her over the river. She crossed that walkway, remembering her footsteps as a child, into the flatlands between the river and the sea.

There were herons there, picking their way along the mudflats. A kingfisher darted, its blue wings close to the brown muddy waters.

She remembered every detail from her childhood holidays, but assumed the tiny, tin-roofed cabin her family had shared would have long been destroyed. By wind and rain and tidal erosion. There had been high dunes, where there was now a flat, rocky shore. She saw a copse of trees then, among the lowland fields and a ruined monastery or farmhouse, and remembered with a shiver the stories told about it. The Taw Wood, they had called it, inhabited by

Captain Mildew, a figure made out of the furred bark of trees and the strange mushroomy growths around their roots and clad in dead mildewed leaves with moulding twigs for hands and a mouth of old man's beard. Those mildewed webs that were his would entangle the careless ones; the roots dragged only downwards, towards the toadstool growths beneath. He was a shapeshifter, though, and some of the stories had him in a more forgiving light, a resplendent youth this time, lithe and muscular, naked but for a covering of green moss all over his mysterious skin. Girls would tease each other about him, daring the bravest among them to enter the Taw Wood, lie on the dead leaves and suffer the Captain's embrace. And when once a local girl fell pregnant, rather than point the finger at a local boy, the rumour grew that Captain Mildew was to blame. She stared at it now, from the mudflats, and wondered at the fact that they had called it a wood at all. It was a thick, unsightly gathering of trees, hedged round by a ruined wall. She remembered the terror she once felt, her friend Daisie May's hand curling round hers as they approached it, daring each other to enter. A boy had enticed her in there once and once only; Jimmy Banks was his name and he used her terror of the Captain to make sure she clung relentlessly to him, her arms tight around his waist while his hand played with the elastic band of her summer skirt. He drew a kiss from her by a tree with long curling shreds of bark and she could still remember the ecstasy before she broke free and ran back out through the Taw Wood, leapt the wall and only felt safe again when the wet sand of the mudflats curled between her naked toes. She went barefoot the whole summer then.

And she took her shoes off, an adult now, the young girl just a memory, and felt the sucking damp of the mud between her toes. She made it to the grassy bank by the crumbling wall and entered the dark copse of trees. And once inside there the world seemed to have fallen away; she could have been a young girl again. Nothing had changed. The curling shreds of bark were still hanging from the tree trunks. The overhanging foliage still worked its dark magic, creating an umbrella of deathly quiet while the breeze from the river soughed outside. She rubbed her shoulder blades against the bark and arced her head back and stared upwards, at the gnarled ascent of the tree trunk that grew ever more slender, like a long uncertain finger, reaching towards the foliage above. The sunlight came through it, in shimmering darts of silver. She saw a bank of moss against an old fallen log. It had an indentation in its crest, as if a hand had scooped out the hard wood hidden by the moss, or as if generations of wanderers, like her, had lain there. She sat down on it, and felt the moss give way beneath her buttocks, like a soft cushion. Then she laid her head back, and imagined her hair, dangling backwards towards the dark grass below, as if she was outside herself, hidden amongst those shaded trees, observing. Where the bee sucks there suck I. In a cowslip's bell I lie. Were there cowslips around, she wondered, hidden in the thick, lily-like grasses that must never have caught the sunlight? That was a quote she remembered from a school play, and she had played Ariel and the same Jimmy Banks had played Ferdinand and she remembered now the passion with which she had hated his Miranda. Geraldine was her name, Geraldine Dukes, a small, too-well-shaped girl with a much-envied bosom. And it was the same Geraldine, she remembered, that had dared her enter here with the same Jimmy Banks, and as she felt her body now ease into its bed of moss she remembered the childhood wonder of it all, only marred by his incessant attempts to pull at her underthings, attempts that she never quite rebuffed, since the ripple of his uncertain fingers was after all part of the thrill. She must have fallen asleep then, lulled by the gentle winds through the late-spring foliage. And the last thing that ran through her dreamy mind was the word that the strange salesman had repeated: specific. The salesman from Blackpool, Liverpool, Hartlepool, though he didn't look like he came from any of them.

When she awoke, everything had changed. It could have been minutes, it could have been an hour later. There was a hard wind ruffling the foliage above her. Her hair was dirty with moss, her head was splitting with an ache and there were goosebumps of cold along her naked arms. She felt all of the terror of childhood and gathered her shoes and ran and only stopped running when she felt the mud squishing once more between her toes.

She washed her feet in the sandy shallows of the river. She walked back, then, barely making the next train. She managed her appointment in the clinic and slept, after the treatment. She dreamed of mossy arms embracing her, the bark caressing her face while leaves above her shifted, like faery fingers. And two weeks later, the pregnancy stick turned pink.

And maybe that was what the darkness was about, she thought, as she retrieved the half-burnt bread from the yellow toaster, stuck in two more pieces and slathered the burnt ones with butter. She could never quite free the memory of her pregnancy from a niggling, subterranean feeling of guilt. The salesman, with his mirrored scarves and his absurd mirrored ball. She had done something, and wasn't quite sure what it was. She had paid him, for services rendered, for a prediction that she knew he had made from the mantelpiece brochure. But still, she had paid him, as if his nonsensical patter had some hidden value, unexpressed. That afternoon nap, in the train that led to her childhood station. She had departed from the normal progression of things in some shocking, unwarranted way. She had never told Jim, with his naive, bland hopes for a family, about that lost afternoon in the Taw Wood. And when her child was eventually born and the quite wondrous Andy arrived, she always felt undeserving of him, as if he was an unwrapped parcel, an unwarranted gift that would someday be snatched away from her.

He had grown, though, quite happily, and not at all unlike normal boys. Grimly attached to her, and vaguely tolerant of his father, with his odd obsession with the different varieties of marmalade.

'What will it be this morning, son? Thick-cut tawny? Or the lemon-zested thin Seville orange slice?'

He could be forgiven this obsession, since he worked as a sales rep for Intercontinental Preserves, travelled widely and often, plugging their wares. His absences weren't unwelcome to her. They would make quite a comfortable, shadow-wrapped pair while he was away. Andy would help her cut the privet hedges back, which always seemed about to overwhelm the gardens of their little bungalow. He would abandon his group of rough neighbourhood friends and spend every moment with her. What kind of boy is it, she sometimes wondered, that would walk the streets clutching his mother's hand, clinging to her bathing things while she swam in the river, nurturing every possible moment they had alone together? And that closeness would retreat then, back into invisibility, when his father returned.

What kind of boy, she wondered again, cutting the slices of Edam neatly on to each buttered piece of toast and placing the finished sandwich under the grill.

He was standing in the darkened hallway, not quite looking at her every time she looked at him. But every time her gaze left him, she felt his gaze return. He had always welcomed her matching glance before. Whenever their eyes had met, while her husband dozed by the fireplace or nattered on about marmalade sales, it was as if on an agreed signal; they had looked at each other just so, just then, from an instinct that only they understood, that only they shared.

Whatever that closeness was, it had vanished now. And something about his stillness told her it had vanished for ever. There was just dark and light in that hallway, as if all of the shadows had defined themselves clearly, all too clearly.

Had something happened, during those lost hours in the mirror-maze, something that could never be spoken of? She thought of carnivals and predators, of the upturned face of the smiling clown, how the smile was painted over his lips and could well have concealed the grimace of . . . the kind of man that lurked around fairgrounds, she supposed, around children's playgrounds. And she thought of other things that couldn't be spoken of: her lost hour in the Taw Wood, for instance; was it similar to her son's lost hour in someone's amazing Hall of Mirrors? What was the name on the neon sign? Burleigh, she remembered. She imagined a Hall of Mirrors then, diminishing her child into infinity. There was a question she should ask, she felt, but she couldn't find the words. And then again, she thought, and felt the tears welling in her eyes once more, every boy grows up. And she couldn't stop the tears flowing and couldn't blame the onions.

8

IT WAS DARK NIGHT by then, all across the land, with one of those gentle summer mists, created by that small difference between the heat of the day and the chill of the evening. The convoy of carnival flatbeds and trucks appeared out of this mist and vanished back into it, the headlamps scouring the suburban wastelands. Like lighthouse beams, distress flares, gigantic glow-worms.

Mona had repaired to her hammock that swung gently with the convoy's movement and every now and then bumped into the adjacent hammock, Paganina's.

'You want me to braid your hair?' Paganina asked, drowsily.

'I don't mind.'

So Paganina reached her feet across the hammock spaces and began untangling Mona's ponytail. She did it deftly, big toe, little toe, all of the tiny digits working like fingers. With her free remaining foot she massaged Mona's temples. They loved each other dearly and it was a love that expressed itself in toe braiding and foot-to-head massages.

'I've found a boy,' Mona murmured.

'Yes, I noticed. In fact, we all of us noticed.'

'In the mirror-maze.'

'Aha. So it happens still.'

'This one did.'

'That mirror-maze,' Paganina mused. 'We should have let it go with that Burleigh.'

'But we didn't. And I can't say I'm sorry.'

'It could be called snatching.'

'But it was no snatch. All that's long gone.'

'But at times, the urge is overwhelming.'

'He's so sweet. Strong and sweet. He was a reflection, you understand. Until I pulled him out.'

'And the real one?'

'Well that's the question, isn't it? The question Burleigh never answered. Which is the real one?'

'All right. The other one, then. Where did it go?'

'Where did it go? Where other ones go. Back with his parents, I suppose.'

'Poor thing.'

'Poor thing? I'm not sure. Would it be so bad? The same bed to sleep in every night. All those comforting childhood things.'

'So what's he like?'

'My boy?'

'Already yours, is he?'

'Finders keepers. And I'm not letting him go.'

'How did you find him?'

'The strangest thing. I was pulling down the shutters and I had the uncanny feeling of being looked at. I turned off the lights and there he was, behind the glass.'

'So you—'

'Yes, I helped him out. I could only imagine the feeling. Trapped behind that glass.'

'Terrifying.'

'Well, blame that old Burleigh.'

'Must we blame everything on Burleigh?'

'He made it. He built it. He found that old Rotterdam gold.'

'He had a plan.'

'Probably still has. So if he ever turns up, keep mum. About Dany.'

'Dany?'

'Andy, Ynad, Nyad. I took the letters, turned them into Dany.'

'Burleigh won't turn up. And if he does, I'll skewer him.'

'Skewer him? How?'

'With an arrow.'

'Like in the old days. But they're long gone now.'

And Paganina's toes commenced a head massage and a delicious languor spread through Mona, from the crest of her ponytailed crown.

Paganina's feet had achieved this level of dexterity more years ago now than she could count. It had begun with archery. The kinds of truculent bows that required a Mongolian giant to bend yielded, quite easily, like a sapling just threaded by a teenage boy, to those pneumatic digits, the balls and arches of which could curl and twist like a newborn baby's palm. She would lie backwards, the bow clutched by her amazing feet, the arrow steadied by her teeth, the string pulled back by one or both hands, and send the missile flying to skewer one or many of whatever adversaries faced them on the faraway steppes. But those days were long gone. The kinds of wars that demanded strength, sinew and such uncanny dexterity had been replaced by mechanised affairs of industrial carnage. She had realised this one afternoon, on a Greek isthmus churned into mud by the toy-like silhouettes of grey battleships beyond the reach of arrows, on a horizon marred by small puffs of smoke, the crushing booms of which reached her many seconds later, along with the whistle of the huge airborne projectile. She would duck, anticipating the explosion and the cone of mud thrown heavenwards, and one hot, smoke-filled deafening afternoon, she ducked and fell into a blasted trench. There was a dead Turkish officer with a violin in his cold hands and she busied herself with this instrument while the bombardment continued above her, unabated. She plucked out Persian tunes she had learned from her mother, who herself had lived more years than she could remember. And when night came down and the bombardment faded, the ghost-like, shellshocked figures of Turkish, Armenian, Georgian and Scythian troops rose from their fox-holes, followed the hesitant scratching of the violin and were amazed to see the mud-smudged beauty lying back in the trench, bowing the violin, which was tucked into her midriff, with her feet. The scratched sounds emerging could barely be called a tune, but maybe it was this very lack of recognisable melody that made them imagine they remembered it. And so the slow, mournful chant began, around the blasted fox-holes and the collapsed cemeteries of trenches, of the anthem that had brought them here:

Inside Cannakale
In the mirrored bazaar
Mother, I am going against the enemy
Aaah, alas, my youth!

And thus her career as Paganina began. She picked up the melody, embossed upon it, travelled from camp to camp, improved her technique so she could play standing, one foot perched stork-like, the other clutching the bow in its dexterous digits, the instrument itself tucked beneath her chin, while her left hand flew over the fingerboard. Paganini, she was told, was a violinist of such brilliance the devil himself was rumoured to have accompanied him, so she chose the name Paganina. The war ended, she joined a travelling Romanian circus troupe, and when rumours of war circulated once more, two decades later, she retreated to the rocky outpost that had declared itself neutral and found a carnival that needed her talents. She learned jigs and reels, with titles that always bemused her: 'Banished Misfortune', 'The Mason's Apron', 'The Priest in the Barley Field', 'The Windy Gap'. And so she travelled now, massaging Mona's head with those same feet, rocking gently with the trailer's passage through the mysterious night.

It was thirty vehicles strong, the carnival convoy, and it obediently did what ordinary vehicles do. It stopped at traffic lights and level crossings, but anyone who had seen it pass would have no memory of it. It was happiest in the shadows, belonged to them and only retreated from them when it had set up its next, public reiteration. And when it stopped, all the vehicles braked as if by common accord, as if a secret signal had been given. But no secret signal had been given, since, as the carnies would have told anyone who asked, they set up where they had to, in whatever abandoned piece of waste ground was available.

9

DANY WAS ROCKED BACKWARDS and forwards by the swaying movement of the lorry that trundled through the misted night. The straw pricked against his cheek, tiny spikes of it crept up his shirtsleeves and even small microbes of it crept into his nostrils. This bed was most unlike his own at home, with the dormer window peering down on the silent garden, through which every now and then he glimpsed a fox, strolling towards the other gardens of the other bungalows, all alike, in the little cul-de-sac that led to nothing in particular. That bed was always cold, no matter how much warmth his mother implanted in the goodnight kiss; the telegraph wires outside his window would moan softly with an unseen wind, etching a tangled scrawl against the night sky, a message in a dead language he could never decipher. So there was much to be said for his new situation. There was definite life here, in the low throb of the distant engines, in the shifting straws underneath him, in the strange, feline odour that seemed to hang in the air around him. If he ever had a grandmother, he imagined she would smell like that. And while he knew he must have had a grandmother – in fact he had seen pictures of her dim and smiling black-and-white face in the family album – he had never known her, and more to the point, never smelt her.

So he slept, eventually, and happily. And the animal odour that he had noticed seemed to wrap itself around him as he slept, cocooning him in the sweetest of dreams. He dreamt he was walking through a forest with giant slender trunks and a huge panoply of leaves overhead and he was with a grandmother; indeed he was holding her hand and the straw skirt she wore, like those Polynesian islanders, kept rubbing off the back of his hand. Her other hand wrapped around a sleeping cat. She had a kind of necklace of dried flowers and was explaining the varieties of jungle flora to him – and flora meant flowers and plants, he was proud to remember, while fauna meant rocks and shells and other dead things – when they were both rained upon from above. He raised his face to the panoply of leaves above and found it washed in eucalyptus-odoured drops.

And he awoke then to find a lion pissing on him. There was no cause for alarm, the lion being separated from him by rusting iron bars, and Dany, whose eyes had become accustomed to the gloom, noticed for the first time that the trailer was neatly divided in two. He occupied one straw-filled half, while the lion occupied the other and gazed at him with dim, grandmotherly eyes. But it was no grandmother, it was a lion, no doubt about it, one leg lazily raised to direct a stream of urine on to the bed of straw upon which Dany had been sleeping.

'Come on,' the boy objected and shifted in the straw, away from one last, contemptuous spurt.

But the lion didn't reply and the boy was oddly relieved. So many strange things had happened, a lion that replied would have been much too much. So he rolled himself in the bales of unurinated straw and considered himself lucky. And he laid back his head, to wrap himself in one more precious swathe of sleeping.

Meanwhile, and it's a word one should never use, meanwhile, since there is no meanwhile, there is only time, doing its mysterious thing in its infinitude of ways. But, as Dany was sleeping, the other we call Andy now lay in what used to be his bed. The telegraph wires made soft, rhythmic clicks against each other, moved by the wind outside that created an eerie mechanical hum. He seemed to be waiting for something, rather than sleeping; his eyes blinked occasionally, as if to keep time with the scraping music of those wires outside.

It was all activity and roustabouts bellowing, the short squat ones uncoiling huge mounds of light bulbs and wires and the tall thin ones throwing down scaffold poles, frames, huge wooden trunks with screws attached, trapeze wires and cables, unrolling of whole acres of dirty white canvas and the huge mechanical arms that carried the chairoplanes angling their way towards the dusty blue sky. He felt some odd responsibility for Burleigh's Amazing Hall of Mirrors, since, after all, he had come from there. So he did his best to help as it was manhandled out of its protective boxes and slotted into place piece by reflective piece. And he proved himself so busy with this that time performed one of its odd tricks again; the sun was well up in the sky and diminishing its shadows by the time he discovered it was finished, the neon sign above the entrance, useless in the midday glare, reading, for those who squinted their eyes, 'Burleigh's Amazing Hall of Mirrors'. And he turned then to see the carnival once more in place, in another piece of waste ground he knew not where, the rollercoaster curving above the horizon line of the sea, the distant cone of the circus tent beyond it, and the ghost train and the shooting range and the other carnie delights he didn't yet know the names of creating a maze of what were very like little streets, caravans with their flaps open, tents with their flaps closed, advertising strange and clairvoyant revelations for those who had the courage or the coin to venture in to the gloom inside.

It was a village, he decided, more than a carnival, a miniature town indeed, and he wondered should somebody, maybe even him, give these ersatz streets proper names. Then he remembered that it would someday, maybe someday soon, pack up and move again and what good would street names be for a travelling village that had to periodically reassemble itself? And he was thinking imponderable thoughts like this when Mona came up behind him and asked, 'How's she cutting?'

She had been observing him for some time. Watching her Dany, and she felt the name bubble inside of her as if he was truly hers, her chosen one, already roustabouting with the roustabouts in the chaotic business of assemblage. He was proving himself indeed a capable lad, a useful pair of hands. Her chosen one, she thought again. And the term, the name, seemed both wrong and right. She had chosen nothing; she had found his reflection and pulled him into the real world, the carnie world, the only world she had ever known. And yet when she watched him make his way among the stunted roustabouts, hardly bigger than them himself, as yet unsure in his new environment but adorable, simply adorable, in his oddness, his unfamiliar gait, he could only be her chosen one. If she had ever been given a choice, she would have chosen him. And any panic he felt – and there would be panic, she was sure of that, no one leaves a mother of fourteen years without some sense of displacement – she would make it her job to soothe it, to quell it, to put it to rest. She would place a comforting hand on his, catch his turbulent gaze and reassure it with those azure eyes of her own. If she had ever wanted a child – and that was a want she never allowed herself to entertain; she knew how impossible it was – it would have been that one, there, unpacking the same mirror-maze that had brought him here, as if he knew the drill and had always known it, his thin, gazelle-like form working hard to keep up with the dungareed roustabouts, and she resolved then and there never to let him wear dungarees; he was made for better things. So she came behind him and felt his body feel her approach, his shoulders tensing and his eyes in a panic meeting hers, and she said the first thing that came into her head: 'How's she cutting?'

Easy, her eyes said, easy, it's only me, you're at home now. And she saw the shoulders relax, saw the tiny shiver of acceptance come into those flecked brown eyes, or were they green? Brown, she saw now, brown and the flecks were green.

Maybe it was luck, in the end. Luck that brought him here to be her chosen one. Burleigh's expulsion had been a long, loud and painful affair, his cries of anguish had seemed to echo round the empty carnival long after he was gone: Why me, why me. He knew of course why him, the Rotterdam gold was only part of it. His absurd claim, to provide a solution to the changeling problem. You broke more than the rules, old Jude had told him and would have shattered his Hall of Mirrors into a million tiny pieces had she not been reminded that it would bring a million years' bad luck. So they cast him out, like old Adam or the one in the vineyard whose name always escaped her. And Burleigh's Amazing Hall of Mirrors had lain fallow for years, until yesterday's miraculous event. As you sow, so must you reap. Or something like that. What was this with the biblical stuff? And why was she bothered about Burleigh? Let him wander in the cold world outside, with the moan of the winds of sin and death and the clouds of nonbelonging with no hope of return to the Land of Spices, and let me deal with my chosen one.

So she smiled, with all of the winsomeness that only she could put into a smile, and she was happy to see him smile back. She took his hand and felt the tingle ripple through it, felt the adolescent hairs stand to attention, as if at her command.

'You did well with the rousties.'

'Did I, indeed?'

Indeed. The old-fashioned tenor to the word. The archaism, the use of a question to answer. And she felt a surge of irrational hope, was it, or promise, that maybe he could be one of them after all. But then she banished the thought, as they had banished old Burleigh. Better not, as the young ones tell it, go there.

'And rousties can be hard to keep up with.'

'That's what you call them? Rousties?'

'Roustabouts. And a good roustie can balance a circus pole on his chin.'

'His chin?'

'No women allowed. But you, young Dany, were made for greater things.'

'I was?'

'No dungarees for you.'

'No?'

She caught the sound of disappointment in his voice. Of course, she thought, the sweat, the muscle, the boy-mannishness of roustabouts. 'What is for me then?'

'Sawdust and tinsel and a touch of greasepaint.'

'I don't understand.'

And he didn't. It was all a mystery to him. This small, pert girl – almost a woman, really – with her perfect posture, toes constantly stretching from the ground as if she wished to be airborne. She was wearing a dirty gabardine coat that hid something that glittered. Behind her a mélange of carnival activity – huge metal pegs being driven into the unwilling earth by hammer-wielding, muscled arms.

'Come with me.'

She tightened her hand on his. Pulled him gently away, from this masculine world. She was determined. No dungarees for Dany. She traced a route through the alley-ways of sideshows as if she had known it all her life. As, of course, she had. She knew every atom of this carnival, no matter how it rearranged itself, and she greeted the stallers as she went.

'Good morning, Zaroaster'.

Zaroaster gasolened a bubblegum of flame back at her.

'Virginie, what a divine setting.'

'Alaister, my dear, no tricks, it's far too early.'

'Monniker, how goes it?'

It was going well, it seemed, as Monniker was already squeezing his agile frame through a tangle of ventilation tubing.

'Jude, my love—'

She passed the aged lion, being led by what looked like a dog lead, towards an assortment of cubes and hoops laid out in one of the few empty spaces left.

'—oh my goodness, they already know each other—'

And they did. The lion nuzzled his tawny forehead against Dany's hip, while Jude, his ageing mistress, pulled him gently away.

'Dorothea, I don't want to know.'

But Dany did. He saw Dorothea in the triangular gloom of her stall, a gleaming ball in her hand. He very much wanted to know what the future held. But they were already moving on.

Past Bulgar, flexing his muscles in a leopardine one-piece.

'Oh all right, Bulgar, we will oil you if we must . . .'

Oil. From a small, twisted jar, he noticed. Tangled, as if wound into many circles by a four-dimensional hand. He had never seen a jar like it. And the oil that Mona shook from it had a smell like camphor, a sweet stinging sensation that flared the nostrils and teared the eyes. Like the onions that made someone cry. Someone? And he was spreading this oil over the mounds of muscle that were Bulgar's back when he remembered who. His mother. The tears streamed freely then, and mingled, when all of a sudden Mona dropped the jar in the stunted grass by the odd-shaped assortment of weights and drew him on.

'The oil,' she said, 'not sun cream, can't buy it, grade it, trade it, but the small tincture of spice can make the eyes stream.'

'Spice?' he asked, and she looked at him as if she wished she could swallow the word.

'You're crying,' she said.

'I was thinking of my—'

But before the word 'mother' emerged, she clutched his hand once more, drew him, step by step, over the enormous guy-ropes that led like parallel strings on a concert harp to a canvas entrance beyond. Some words were forbidden here, it seemed. Mother and spice amongst them. And he was remembering a nursery rhyme, when the curl of her hand diverted him once more. Mother and spice and all things nice. No, it wasn't mother, he fretted: sugar – sugar and spice – when her fingers rubbed off his palm and he felt that tingle again and was confronted with yet another reality.

This carnival kept doing that. First one thing, then another.

And this reality was – a triangle of dark exposed by two flaps of pinned-back canvas. Head-height. A sound, from inside, of a lonely trumpet. He had never heard anything sadder than that trumpet. It made him think of onions again, and flowing tears and that word he was struggling to pull back to his brain, when he felt a hot breath close to his ear and another word took over.

'Tango.'

'Tango?' he repeated. It seemed safest, again, to repeat things. There were so many things he didn't know.

'I swing,' she said, 'to a tango. Come inside. Have a look.'

And she led him in, into that dark triangle, where his eyes gradually accustomed themselves to the gloomiest of glooms. The trumpet still played, and as the darkness slowly became visible, he distinguished a small man, far far off, in a spotted white suit, with a conical hat on his head. Something gold to his lips, which must have been a trumpet. Because the sound of it soared now, all around him, and he could detect just the hint of a dance in the air. As she had whispered, a tango.

'A dance,' she said, 'is best with a touch of swing to it, because that's what I do, after all. Dance.'

He could distinguish the shape now, the huge conical funnel, leading to an apex of thin sunlight at the top. So there was light in here after all, he thought. Quite a lot of it. Early-morning light, coming through the various blighted holes, in trembling, hesitant fingers. He could see hanging wires, trapeze bars in the upper gloom, a small platform, circling the central pole.

'You be my hauler,' she said and withdrew her curled fingers from his. 'Hauler today, maybe catcher tomorrow.'

He said nothing. He was becoming adept in these transitions. Pretend to understand, he was thinking, and understanding just might come to you.

And she raised her two hands to her shoulders and, with two deft flicks, threw the canvas-coloured garment to what he now realised was a sawdust floor. He watched it fall, some kind of gabardine, and it seemed to descend in slow motion, to raise a whorl of misted dust from the curls of old woodchip. It fell beside her two dark pumps, which he saw now were sparkling with tiny specks of diamanté or glass. Spangled slippers, he would have called them. His eyes followed her ankles, her thin, muscular calves, clad in fishnet tights, up to the body-hugging tutu with its golden bustier, stays and angled shoulder pads. Circus garb.

Of course, he realised. There had always been something airborne about her.

She pressed upwards on her toes again, as if stretching towards the narrow beam of sunlight at the apex. Then she walked on those spangled slippers across the sawdust floor to where two ends of rope dangled down from some beam in the heavens. They swung gently, neither touching the other.

She wrapped an arm around one, deftly, making a snake of it, and looked back at him.

'The hauler pulls,' she said. 'Pulls the artiste.'

'You're the artiste.'

She nodded. She had a small dimple, he realised for the first time, below her smiling lip.

'Be my hauler.'

'I could never hold your weight,' he said.

'Aha,' she said and she smiled and her green gaze swooped to meet his. 'You've a lot to learn.'

'About what?'

'About carnies. About Mona. About tangos.'

And she wrapped the rope around her body in one feline move, crooking her slim knee above it, snaking it round her waist and upwards towards her breast, her left hand twisting above her like an open-mouthed cobra.

'Now pull,' she said.

And the boy obeyed her. He would always obey her, he realised, whenever she wrapped the rope around herself like that. He gripped the other end and pulled.

She seemed weightless. More than weightless: she seemed to have an inner force that propelled her upwards. She soared with the force of each tug of his, up, up and up into the blaze of that beam of light that spilled down from the centre hole.

'Now loop it.'

He began to swing the rope, in successive loops that grew ever more large, widened in that element, that term of measurement that he could never remember from school. Although school felt very far away now. And as the trumpet soared, in its tangoing dance, he remembered. Circumference.

And up above she began to spin.

And down below, he was reminded of many things.

Of the silver angel on the Christmas tree that his mother unpacked every December.

Of a toy windmill, whipped by an invisible wind.

Of a devil stick he used to play with in the garden of the privet hedges, which he would practise twirling until it became an indeterminate blur.

He whipped the rope around, saw it widen above him into a similar blur. The shape of Mona, her leg and arm crooked around the rope, seemed to lose itself from any sense of the real world. He was spinning a top, the handle of which was a spinning girl, Mona, and as she spun she became a feather-like thing and he felt, as he spun her, that the twirling rope was some kind of pretence and its real purpose could have been to keep her earthbound.

He dismissed this thought as soon as it occurred to him. It seemed absurd, and somehow forbidden. And he felt his mother's absence with a real pain, as if some strange animal was sifting inside him. He missed his mother then so much, he felt the pain so keenly, he had to forget her. And the only way to forget her was to look upwards once more at the blur of those twirling legs.

The tune ended and he saw the small spotted figure across the sawdust circle remove the trumpet from his lips. He pushed the conical hat back on his head, and shook the spittle from the golden bowl. Dany stopped his twirling but the rope didn't. Its momentum kept her going, far above him, and its circumference only gradually lost its bloom.

11

HIS MOTHER, MEANWHILE, MISSED him. But it was a peculiar kind of missing, because Andy was there in front of her, sitting on the wooden chair that was half sofa, the light of the television whitening his face, with a fly swatter in his left hand. Where the fly swatter had come from, she had no idea. Probably the garage, she imagined, where her husband's condiment samples and the empty jamjars he used to experiment with mixing tended to attract flies. And now that she thought of it, too many things in there were coated in an invisible, sticky essence, even Jim's carpentry table, which was one of the reasons she rarely ventured inside. But she resolved to do so now, and give the place a thorough cleaning. She had been neglecting things of late, and obviously had taken her eye off her growing boy, given the evidence of this apparent stranger in front of her. They don't develop in an ascending curve, she remembered the teacher saying, they tend to make quantum leaps, from one state to the next. But what was a quantum leap? she wondered. She had been bored by physics and tended to think of scientific parallels with life itself as so much mumbo-jumbo. She had not done badly, she hoped, given the stresses of conception. And she shivered a little at this memory, and looked once more at the fly swatter, banging against the upturned sole of his shoe with an annoying persistence and a persistent regularity. It was like a metronome, set to a fast rhythm, too fast for whatever tune should have accompanied it. Her boy seemed to have vanished, and yet there he was. And she thought some more about quantum leaps then, something to do with particles that didn't behave the way they should have, but jumped from one level to the next. Like the stairs that led to the dormer bedroom. Was the movement always upwards? she wondered. Could he take a quantum leap back, to the state she so loved?

Because she had always relished these moments, just with the two of them, kneading dough or washing dishes, when whatever spell the television had cast was broken and her son would turn and join her at the sink and take the sudsy dishes in his hands, washing them clean with the damp towel, or cutting the pastry into starfish that would later become baked biscuit, both of them covered in flour from fingertip to elbow. She would never have to vocalise it, the invitation to join her and help, at the dough-covered table or the sink; she would do her thing patiently, knowing the rhythm of her work would gradually draw him in, make him turn and utter the magic phrase: 'Hey Mum, let me help you with that.'

She switched her attention from the fly swatter to a panel show with those witty comedians, which only tired her brain, but he would watch, even while thumbing his phone or his game console. 'Mongolia,' the dickie-bowed host was saying, 'is famed for many things, but rarely for its popular singers. And can anyone give me the Mongolian name of the following member of the boyband—'

She moved past him, through to the kitchen, expecting a word, at least. But none came. A glance was all she got, and a brief grimace which could have been a smile.

And she knew then she wouldn't hear that phrase, 'Hey Mum', maybe not that evening, or the next. Mother was what he had called her, coming home from the carnival.

It seemed a word from a different boy, in quite a different home. In fact she knew something worse. She knew she didn't want to hear that word, mother, and again that foreboding licked at the edges of her consciousness, where understanding lay over the illogic of dreams. Night would fall, sooner or later, and the shadows would be all the darker for it. And the only respite would be the return of her husband, the rattle of his briefcase off the front door, the metallic series of clicks he made as he tried to extract his front-door key.

There was a sound at the door now, and she saw the boy's head turn. Not the sound of a key, or a briefcase, but the rat-tat-tat of the doorknocker and the drumming of fingers on the door that only a boy's hands could make. And she had to remind herself that Andy had friends. Friends that she could see through the hallway, their faces pushed against the bubbled glass. She recognised the tousled head of Darragh, the short spiked hair of the one they called, for some reason, Drum. She walked down the hallway, opened the door and saw four of them there. 'Is Andy in, Mrs Rackard?'

'Yes, he's watching television.'

'Get him to come out, Mrs Rackard, he'd kill us if he missed this.'

'Missed what?'

'The rats. They're pulling down the trees, below the football pitch.'

'Rats?'

'Rats everywhere, coming out of the roots.'

And he was behind her now. She felt this, without turning. She saw their eyes register him.

'Come on, Andy. They'll be all done if you don't hurry.'

He walked past her to join them. She observed the slaps, the high-fives, the knuckles meeting knuckles.

She watched them run, like a gaggle of boys again, along the cement path past the privet hedges, and out of sight. He quickened his pace, to keep up with them.

What was this about rats? And she heard the groan of a great earthmover, and found herself following.

Down the pathway, to the right by the creaking gate. He seemed to be the son she had known again, running with the bunch of them. There was another posse of kids coming up from the sea road. And from the end of the football pitch she saw the top of a huge, gnarled beech tree quiver and tumble out of sight.

She walked past the bus stop, down the slope past the other bungalows that she knew so well, each not too dissimilar to her own. There was a fresh wind blowing, and the distant caps of white showed on the horizon. She hardly noticed them today, though, since the groan of unseen machinery and a slight trembling in the earth – she had crossed from the bungalows to the grassy edge of the pitch – seemed to herald what was the event, as yet out of sight. She followed the smudged white line, the crushed cider bottles lying in the longer grass, and only when she reached the sagging goalpost could she see what all of the excitement was about.

The tangled slope of undergrowth and ancient trees was being cleared. One huge beech tree was down, and the others would soon follow. There was an immense earthmover, with metal cables running from it to the next tree trunk, on the slope. A man with a high-vis jacket and a yellow hard hat was clambering down to the base, spikes on his reinforced boots. He stood back and gave the earthmover the all-clear. The rusted chimney belched smoke, the tracks churned up the ground beneath them and the beast moved. The trunk began to give way, not in a regular curve, she noticed, but in jerked stages, like the quantum leaps the teacher had mentioned. Eventually the huge beech tree fell and was dragged towards its companion, on the safe, flatter ground. It wrenched its huge roots from the earth and from the dark wound left behind came the surge of rats.

There must have been hundreds of them. A seething mass that could have been grasshoppers from her high vantage point. She had to suppress a wave of nausea. They seemed to foam from the jagged hole like maggots leaving a cadaver. But there was no doubting what they were, as the adolescents all around reverted back to unruly, childhood, chasing them with sticks, broken pieces of branch, concrete blocks, held aloft, ready to crush the squirming rodents below. And among them was Andy, who seemed just like a boy again.

12

A WOMAN STOOD WATCHING IN the triangle of blazing light by the entrance, as Dany slowed the circumference of his twirling rope to something near zero and as Mona began her feather-like descent. As the trumpeter, whose name was Piertro (his name had once been Pierrot – appropriate, given his spotted costume and his conical hat – but names tended to get mangled in carnieland), pressed soundlessly on the valves of his trumpet, still shaking the last drops from the mouth. This woman smiled wistfully at the spectacle of Mona floating down, as if on gossamer wings, almost into the arms of the puckish figure that stood waiting below. The rope joined them, an umbilical cord in everything but name, and Virginie felt a pang, of longing and remembrance. She had done her share of snatching in her time, but many decades ago, when children were mostly unwanted and much more numerous than now. In fact some of her swains inhabited the carnival and one of them, Cederick, kept jealous and watchful suzerainty over the ghost train, a stance more understandable when one considered the fact that several of his siblings resided inside. But that was a long time ago and memory had done its thing. If she took her seat on one of the ghost-train rides, Cederick would barely return her glance, and once inside, in the enveloping darkness, when the wraiths of the apparently dead ones loomed forward to terrify, to chill, to amaze, she recognised faces she had touched with an affection that surprised her, many, many years ago. But there was little of that now; time had done its blundering work and what it didn't do to hands and faces, it did to memories, and memories of memories.

And she was experiencing just that now, a memory of a memory. She saw the boy hold out a quite unnecessary hand to aid Mona back on to the solid ground of the sawdust floor. She was on a ship, more like a floating city, remembering a boy she had left on the crushed grass of a Kerry fairground. She had left him, knowing the time for fairgrounds was almost over, for summer races by the strand at Inch, for the tick-tack men and would you grace my palm with silver, sir. With a variety troupe, on the Cunard Line, more burlesque than variety if Auberon Smythe had his way, the actor-manager who had enticed her from the booth at the Listowel Races with promises of a season on a place called Broadway. She last saw him at New York Harbour disembarking with the first-class passengers while she was bundled with the rest of steerage on a barge bound for Ellis Island. She had never been as close to human bodies as then, their gaseous odours, their tooth-rotted breath, their phlegmy coughs and open sores. She received a swift and singularly clean bill of health, and on the ferry to Manhattan, as she saw the towers of the city pitching towards her, she was filled then with a longing she had never experienced before; a longing for a home she never knew she had had, and a longing for that boy, almost grown enough to be inducted, that she had left on the Waterville shore. If she had a heart, she remembered thinking, it would have broken then.

Then, and maybe now. She saw his hand grip Mona's, she saw Mona's arched feet touch the sawdust floor in their black spangled pumps; she saw that moment of gladness, of pride, even, with which he greeted her, pride in a job apparently well done.

She clapped. Two small, unblemished hands striking off each other. The sound echoed round the voluminous tent. She saw Mona turn and curtsy, gesturing at her charge to do the same. 'Then, the bow,' she said.

'The what?' He knew what she meant, but the repetitions were becoming a matter of rote.

'The nod, the bob, the curtsy, the hand salaam—'

Mona gestured, her right hand tracing invisible arcs in the air.

'Why?' he asked.

'Because,' said Mona, 'the applause will be thunderous. And as my hauler, you're part of the show. Am I right, Virginie?'

'Mona's right,' said Virginie, walking forwards. 'And you should let him know there's no why, there is no because, there is just the show and he's part of it now.'

And he turned towards her, inclined his head towards the sawdusty floor, traced an invisible coil with his boyish hand, as if he had been doing the same all of his boyish life.

How many mothers could a boy have? Virginie wondered. But she already knew the answer. Mona would keep this one bound to her like a newborn kangaroo; if she had a marsupial pouch she would have kept him in it. The best she, Virginie, could hope for was the privilege of sisterhood. So she wound one arm around Mona's as they left the inside for the bright outside air, as if she had always been a soul sister to Mona, and an aunt of kinds to him. He had parents, she assumed, but if he was missing them it was yet to show. And when the time came that he missed them, she could put her sisterly virtues and her auntish instincts to work.

'Have I met you before?' the boy asked, as they threaded their way through the fairground caravans.

'Virginie,' said Mona, a little unwillingly, since she already sensed the incipient rivalry for his affections. 'She's an equilibrist, of some note and fame.'

And Virginie was that, and more. She could balance many things; she could balance decades in her posture and continents in her soul. Like Mona, she could defy the laws of gravity and, like Mona, she had long managed to keep it secret.

They negotiated the warren of stalls and tents through which the trickle of punters was already beginning to stroll. They moved from the waste ground of the carnival on to the promenade, where the salty wind began to whip their faces, and on the way, almost without him noticing it, Virginie had managed to change places. Her arm threaded through his arm now, whereas before it had linked Mona's. So he walked with two girlish women on either side of him, through the promenade crowds. There was an unmistakable aura to them, he felt, something eastern, something old, something gypsy, as if all three of them had stepped out of the pages of *Arabian Nights*. He saw another boy walk towards them, hand in his mother's dowdy pocket, turn his head backwards until his mother chucked him onwards, muttering, 'Leave them be, they're carnies.' He felt a flush of strange pride, to have become so noticeable all of a sudden. And then he remembered it wasn't sudden at all; it had been two days at least since he'd walked into Burleigh's Hall of Mirrors. He realised he hadn't eaten and as he realised that he got the whiff of chips and saw a fish and chip stall up ahead, with an ice-cream vendor beside it. He had no coins in his pocket and to ask either of them would have seemed indelicate, but as he passed it he couldn't help looking back.

'Either he's hungry,' Virginie said, 'or he misses his carnival already.'

Was it already his carnival? the boy wondered. But she was right about one thing: he was hungry. And he was more than thankful when Mona turned, drew their small threesome back to the chip stall. More of a van, really, with the car that drew it missing, with the axle perched on a stack of breezeblocks. They bought him chips, and a fresh cod and batter, and when they raised their eyebrows at the ice-cream vendor adjacent, he shook his head. He had his hands full as it was. They sat then, on the concrete parapet, and watched the silhouetted figures of the strollers passing by.

So Dany ate, staring at Virginie's small, pixie face, with the brown hair falling in old-fashioned ringlets round her cheeks. As the chips and battered cod did their work on his hunger, he couldn't shake the feeling that he had seen her before.

The truth was that he had, he had seen her before, many times and always on a television screen. His father's favourite Sunday-afternoon indulgence, old reruns of black-and-white movies on the Turner channel. The small tramp, with his twirling stick and his bowler hat, the pitiful waif on the pavement, the look of wonder and longing, the pratfalls then, the car and constabulary chases, all designed to keep them apart and eventually bring them together. The waif had Virginie's pale face and brown ringlets. Because, for a time, Virginie was her, and she was Virginie.

Mona watched him watching her and knew the feeling. They were a watchful bunch, these carnies, they had to be. And Mona remembered her own reacquaintance with Virginie, in one of the new-fangled theatres in the old St Louis, where she saw the staggering clown with his bandy legs and his twirling stick and his lovestruck gaze for the blind girl at the busy street corner, and, like the boy now, she recognised Virginie. The same pale face, the same twists of hair nudging the cheekbones, the hand in which she had once read no future, begging for spare change.

But that was many years ago, in another country. Another continent, indeed, divided from this one by the ocean she had first crossed in a coffin ship. She would journey over it many times, always in different guises; indeed she would become a fixture on Atlantic crossings, performing in the floating theatres of first-class decks of the White Star Line. But she would never forget the first.

Mona had memories, too many memories, a whole cacophony of them, that in the carnie way she did her best to forget. At times she felt like the keeper of a whole genealogy of memories stretching back to the Land of Spices itself. But that was impossible because Mona herself had been snatched, at a time when snatching was not yet an issue, when children were so plentiful they were given away. Could she remember Keem Strand, seventeen of them packed into a limestone hovel with a straw roof? Hardly. All she could remember was the feeling of loss, when the caravan packed and trundled on its journey to God knows where. And the feeling of relief, of pure, unadulterated joy, when a shawl wrapped round her, when the dark hands lifted her into their painted, shuttered carts. And that joy became confused, over her subsequent carnie decades, with the original memories of the Land of Spices. A girl, wrapped in a cocoon of dreams, rocked back and forwards by the carnival horses. But like most carnies, she did her best to keep memory at bay. Memory was treacherous; it was a shapeshifter, and to be entertained by it would be to admit that she herself had lived so long and to admit in turn the Fatigue, which as a carnie it was her duty to keep at bay. But she could never forget that first crossing.

The Hunger had scattered the carnies like chaff, though they weren't called carnies then. It had scattered the people too, into ditches and byways until those that didn't die in bogs with the paste of green grass on their mouths, or get work on the Meitheal, creating roads that went nowhere through the selfsame bog, crowded on to the coffin ships. They brought with them their pitiful rags, their starving bairns and their native beliefs, which they clung to like sacred talismans, so the carnies, naturally, clung to them. It was a strange kind of clinging. There were no eggs to be despoiled, no milk to be soured, nothing of the land they had left but the fevered imaginings of their hosts, so they survived, barely, kept alive by the bible of superstitions they brought to the unbelieving shore. Mona's coffin ship lived up to its name. It literally became that, a coffin, after the deck hands that consigned the skeletal bodies to the waves came down with scurvy, dysentery, a whole host of diseases that she had known, in earlier times, simply as 'the flux'. So it was a lifeless ship that drifted into New Haven Harbour in late September of the year of Our Lord 1847. The ship was isolated, quarantined, and Mona slipped ashore before it was scuttled and its melancholy load consigned to the deep.

She found herself wandering those cold New Haven streets among wave after wave of immigrants, from corners of the world she had barely known existed. But they all had one thing in common: they abandoned the old and embraced what they thought was the new. She could have died from lack of belief, the absence of a superstitious cloak to coat herself in, but like those new-minted humans, she found new ways to survive.

A stint in a vaudeville theatre, where she had to keep her airborne possibilities in check; several long winters in an uptown brothel, until, like most of her kind, she found her most comfortable hiding place in a travelling sideshow. She endured the gaze of random city folk, looking for freaks and wonders. She befriended gigantic furred ladies, perfect miniature families, and when the travel west became inevitable, the sideshow travelled too, among that vast movement of humanity. There was always the need, she found, for a pirouette, a cartwheel, a backflip, on the windy corner of whatever half-built western town. San Francisco, when she reached it, was in one of its boomtown phases, and she spent most of that boom in a mirrored honky-tonk, as the city around it grew, sucking in money like yeast. She tired of the tinkling piano and the clutching hands and the clanging cash register and drifted southwards, telling fortunes in a carnival booth, into which one day walked Virginie.

Something about the voice in the darkness made her spine tingle, told her she had met another of her own. But she couldn't be sure, so she rattled through the normal rigmarole, a man was waiting, a child would come, when the question seemed to leap out of her painted lips. 'Why have your future told when you know it already?'

'What do I know?' the breathy voice asked back, and Mona elaborated. 'You know already what I'll tell you, time goes on, the years pass away, but for you, nothing changes.'

And Mona felt her own palm turned in the darkened booth and heard the voice she would come to treasure tell her, 'I could say the same for you.'

'Don't cross my hand with silver, then. Buy me a drink.'

So they repaired to the one bar in that one-horse town in the corn-filled wilderness that would some day be a dust-bowl. They drank sharp rye whiskey, two young women who drew glances but knew well how to buffer them. Two carnies, with silk stockings, blocked heels and coloured skirts that revealed too much of their always-adolescent legs.

Virginie was her name, and she was headed for the flatlands of Los Angeles.

'Whatever for?' Mona asked, and felt the Irish cadence immediately flooding back. 'This new-fangled thing,' her new acquaintance said, 'making carnivals and sideshows history. The cinematograph.'

Mona had already noticed them. The flickering shimmer in the darkened tent, the crowds lining up outside while the bearded lady sat alone and unnoticed. She was getting used to change, redundancy, being cast aside like an out-of-fashion coat.

They parted ways that night, and while Mona knew their paths would cross again, she could never have imagined how.

She was in St Louis, in a sideshow amongst the decaying skeleton of what was once the World's Fair. There was a theatre across the way, showing the early two-reelers. A life-size poster of a tramp, with a half-bent cane and an odd top hat. She paid her twenty cents and walked inside.

The theatre was empty that afternoon. She sat alone, with the fake Egyptian pillars all around her, and watched the antics on the screen and only paused her laughter when she saw Virginie, in black and white and ten times larger than life.

She remembered the feeling, as odd, as distant and yet as intense as the feeling the boy must have now. He sat on the promenade parapet, the last piece of battered cod held to his lips, still staring at her. Virginie caught his glance, finally, and acknowledged it, with an intimate smile. Take your time, that smile said, it will come to you. And you have all the time in the world.

The truth was that Virginie enjoyed her time with the Little Tramp and Arclight Pictures. She would work all day and vault back in over the lot perimeter at night. She'd make her bed in the rigging way above the stages, to be woken in the morning by the rattle of chains, the strange whine of the arclights as they came up to heat. It had the added advantage of always making her on time, for if there was one thing the Little Tramp insisted on, it was punctuality. She made the imagined world her real one and wandered the backlots at night, finding herself now in an ancient Egyptian city, in an Elizabethan dungeon, then in a fairy-tale castle, all turrets and portcullises and elaborate ascending staircases that went nowhere in particular. She had found a home of kinds, like her carnival home but with its own predicaments, too. And the predicaments were these: the Little Tramp, first of all, and his insatiable need to bed any female that came within his range of vision. She would hear the sounds of his passionate engagements in the make-up trailer, in the vast office he had made his own, in the barn of the Ruritanian village with its quaking geese and mooing cows, everywhere in fact, except on the stages where he twirled his comical cane and photographed his gags. She knew that his wet brown eyes would one day fall on her and prepared herself. The space between her legs had almost forgotten what penetration was, so long had it been. But with the help of a lubricant, and an oratorio of delighted sighs, she managed the experience when his eyes did make their landing. The small moustache was wet around her lips, the baggy pants crumpled round his ankles, the event itself happened on his overflowing desk soon after lunchtime, and his postprandial bowl of fruit was trodden to a pulp by his patent-leather shoes. Ah, he muttered, my dear, in that voice, mellowed by the streets of east London, which his public would never hear. Because with the arrival of sound, his career ground to its inevitable halt.

The other predicament was success. She had no sense of it, no knowledge of it, since she rarely, if ever, ventured outside the back-lot gates. But it arrived all the same, like a small glittering tributary to the raging torrent of his global fame. With it came requests, for publicity, for public gatherings, for a place in that huge, pulsating world outside that she knew never could be hers. So one day, after the last reel on the last picture she would make with him, she quite simply vanished. She packed her few small belongings in a diaphanous bag, and made her way, under cover of darkness, to the carnival wastelands round the beach they called Venice. She wandered through the stalls, the circus tents, the rollercoaster, searching for one of her own kind. And she found them, as she knew she would. She adopted a new name, Indira, wore a gypsy headscarf with a diadem of thin gold coins, and read the palms of those whose future was a readable map to her, a map she tried to keep hidden from them.

Their paths would cross again, many years later, on the craggy Atlantic coastline of the West of Ireland. The little tramp, by now a revered, white-haired clown, came to her circus tent with a daughter and three grandchildren. She was a contortionist that day, and twisted her lithe, still-young body on a glass table above him. She bent backwards, caught a rose with her teeth and caught those brown eyes again, everything around them bent and arthritic, a gleam of awakened lust still there. Did he remember? she wondered. She opened her mouth to the stem of the rose, and brought one lithe, adolescent leg in a straight line towards the ceiling of the bell tent. She heard the crowd gasp; her balance seemed barely human, and inhuman it certainly was. She saw his moustacheless lips open, and the clown's ancient tongue emerged, to moisten them. She remembered that tongue on hers and wished she didn't.

13

EILEEN LEFT HER SON playing with the scarpering rats, as the man in the high-vis jacket wound the cable round the trunk of yet another beech tree. The rats disturbed her, but every boy in the cul-de-sac was involved in the chase. And playing, after all, was what boys were meant to do, even boys who were crossing the threshold into something else. He was growing, a little taller now than the others of his gang, but it was sweet to see him become the boy she remembered once more, even if it took the game of Rat Catcher, Rat Pulveriser, whatever they would call it, to do that. She crossed back over the football pitch to her bungalow, among the privet hedges by the number 30 bus stop, and began to prepare dinner.

She started to peel potatoes to cut them into chips. She thought chips might work the same trick, remind him of the boyhood he was so obviously moving past, bring him back to it, albeit just for an hour or a day or two. Beef stew was the normal dinner on a Thursday, but she knew that chips, beans and sausages were the boy's favourite, and thought to surprise him with just that dinner. And if the wind died down, perhaps after dinner they would both of them walk down to the bathing place by the concrete wall and swim. The day was hot enough, the sun was shining; it was only the wind that gave that unseasonal feeling, brought the white caps to the sea on the horizon.

They had always enjoyed the closeness of that ritual of theirs, the stroll down by the inlet, the walk over the wooden bridge, then the strange business of undressing, she in the women's shelter, he in the men's. She kept a watchful eye on him there, since she had heard stories of the adult males who swam there. Some of them she knew by name, hardy perennial types like her who swam throughout the winter, but others came and went, sat in the shadows of the curved concrete shelter, and seemed more intent on gazing on lithe young bodies than immersing themselves in the waters. She had heard stories; she didn't fully believe them, but yet. But yet. Grown men could do strange things, things that were unwritten in her book of life. A neighbour's child, for instance, had transformed from a charming freckle-faced boy into a sullen, withdrawn adolescent, and it was only after his death, in a stolen car crashed on the way towards the West, that rumours spread about 'the incident'. Eileen didn't know, and didn't want to know, the details of the incident, but it involved the sand dunes beyond the shelter, and some acquaintance that started here, inside it. Some acquaintance with what was termed a 'stray man'. The word 'stray' affected her deeply, so deeply she refused to think about it. So whatever the pleasure of their swimming rituals, she kept a watchful eye on him at all times.

Jim wasn't one for swimming, she reflected, as she heated up the corn oil for the chips, and sliced the cellophane wrapper on the Denby's sausages. A little self-conscious about his pale skin, he would cover his body in a veritable burka of towels before emerging in the old-fashioned Speedos he would never let go of, the red bolts of lightning decorating the sides of the hip. He would stand in the shallows, contemplating things, before finally making what he called the 'corpus immersus', splashing around in one or two strokes, then retreating to the cement steps, where he would begin a series of Boy Scout stretches.

So you can imagine her surprise when, after Jim had returned and Andy blundered in from his waste-ground antics, after all three of them had consumed the unexpected treat of chips, beans and sausages and Eileen suggested a walk down by the sea wall and maybe a swim, Andy nodded gravely and Jim took a last gulp of tea and came out with an enthusiastic, 'Absolutely!'

So, absolutely it was. She removed three towels from the hot press and wrapped their swimming things separately in each of them, handed each of them their rolled bundle and in no time at all, all three of them were walking down the gentle slope from the 30 bus stop to the vista of sea below.

The wind had died a little, the sea was an uncertain sea-green, but there were no white caps, thank God. She could do a slow breaststroke without those flurries of blinding spray in her eyes.

She took Jim's arm and slipped her hand through the elbow of her growing son and found that, to her quiet surprise and delight, he didn't flinch or withdraw in that adolescent horror she had read so much about. No, he allowed her arm to sit there, quite happily in the crook of his, the only resistance being the gentle rocking of his gait, the soft scrape of his hoodie.

So they were a family again, a proper family, she was gladdened to think, and she wondered how she could have imagined it otherwise. He was a growing boy; some kind of withdrawal was what Jim would have termed 'par for the course'.

So they walked. Jim talked about oranges from Seville, apples from New England, strawberries and raspberries from Donabate and Balbriggan, about a new contract

Intercontinental Preserves was managing for the SuperValu chain. And it was odd, Eileen thought, the attachment he had forged with his employers, as if their brand, their values, their future even, was interconnected with his. They were just his employers, after all, and she could even now remember a time in which he didn't go on so much about marmalade. Marmalade and jam and various brands of fruit curd. If he had found employment in a bank, she wondered, would all the talk be about interest rates and negotiable loans? And she had to smile wryly to herself then and think that, knowing Jim, it probably would. She looked down at his brown shoes, beside her coloured espadrilles, and noticed Andy's boots, moving in time with both of them, and saw flecks of blood on the toecaps.

She had a mental image then, and she couldn't escape it, of a rat crushed beneath his Doc Martens. He had chosen those boots himself, olive-green leather with the wine-coloured stitching. He had wanted the green ones, not the black. Another image came, of a boot flailing through the air, sending a bloodied, broken-backed rodent back to the hole it had scurried from. She shivered, with almost a wave of nausea, wondering what happened to his pride in his Doc Marten boots, the toecaps more than flecked, streaked with lumps of blackish goo.

'They were pulling the beech trees down,' she said, 'below the football pitch—'

Andy finished for her.

'And you'll never guess what came out of the roots?'

'What?' Jim asked.

'Rats,' Andy said.

'Rats?'

'Rats,' Andy repeated. 'Hundreds of them.'

'I suppose it makes sense,' Eileen murmured, 'when you think of it. Those old roots, buried in the ground for a hundred or so years. They would grow their own colonies, wouldn't they?'

And another involuntary image came. Of subterranean tunnels, burrowing rats scraping their way beneath the football pitch, underneath the bus stop, carving a honeycomb of rat-holes beneath the bungalow itself.

'Is colony the word,' Jim asked, 'for a collection of rats?'

And her heart sank for some reason. She recognised the didactic tone. Jim was too old when she'd had Andy. Maybe they were both too old.

'I mean, Andy, you can talk of a flock of geese, a murder of crows, a charm of larks. Collective nouns, actually, are an interesting study, in and of themselves.'

At least he had moved on from preserves.

'But rats? A pack? A plague?'

She imagined tiny feet scraping beneath the kitchen floor.

'It was a whole city of them down there.'

This, from Andy. And his voice had positively deepened lately. Maybe it had dropped, with his other bits and pieces.

'Not only a city. A whole race of them. Big ones, small ones, baby ones . . .'

'The boys had fun, chasing them. But I have to say, Andy, I hope you never touched one of them—'

'With my boot, only. I tried catching them, but Jesus, they were fast.'

'Andy—' Jim remonstrated. And Eileen had to admit, he did give excellent example.

'What?'

'Jesus has nothing to do with rats.'

'No?'

'And I know we don't go to Mass, but there are people who do.'

'Oh. I see.'

'Good. So, back to the rats.'

'Each time a tree came down, they swarmed out—'

'Maybe that's it,' Jim enthused. 'A swarm of rats. We can check when we get back.'

'Check?'

'In the *OED*.'

'What's that?'

'Come on, son, you know what that is. Porcupine, portcullis, Portumna. The *Oxford English Dictionary*.'

And Eileen bit her lip as she walked. She hoped Andy's appetite for reading wouldn't sink and lose itself in this adolescent swamp, which she knew, instinctively, was approaching.

The swim, when they arrived at the shelter, was uneventful. She didn't have to worry about Andy in the men's since she could hear his father huffing and puffing his way through his ritual of disrobing. And when Andy emerged, skinny and light-footed, with the baggy swimming trunks she had bought for him in TK Maxx, she marvelled once more at how this element had entered her life. He had an elegance all of his own; he stood, ankle-deep in the water, with his free foot touching his knee, like a thin stork. And he sank that magical body slowly, the way he always had, one or two intakes of breath, then a rush of rapid strokes that took him far out into the centre of the bay. It was all she could do to keep up with him. But she did manage it, and soon they were both treading water, their backs to the great dockland derricks behind, their faces towards the string of cement shelters, where Jim was only now making his way into the water.

She turned, looked at her son's sleek head disappearing like a seal beneath the waves, and thought she should do her utmost to treasure moments like this. The more the boy grows into adulthood, the rarer they become.

14

DANY WENT TO SLEEP on the same mound of straw, wondering how the strangest things could seem so natural. The lion snoring gently behind the rusted bars, smelling of old fur and faraway toilets, like a tawny grandmother. Though he had no idea, he remembered thinking dimly, how grandmothers smelt. But he awoke then, minutes or hours later, and nothing in the trailer seemed natural at all. The lion smelt of acrid urine; its wheeze was the rumble of a savage beast. The pricking of dried grass on his cheeks, the scent of hay in his nostrils, the irritation down his spine, where the shards of whatever he'd slept on had gathered; all of it itched and none of it seemed right. He stood, and angled his back towards the metal handle of the doorway to scratch it at the places his fingers couldn't reach, and the lion shifted and the door creaked, and he realised his spine must have shifted the handle to whatever was the open notch.

He looked outside, at the oily, downtrodden grass, and felt a sudden pang of homesickness, as if a door to a lost memory had opened of its own accord. And as the lion's eye opened lazily he cracked the door open further. The door creaked, the way his own kitchen door at home once creaked. And the eye watching him had a dull certainty about it, as if the lioness grandmother knew about that kitchen door, saw in its inner eye the lozenged pattern of the tablecloth, the living room beyond, with the embers still burning in the fireplace. Does a lion have an inner eye? This one seemed to, an eye inside the eye that watched him now, that knew everything about him, as he put one foot on to the metal step outside and gently closed the door behind him and saw her eyelid close as well before the door handle clicked home.

Home. He was going home. This carnival adventure suddenly seemed like a dream to him, a dream from which he had now woken. And when Dany walked through the shuttered carnival, he had that half-awake feeling, that yawning stretch about his body, and he shivered, as if to dispel the admittedly pleasant dream he had been in. The sliver of moon above the pennant above the big top, a fox slinking between the empty alleyways. It had all of the transience of a dream, all of the unreality, all of the shimmering quality, dispersing now, with the mist around the caravans. The real him needed to be back where it always was, in the small bed beneath the dormer window, with the sweaty wheat-coloured pillow that he used to think of as his own.

For that was his plan now, to find his way home, back to that proper bedroom, to the mother with the flour-dusted apron that he missed as he would a missing limb. So if his plan was a return, why did he feel that he was running away from something already like a home? It was confusing, the pangs he felt, for a return and an exit, the image of a mother that drew him and of the moonlit carnival that he was somehow betraying by his leaving.

He ran when he came to the tangled grass before the lip of cement that divided the caravan fields of the Tuileries from the road. One slow car coughed down it, headlights illuminating the road before it like a melting cone. He ran past the car to the train tracks, since he knew the tracks would take him back towards the city centre, the river and somewhere beyond it, the northside suburb he had grown up in. A train ambled past him, a long clunk of orange and black, and he ran behind the last carriage, grabbed the metal buffer of the end, felt his hands slip in the grease around it, his shoes scuffing the gravel between the sleepers. He hauled himself up then and sat as the train gathered speed and the sleepers flashed by. Small squat grey buildings flew by, and then an empty station and more sagging concrete posts and chicken and razor wire, and then an abandoned baths, a Victorian pier reaching out to curve its granite arm around the sea and another empty station, and he realised he was seeing the city he had lived in from another perspective, the perspective of a speeding goods train. Then came the vertical and angled hawsers of the bridge across the river; he had only ever seen it as a tunnel of rusted metal that his mother or his father drove through and here he was inside its armature, as the towering cage of girders thundered above. If she missed him the way he missed her she must be hurting terribly, he realised. And he felt another pang of guilt, of panic. He thought of his father, working the carpentry bench alone, saying, 'It's all right, love, I'm sure he'll turn up,' as if he were a set of car keys that had unaccountably gone missing. He saw his mother's hands pushing the buttons on the phone, making call after call to his round of friends. And his friends, what about them? Did they notice his absence in their forays through that bank of daffodils that led to the scum-covered artificial lake? He saw his feet dangling over the railway sleepers flashing beneath them and he wondered would they be kicking a ball again tomorrow, against the cement wall behind the cul-de-sac, or would he be confined to his room.

The train stopped at a level crossing and he took the opportunity to reacquaint his feet with the gravelly ground between the sleepers. It felt strange and weighty somehow to be walking once more and as he was getting used to the feeling the train pulled off again, too quickly for him to scutch back on.

So he clambered down to the roadside below and he knew where he was immediately: not in his street, not in his suburb, but in the suburbs that led to his street, through identical red-brick houses, a public park, a series of football pitches and the last one, across the roadway from the bungalow with the privet hedges.

He walked. Past the tangled shadows of old beech trees, down a long avenue, across small forests of bamboo and holly, to a bus stop, by a row of small bungalows along a road that descended towards the sea.

And there it was: his house. There was no moon above it, just the brown clouds of the night, lit by an orange glow from the city beyond. He knew every feature of it, every detail of it, like a toy house that he had built with a carpentry set and inside this toy house was another carpentry set in the tiny garage through the window of which he was gazing now. He could see all of the details inside, the Cortina beside the worktable and he could even imagine the patch of oil below it, where the sump wouldn't stop leaking, but they were the features of somebody else's house now, a house he knew intimately without knowing why. And he climbed on the garage roof then, walked over it to the dormer window and looked inside his bedroom and suddenly knew, or remembered, why. Why he knew it so well and why it couldn't ever be his house again. Because there he was, beneath the canvas-coloured coverlet he had chosen himself, sleeping in his own bed as if the boy outside, fingers clutching the cement windowsill, toes stretched upwards to get a better look, was being dreamed by the boy, fast asleep on the bed inside.

Did it make sense to him? No. And he knew, somehow, standing on the tar and gravel surface of the garage roof, a surface that he had helped his father clad the roof in, with much bubbling of tar and asphalt and a sulphurous smell that the masks over both of their faces couldn't quite dispel, that nothing would ever make proper sense again. He was sleeping inside on his wheaten-coloured pillow, and he was standing outside on the garage roof. The wind was by now scudding clouds over the waning moon. One of them was an interloper and he didn't know which. One of them was unreal, and the other wasn't. One of them could even have been part of the other's dream, or nightmare, but if he was being dreamed by the sleeping head inside his bedroom window, why did the goosebumps covering his arms and hands feel real, why did he shiver in the cold wind coming from the neighbour's yard? And suddenly his home felt most unhomely to him. It was someone else's home, no longer his. He felt a vast ache inside him for a home of his own, any home, and he jumped, in one supple move, from the garage roof on to the grass below, and began to run, blindly, in the direction of the carnival he had left.

He ran past endless cement shelters that he seemed to remember, past dockland derricks that reflected in the sea waters below them, over the metal bridge that he had crossed in the train, and he ran then alongside the same tracks, with a power and a force he never knew he had before, as if he was running from something he could never again think of, talk of, or truly imagine. He found himself back at the unkempt fields of the Tuileries before the sun came up and followed the creaking sound of an old rusting metal container door and crept back inside.

15

IT HAD BEEN A pleasant enough day, all in all, she thought, lying beside the sleeping mound of her husband. And with any luck, tomorrow might be just as good. But she had woken, suddenly, in that godawful time of night that could have been ten minutes after your head touched the pillow, or ten minutes before dawn. So she lay there, fretting, praying for that blessed wash of oblivion, her only trouble being that she never knew when it would come. The least small sound, the tiniest of distractions, and sleep would be a forlorn hope for her, without the help maybe of a couple of Kalms, or in the worst of circumstances, a Stilnoct. And she could hear something now, behind the soughing rise and fall of her husband's breath. It was a banging, gentle maybe, but loud enough to keep her awake if she didn't investigate its source. So she rose, and wrapped her dressing gown round her and edged the door open. The hallway was quiet, as was the kitchen, so it must be from Andy's bedroom, the one facing the cherry tree on the lawns, with the football pitch across the road from them. God forbid it would keep him, like her, awake.

So she climbed the stairs softly, opened his bedroom door and could see the curtains blowing from there, and hear the rhythmic banging of the loosened window, like the introductory beats before one of those metal tracks he played so often. She walked quietly through, careful not to wake him, and it was only after her feet had touched the patch the streetlight left on the carpet that she turned, realising there were no sounds from his bed. There were no sounds, because there was no one in his bed. She turned in panic, back to the window, and was about to pull it closed when she saw a figure, through the gently blowing curtains, at the far-off goal of the football pitch, making a stark silhouette against the dawn sky, where the beech trees once had been. So it was almost morning. It shouldn't have been, but it was. And there was her son Andy, in the hour before dawn. Alone, vanishing from sight now, down the slope towards the waste ground and the sea.

He had slipped out, of course. Opened the window for some adventure in the dark wood beyond the pitch and the waste ground below it. Through some arrangement with his friends, maybe, or perhaps, God forbid, a girl. All behaviour to be expected; age-appropriate, as the developmental books said.

But still. And here she was moving back down the stairs, towards the hall. She wouldn't wake Jim: he had to work in the morning. But still. There were strange men in the park beyond. And a night-time woodland was a place to be feared. She remembered the childhood legends about the Taw Wood and knew none of them would dare to approach it, let alone enter into it at night. So she opened the door and walked in her bare feet across the street, through the line of sad poplar trees that divided the street from the football pitch. A neighbour could see her, maybe even the early-morning driver of the 30 bus, but she didn't care. If something was wrong, and her common sense told her nothing was, but if something was wrong, she had to know. She could feel the dewy grass beneath her feet now, and was amazed it felt so fresh, so natural and good. And maybe it was a girl he was meeting, a local girl, and she thought of notes exchanged and text messages and she felt wistful, and a little sad, at the thought of both of them lying in the same damp grass. He could catch cold, she thought, as she passed the goalpost and made it to the rougher, uncultivated grass beyond. Where the discarded cider bottles and the Heineken cans resided. And she felt something rustling past her bare feet and knew she should take care, as some of this glass was broken. She looked down and saw brown shapes burrowing through the grass. There was one, followed by another, then another. Rats, she realised, and almost screamed, but however terrified she was, she didn't want her son to hear it. And she needed to find him now, desperately, because something untoward was happening. Something not to do with calm moonlight, bare feet and dewy grasses. She walked to the edge of the lip of ground, where once she could have reached and touched the upper leaves of the now-vanished trees, and she looked down and saw them everywhere. Rats, scurrying down the broken slope, up from behind the upturned roots of the once-great beeches. Rats, displacing the earth in small flurries, as they squirmed down. Rats, advancing across the caterpillared tracks of the earthmover. They were returning home. And home was the great gaping wound beneath her, with the exposed tunnels the sycamore tree had once lived in. The huge root loomed above that hole, tendrils quivering in the night air. There was a boy sitting with his back to it, his feet idly swinging above the surging rats below. And that boy was her son.

'Andy,' she called, with a kind of chill, wondering did he need another name now.

'Mother,' he answered, as if his presence there was the most natural thing in the world.

'What are you doing, out like this?'

16

'DOES HE HAVE IT in him?' Virginie wondered aloud.

They were sitting in the awning of Virginie's caravan, their eyes shielded from the late-afternoon sun. He was playing football with the roustabouts now, before the evening rush and influx, and they could see him appear and disappear in the gaps between the tents as the ball took him hither and thither.

'*An bhuil an sult aige?*'

Had he got the stuff, the shine for it, the guts for it, the blood for it; there were many ways of asking the same question, all of them old, almost dead now, as it was so long since the question had been asked.

Mona didn't reply. It was so long since she'd dreamed of a child, she had almost forgotten what the want was like. And now there he was. A son, on the cusp of his teenage years, the down barely formed on his cheeks, with that lightness in his step, that way of pressing up his arches as he walked, as if he was stretching already to be airborne, to be higher than he was. There was a grace to him, like a gazelle, a sudden darting quality in the eyes and an exquisite sense of sadness, even loss, as if the full melancholy of the world would never be felt as strongly again. There are tears in the heart of things, she had heard once, a saying from long long ago, and Dany reminded her, almost painfully, of that phrase. She could never imagine bearing a child, the way women of the world were so anxious to do; the weight of another in her precious stomach, the blood pulsing, the pushing, then the mewling infant that hungered for the breast. No, her breasts were her own, always had been, always would be. But the arrival of a fully fledged son was a gift too perfect not to grasp, to keep, to have and to hold.

'Will he have the shine for it?' Mona repeated the question now and wondered. Or would he be thrown into that all-too-human panic by the knowledge, when it came?

'That depends,' Virginie hazarded.

'On what?' murmured Mona.

'On what he's made of.'

'Only that?'

'And on how he hears it. All at once, or in bite-sized stories.'

'Like Bible stories?'

'Kind of. If there was a carnie bible that we all could agree on.'

'Good luck.'

'In the beginning, kind of thing.'

'No one agrees on the beginning.'

'But we all agree, there was a beginning.'

'We do that, because we have to.'

'Bad cess to the beginning then. Take it back to the Hunger.'

'That did change things.'

And yes, they both thought, and for a long summer moment they had the rare carnie pleasure of sharing the same thought, the same long surmise, turning round in their minds like a daydreaming apple, the Hunger did change things. After that, nothing was ever the same.

They could do that Bible trick with it, BC and AC. BH and AH. Before the Hunger and After the Hunger.

In the BH times they had been the stuff of legend, myth and fairy tale; they had hardly needed a name, so many names were thrust upon them. Ghoul, pooka, gnome, fairy, golem, banshee, nymph and dryad; the list goes on. Any hint that there was a separate race, living and breathing amongst the mortal ones, was covered by a fiction, a tale of otherworldly wonder and horror that was given the status of legend, remembered, retold, but hardly ever invented. So they cloaked themselves happily in these absurd tales, went about their lives, collecting their precious spices, were content to let any sighting be attributed to whatever legend fitted, golem, pooka, troll or banshee. In fact they were never averse to playing along; when a crop went bad or the milk turned sour or a drunken farmer happened upon one of them, at night on the lonely road home, or by a moonlit graveyard, they inhabited the legends and in time the legends inhabited them. There was a word for it, Mona remembered, a complicated word, that her Dany, with his predilection for many-syllabled words, would probably know: symbiosis. In fact there was a theory among the original carnies that they invented the legends, even propagated them, to explain their presence, but that was one too far-fetched for Mona.

But then the Hunger came and changed things. Changed everything, in fact. It was the carnie biblical flood, the great rupture, after which nothing would ever be the same again. With the deaths, the scattering, the coffin ships, the half-living ones blown like useless chaff so far beyond their homeland, the legends, inevitably, faded and died. And they were scattered in turn, without the cornucopia of myths and legends to hide behind. They hid themselves instead in sideshows, circuses and fairgrounds, stages on which wonders, monstrosities of height and girth, death-defying balancing acts, feats of inhuman strength and contortion would be seen to be the norm. The gravitationless ones had to pretend to be earthbound, to be obeying all of the tiresome Newtonian laws. Their feats of impossible torque and balance had to be seen to be, just as the term implied, feats.

He flies through the air
With the greatest of ease
That daring young man
On the flying trapeze.

And so the carnival began and the term carnie came, and stuck. Mona slowed her passage through the air to catch one more trapeze handle. Virginie teetered on the pole balanced on Monniker's ample chin when she could have simply stood. Dorothea murmured platitudes about dark strangers and government men and pretended she didn't see every detail of the future in the glass bowl beneath her painted fingers.

Mona rose now and walked through the channel of stalls to the roustabout game and, as she stepped through it, caught the ball on one angled back heel, tossed it from head to toe and back again, and as the ball made one parabola, she made another, twirled into a cartwheel kick and made the ball soar towards her Dany, who headed it into the space between the orange-painted trailers that the roustabouts called the goal. There was an ironic roustie cheer, and she bowed and walked on.

She made her way through the zigzagging maze of the trailers to the rusting door that Dany had lately thought of as home.

She opened it and saw the dust wheeling in the evening sunlight. The lion padded backwards and forwards beyond the bars, on the other side. There was hardly a need for those rusting bars, she thought, as this lion was beyond anything now but dreaming. And she lay down in the mound of hay that must have been her Dany's bed, because it still held something of his shape. And of that sweet adolescent smell too, she realised. A young boy's sweat, stronger than the odour of new-mown grass. She nudged her head against the old lion's mane, looked into those yellow eyes and again asked the question. Does he have it in him?

The lion soughed gently and seemed to think he had.

17

SHE HAD THE CAR to herself the next afternoon, since Jim would take the train to a conference in Drogheda, so she asked Andy did he want to visit the Roebuck Centre.

'The what?' he asked.

'The whaddya kids call it – new mall.'

'What mall?' he asked her and once again she wondered what universe he'd gone to. What kid doesn't want to know about the new Starbucks with the whipped-cream lattes, the 3D screens, the shining escalators, and for a moment she was transfixed by an image of one, a glittering silver thing, ascending into some heaven or descending into hell.

'The Roebuck Centre,' she repeated. 'We were on our way there when we got diverted by the carnival. The one with the new cinema. Sixteen screens.'

So she drove with Andy, but her real intention was to revisit those carnival fields. She had a knot in her stomach as she drove, a feeling of dread. She remembered the clown with the painted face, calling out, last chance to see Lydia on the high wire, rattling his half-empty plastic bucket. She could see the neon sign against the late-summer sun, somebody's amazing Hall of Mirrors, and she tried again to remember whose. She asked Andy, beside her, as she drove across the river, 'What was the name, love, of that Hall of Mirrors?', and he shrugged, as if nothing could be less important.

'Where are we going?' he asked her, as the Pigeon House sped by.

'I have to pull by the carnival,' she said.

'Why?' he asked.

'I might have lost something there,' she lied.

'What?' he asked, and she invented a story.

Why she was inventing it, she had no idea. Other than that to reveal the true purpose of her journey would have been impossible for her. She came up with a tale of a ride they had both taken while their darling son was in the Hall of Mirrors. One of those whirling things that turned you upside down, which she had always dreaded, and now she knew why. Because Jim's wallet and coins had tumbled from his pocket, along with his membership card to the Lions Club. And while they had retrieved the wallet and coins from the grass underneath after the ride, they hadn't noticed the missing card until later.

'The Lions Club,' Andy repeated.

'Yes,' she lied, and blushed, realising she had no idea what a Lions Club was. She had been invited to a dinner-dance once, on behalf of it, but had no idea what the club was, or did.

'And you think they might have it?'

'Why not?' she said brightly. 'Even a carnival has to have a lost and found.'

So she drove back with him towards where the carnival had been, behind the large industrial container park behind the train tracks. She sat in the car by the level crossing as another train trundled by, and waited until the barrier was lifted and then drove through the tiny streets behind, but she could hear no cries of mock terror and delight and she could see no pennant fluttering above the tiled roofs, so she already knew, before they reached the fields behind the container park, with the crushed grass and the muddied tyre tracks, that the carnival was over, here, at least.

'It's moved on,' she said.

'That's what carnivals do,' the boy said. 'They move on.'

'I wonder where?' she asked him, abstractedly, walking round the muddied field, wondering how he knew so much about carnivals.

'Does it matter?' he asked.

'No,' she answered, 'I suppose it doesn't.' But she knew inside that it did. It mattered hugely, and she didn't know why. She felt such a sense of loss, in that crushed field, that she reached out and gripped his hand. She noticed a crane or a heron picking its way through the muddied pools the carnival lorries had left behind. And he pulled his hand away, out of natural embarrassment, and she had to remind herself that he was no longer a child; he had become this thing, this adolescent stranger, and if there was a moment where the change became apparent, that moment had been here.

'Clothes,' she said, absurdly, 'you're growing so fast. We must get you some clothes.'

'In the Roebuck Centre?'

'TK Maxx.'

So she drove towards the centre, which, for a time, seemed even more elusive than the missing carnival. A gaudy shopping sign led her one way, then a road sign another, and eventually it loomed up before them in the windscreen, so unexpectedly that she almost missed the turn. She drove in hard then, through another barrier into an underground car park with separate caverns painted orange, green, blue and red, and she parked in one of them, took a series of escalators upwards into a gleaming interior and found herself among crowds of adolescents, a little older than him, but in their air of removal, abstraction, in their constant glances at the glowing screens of their telephones, just like him. It was a communal virus, she realised, that came upon beloved children suddenly, removed them from whatever emotional realm they had inhabited, with no hint that they might ever return. So she did what mothers all around her seemed to be doing: she bought him things. A pair of jeans that would accommodate his stretching limbs, a dozen T-shirts with incomprehensible slogans printed on them, a pair of new, gunmetal-grey pyjamas, since his old ones, with the grinning dinosaurs, were part of a vanishing childhood. And afterwards they ate hamburgers in a neon-lit American-style diner, before heading back to the car park, and home.

She paid her ticket, and realised she had no idea where her car was. And she understood, too late, the significance of the caverns of red, green, orange and blue. One was meant to memorise them, the colour and the number, and she was lost now, in a colour-coded maze.

He walked away from her without a word. Down a pathway banded with orange, down a small slope, which headed down a curving slope to another level. She watched him go, clutching her purchases, sweating and angry at him, shopping malls, car parks, everything. 'Andy!' she shouted, and he replied, 'Just follow me.' So she followed, and saw the orange band give way to a band of red, then a band of green, then in another level below, to a band of blue. He stopped by a number, 7,462, and there was her car, behind a concrete post.

'You have to remember these things,' he said, 'Mother.'

'Of course,' she said, wondering how he did. 'I do, and I will.' She drove out again, hearing her tyres squeal on the rubberised surface of the car park. She knew she should be thankful, that one of them remembered. But once again, she missed the term 'Mum'.

'Burleigh,' the boy said, at dinner that night. Jim had cooked it, coming home earlier than both of them.

'Burleigh who?' Jim asked, his mouth half-full of spaghetti.

'Burleigh's Amazing Hall of Mirrors,' the boy said, and forked some bolognaise sauce on to his pasta.

'We went back to the carnival,' Eileen told him.

'To look for your—'

'But it was gone,' Eileen interrupted.

'That's what carnivals do,' the boy said. 'They move on.'

'So we went to the Roebuck Centre, instead.'

'Ah,' her husband murmured. 'Where we were headed, the first day.'

'Yes,' she said. 'I bought him jeans and T-shirts and—'

'We got lost in the car park,' the boy said.

'And if it wasn't for you, we'd still be there . . .'

The boy stood later in his darkened room. He could hear voices from his small room above. He knew the voices were discussing him. He knew it was true. If it wasn't for him, they would still be there. Wandering through the car park, looking for a lost Cortina. Or locked into a giant carnival arm, in some endless gravitationless swing. The only light came from a streetlamp through the soft window curtains, from a lamppost across the L-shaped garden beyond. There was a threadbare rope tied to a leafless tree, a rickety bird hut on a pole and the ochre-coloured roof of another bungalow beyond the privet hedge. How alone he felt, how estranged from everything that should have made him feel at home. A vast turbulence inside of him, the turbulence of waves, slapping off against each other, reflecting each other's ceaseless movement, in broken infinite shards that never seemed to settle into a circle or a curve, that peaked and troughed and went on forever. He was Burleigh's triumph, Burleigh's creation, even, and was made of stuff that even he, when he would come into his full and awful glory, could never have imagined: the Rotterdam gold that gleamed somewhere within him, that enabled that dreadful and final separation of reflector from reflected. He was someone else, he felt, as he brushed something with his toe from the carpet beneath him and recognised the remnants of mud and rat shit from some nights before. He stepped out of his clothes, pulled on his new pyjamas and dropped his old clothes on his reflector's old pyjamas, and the dinosaurs grinned up at him, reflecting some childish world that he should have known. He felt a shiver, and wondered did others of his age feel like that. As if they were someone else, someone they didn't know; they were growing towards a shape, a definition of themselves that they would only recognise when they met it, in some distant future. And the future is always distant, he realised; tomorrow morning could well be a tomorrow two years hence, since neither of them had yet arrived. But one thing he did know. There was something out there that he would recognise when he finally met it. Some shape, some destiny, some avatar that would be familiar, instantly knowable as his own. But for the moment, he was this thing, whatever it was. This boy, and his name was Andy.

He pulled the curtains over the streetlights, crawled into bed and tried to lose himself in someone else's dreams.

He dreamt of his thumb, severed. It was severed very neatly, with very little evidence of blood, and as to who had severed it, he had no idea. But he dreamt he woke, then, in that bungalow, which seemed stranger than ever to him in his dream, and walked from his bedroom to the living room where the gauze curtains looked out on the front garden with the privet hedge and the bus stop, the streetlamp beside it surrounded by a penumbra of mist that seemed absent from the street below. The streetlamp alone gave evidence of the mist that he knew cast its pall over everything: the football pitch beyond, the ancient beech trees (they were still there) beyond the far goalpost, the cherry tree in the garden with its circle of absent lawn around it. Everything was absence, he knew, and only the mist gave the illusion of presence. He also knew that the cherry tree that had been planted on the day of his, or someone's, birth, would one day lie on that lawn severed, like his severed thumb. He saw his bloodied father, the loose skin clinging to his face like some badly made Frankenstein's monster, digging methodically where the cherry-tree roots once were. There was another father inside his father, a far more urgent, primal one that had coated himself in his father's bloodied pelt like an otherworldly breath that needed a human skin. The mouth opened as if it had just learned speech and the whole of human history was compressed into the words that came out. But there was a dissonance behind the words that thrilled the boy's soul. It was an echo from an infinite well. It was a sonic boom, across time. And there was a screech of tyres then and his mother was backing the Cortina towards them both. He reached out with his hand and lost his thumb in the knuckle of the rear-view mirror. And he was looking at his thumbless hand now, wondering where the pain should be.

And he wondered then, had he ever truly woken up?

18

DANY MADE HIS DEBUT on 14 September 2016, or on carnie day 347,683, year 166. But to call it a debut is to imply a glamour that was hardly there, given that the audience consisted of fourteen random families and a raucous party of seven-year-olds. The carnies didn't seem to mind. Did carnivals always have circuses attached? he wondered, as he walked through a warren of stalls towards the fluttering pennant of the big top. A circus was one thing, he remembered from what he was already beginning to think of as his distant childhood, and a carnival another. But it made sense, he supposed, given that the carnie personnel could double from one to the other. And as the daytime business of the carnival wound down, the night-time business of the circus wound up, so to speak. He allowed Mona to lead him through the maze of haphazard carnival attractions, the old gabardine coat wrapped round her circus garb. They had dressed him, Mona and Virginie, in a kind of glittering boiler suit, a one-piece that zipped right up to his Adam's apple. He had cringed with embarrassment at first, until Mona led him back through Burleigh's Hall of Mirrors and he felt a shiver of déjà vu, entering the mirrored womb where it all began. He saw the long and the short of himself, the squat and the thin, the multiple reflections of himself, and he had to agree with her that it didn't look bad at all. And a costume was essential, some kind of costume since it was a show, after all, and a glittering boiler suit could well be the best option – much better, he felt, than the body-hugging leotards that the gymnasts wore. They were involved, he saw, as they entered the dark tent with their acrobatics and their tumbles, in quite amazing feats of physical agility and each time they arched their backs to take a bow, he could see the pitiful protuberances between their legs, like ballet dancers in a version of *Swan Lake* he had seen on television, and he muttered a silent prayer of thanks that he had been spared embarrassment like that. So when his time came, after Alaister the clown had exhausted the peals of laughter he could wring from the children, he didn't feel too bad at all in his choice of costume. He followed Mona out to a drumroll, was surprised by the glare of a spotlight from above, and, to the sound of Piertro's mournful trumpet, began the strange business of pulling her to the heavens.

He pulled and she soared, though at times her upwards trajectory seemed to burn his fingers with the rope. And his hands did feel scalded, as if he was bringing them too close to a secret flame, something that burnt white-hot, with none of the attendant colours flame seemed to need to go about its business – pale orange, red, yellow and that flickering, fluttering blue. No, she was propelled upwards by some mysterious inner heat, the way a fragile piece of ash rose with its own displacement of the air around it and somehow retained the shape of the page or the scrap of paper it had once been. Thoughts like this turbined around his brain as he worked that rope. His mind became a veritable tumble-dryer, one image whirling, cascading downwards and wrapping itself around another thought that had barely begun its flutter towards clarity. All the time her legs, jutting out above him in their fishnet tights, one forming a V at the knee of the other, ascended from things that were thigh-strong and muscular into small, infinitely tender things, far far above him. And at this time he was glad of the bulky boiler suit; those feminine leotards would have given too much of him away. A drumroll then and he began to twirl. The rope bellied outwards into a cone or a gyre, which increased in its circumference the more she twirled above him. He thought of the devil stick again, of a heliotrope, and of a girl that he was in the habit of holding hands with, blowing a dandelion pod. She would blow towards him, he would blow back towards her, and the miniature feathered helicopters that flooded her face would bring a peal of laughter from her cherry-coloured lips. Then the drumroll ended and the rope went slack and he saw that Mona, far above him, had already gripped the trapeze bar and was carving delicate parabolas through the upper air. One of the leotarded ones had gripped another bar by the knees and was swinging towards her, arms outstretched. And Mona released her grip, made three backflips in the air, and gripped those same arms, so that this doubled creature doubled the momentum on the swinging trapeze. And another leotarded one had wrapped his knees around her first trapeze, begun a complementary swinging, and she was soon flipped, from one to the other and back again, like a pass-the-parcel in a birthday game. Would the music stop, he wondered, and would she be left up so far above him, frozen, like a fragile butterfly, pinioned by an invisible pin? Or would she fall to the sawdust down below, suddenly burdened by mass and weight and all of those bothersome Newtonian rules he had once learned about in his physics class? Then he realised, in a panic, that there was no net underneath her. If she did fall, some broken, bloodied thing would end up at his feet. Surely an aerial artiste needed a net? And he was resolving in his tumble-dryer of a brain to bring this issue up with her, when he saw the leotarded catcher farthest from him release her, flinging her towards the other pair of outstretched arms, which missed her own clutching hands, to a desperate gasp from the crowd below. She missed, but seemed unconcerned and continued on her trajectory, through the weightless air, tracing a parabola that seemed to defy gravity entirely, and ended up wrapping herself once more in the rope above him. It curled around her like an enveloping snake. The gasps turned to applause and she bowed her head, and he knew without being told that the display was over and it was his duty to bring her back to earth once more.

Which he did. The spotlight followed her downwards until it enveloped him as well in its circular glare. She took his hand, made two steps forward and began the business of what she had called the curtsy, the bow, the hand salaam. Which he did too.

Something changed after his first performance. Something subtle, barely noticeable, but yet something important, permanent and definite. If he was to compare it to something else – and comparisons to other things, he was beginning to realise, were often the only way to understand this carnival, this circus and these carnie folk – he would compare it to the secret understanding that the gang of boys in his cul-de-sac would have about a new arrival on their street. There would be an off-handed refusal to make eye-contact at first, then a ball that was kicked in his direction might one day be kicked back, and the moment would come, during a game of marbles or conkers or McKenzie's Raiders, when the new one was somehow 'in'. There would be no discussion about this fact, no secret handshake, just a common understanding that was palpable now amongst them. He felt the same, as the spotlight swung to another segment of the sawdust floor, as a team of jugglers whirled plates, a tea set and an assortment of wicked-looking knives in the air above them, and as Mona took his hand, led him through the darkness of the bleachers and back to the small canvas flap that opened to the night-time carnival outside.

'You did well,' she said, and then mysteriously added, 'Maybe you have it in you.' He felt a small glow of pleasure and gave her hand a sudden squeeze, and she then led him, as if she was a girl of his own age, or barely a year older than him, to the spinning bowl of a candyfloss machine, and asked the white-hatted operator to 'whirl him up one'. Now candyfloss was child's stuff to him, and he was certain it must be to her as well. He knew her looks told lies about her age; she was older than him, far older, yet somehow seemed of an age to wait, with delighted anticipation, for a 'whirl' of candyfloss. 'And make it spicy,' she said, to the white-hatted one, with a familiar wink. The thought of spice seemed odd to him, with its suggestions of pepper and salt; how would spice of any kind go with the whorl of pink sugar that was already assembling itself around the candyfloss stick? And the tumble-dryer took over his thoughts again, staring at the dull-green metal bowl around which the pink candy seemed to be materialising, as if out of nothing. It looked like the beginnings of clouds, like the flecks of pink wool he once found around a briar tree, and surmised it had been left there by a red-branded sheep. It looked like the dyed hair of a girl who wanted to seem to be a teenager, but didn't quite know how. It looked like the threads of his mother's pink scarf, hanging from the washing line, blowing in the early-spring wind. And with the thought of his mother, a rush of melancholy flooded him once more; he thought of her, standing here with him, watching the pink cloud assemble itself, impossibly upside down, around the thin lollipop stick held in the meaty hand with the smudged sleeves of a chef's coat and he knew, somehow, and with terrible certainty, that that could never now be.

'Here we go,' the flossman said, 'spicy as requested,' and Dany took the stick handle and brought the cloud of pink to his mouth and felt the sudden, overwhelming explosion of taste. It was more than taste, it was a whole world of sensation that pushed the thought of his mother to a distant horizon, where she seemed to perch, with her coloured handbag in her hand and her going-out coat blowing softly in the thermal breeze of whatever ocean she had been spun away to. And even though she was distant, barely a speck on that horizon, he could recognise every detail of her: the brown hair blowing in front of her grey eyes, the rather sad, lost smile that played upon her lips. 'I understand,' that smile seemed to say, 'everything is different now,' and he knew it was different; not only different, all of his feelings of loss and separation were manageable, because, for some mysterious reason, they had to be. Things were as they had to be and his mother sailed off as if she had grown sails that fluttered and billowed in those thermals, and soon she was not even a speck; she was gone, quite gone. Mona was leading him through the circus and carnival stalls towards the promenade, which was quite empty now, apart from night-time couples, most of whom were holding hands, and the others who huddled in the curved cement shelters, wrapped in their overcoats and their embraces.

'We should walk a little,' Mona told him. 'You've been through a lot.'

So he walked, relishing the candyfloss. It was gathering round the perimeters of his mouth in a kind of sticky paint, which would make kissing Mona, he realised, quite out of the question. And why the thought of kissing her popped into his head, he had no idea. Maybe it was those shadowed pairs they passed in the cement shelters. Or maybe it was floss itself, with its taste of something unfamiliar, quite at odds with the texture of spun sugar. It was the taste of something old, something that was beyond age, even, something that Mona knew everything about and that he knew nothing.

'But you'll learn, soon enough,' he heard her say and realised, since he was looking at it, trying to catch the fleeting thought of kissing it, that she hadn't moved her mouth.

'What will I learn?' he asked, aloud, since if there was a carnie talent of communicating without opening lips and tonguing syllables, he hadn't mastered it.

'Everything,' she said out loud this time, and he wondered had he imagined the earlier, silent communication.

'Or not quite everything,' she continued, 'since none of us know everything.'

Of course, he realised and didn't say, since it seemed unnecessary, none of us know everything; knowing everything is impossible and who would want that kind of knowledge anyway?

'And I don't mean everything in that sense,' she continued, just as if he had vocalised that thought. 'I mean everything about circuses and carnies and the original ones and the Land of Spices and—'

'The Land of Spices?' he asked, aloud this time. It was safer to vocalise things, he felt, since it saved him the confusion of trying to work out whether she had read his thoughts or not. He didn't like the idea of reading thoughts; in fact it made him blush to the roots of something, something way deeper than whatever was going on between his hips. And, besides, what mad world had he entered where reading thoughts was even a possibility.

He had finished the whorl of candyfloss now, and had licked the stick clean of its residue of pink, and dropped it in a nearby rubbish bin.

'You're finished?' she asked, and turned towards him, and he became aware of the night-time sea undulating behind her.

'You enjoyed?'

'Yes,' he told her, although enjoyment wouldn't really be his word for it. It had felt more like an explosive pop in his mouth, leaving a taste of something like cough syrup.

'You covered your face in pink,' she said, and licked her own fingers and began to wipe his cheeks clean.

'The spice,' she said, and licked her own finger then as if she didn't want to waste an atom of it.

'What is this spice?' he asked.

She smiled then, took his arm and led him towards the dark grassy slope beyond the promenade.

'Oh, it's nothing really, an old wives' tale, one of those stories nobody remembers where they came from—'

'One of those urban legends,' he said, and tried to think of some examples.

'That's it,' she said, 'the kind of thing one person heard from another that grows and changes beyond all recognition and nobody can claim in the end. Carnie folk,' she continued, and she mouthed the work 'folk' in an old-fashioned, deliberate way, 'can be full of superstitions. Because we move so much, so often, these scraps of stories come to seem like the only real home we have.'

'Home,' he said, 'as in house, place you came from, familial hearth,' and where the word 'hearth' had come from he had no idea, but it had the same resonance of her use of the word 'folk'.

'Exactly that,' she said, and slipped her arm through his and led him towards the darkness beyond the promenade lights. 'Where most folks have a memory of a place they come from, us poor carnies have a story. A whole raft of stories that keep changing, growing as they change, like a—'

'A bacteria,' he said. 'Or a protozoa. Binary fission.'

He had been good at biology at school, and school, he realised, was as distant a memory to him now as all of the others. And that was his tumble-dryer of a mind at work again; he had to stop this, he realised, and clarify his thoughts. But clarity didn't seem desirable at this particular moment; what was most desirable was the continuing conversation with her, which he didn't want to end.

'Something like that,' she said, 'where the real world has life, we have stories.'

'So tell me the story,' he asked her, 'of the Land of Spices.'

'The land of what?' she asked, and he felt a sudden abruptness in her tone, as if the road they were walking on had come to a hedge.

'Spice,' he said. 'You said there was spice in the candy-floss, you talked about the Land of Spices; in fact, I've heard the word on and off ever since I . . .'

'Ever since you what?' she asked.

And he had to think then. Ever since what? Since he got locked in that mirror, since her small, strong hands entered the cracked field of the glass and pulled him from it.

'Since you became part of the story?' she asked, and her gentle, rather inviting tone of voice had returned. He could listen to that voice for ever, he realised; he could sink into it, he could float around in it like a pair of silk stockings in a tumble-dryer; and he realised his thoughts had begun their tumbling again, and shook his head to clear it.

'You can be part of the story,' Mona was saying, 'and never know the whole of it. Do you think that Rumpelstiltskin, for example, or Snow White knew they were in a fairy tale?'

'I'm quite sure they didn't,' he said, but why he was quite sure, he wasn't certain, since the question didn't really make sense. And besides, fairy tales were children's stuff. Like candyfloss, he realised.

And once again, she iterated what he had just been thinking, so he wasn't certain he had spoken the thought or not.

'And don't you go saying these stories are just children's stuff, like candyfloss and twirligigs and why is the sky blue.'

Had he thought it, or had he actually said it? He couldn't be sure now, since he had thought of candyfloss and children's stuff, but twirligigs and blue skies hadn't come into it. He was suddenly so exhausted by the confusion that he felt the need to lie down.

'And if you want to lie down,' she said, 'I second that thought, and there's a mound of heather over here which we can sink into, if it doesn't turn out to be too scratchy.'

She seemed to know the terrain, even though the light was almost non-existent. Almost, because he could see her pale face and lips by the light of the half-moon above, and when she turned, to sink into what she already knew to be heather, he could see her figure silhouetted against the amber lights of the promenade and carnival below. Then she lay backwards, in one simple, supple move, and he was amazed by the fact that she didn't feel the need to use her arms to determine the lie of the land beneath her.

'Not scratchy at all,' she said, delightedly, he felt, 'in fact, just think of it as a cushion of moss.'

So he allowed himself to sink backwards and felt her arm guide his elbow downwards and sure enough was soon enveloped by a cushion of kinds, not prickly at all and with a delicious odour of heather.

'Now where were we,' she went on, as if their conversation had occupied a particular space, 'yes, how would

Rumpelstiltskin know if he was in a fairy tale; well he wouldn't and that's the point, because the story is only there to give him a kind of existence.'

'He has no existence,' countered Dany and felt proud of himself for engaging in such a conversation, 'since he is not really real.'

'So, Rumpelstiltskin isn't real?' she asked. 'What is he, then?'

'He's part of a story,' Dany said.

'And am I not part of a story, no more than you? In fact, how can you be sure that at this precise moment, your story is not being related by someone else, some time, in some place, some part of the present or future?'

'Well, I can't be,' Dany allowed. But the complexities of the thoughts were now tiring him, and he would soon, he realised, allow her anything.

'Those stars, for example,' she continued, and he wondered if Mona had been a teacher in a former life. But no, he realised, if she ever had a former life, and if former lives were admissible, she would have been very far from a teacher. 'Can you name some of them for me?'

He was happy to find himself on firmer ground. And the stars did seem unnaturally bright that evening, sitting in their canopy above the pale half-moon.

'Well, there's Orion's Belt, there, and the Pleiades across from it—'

'So there was someone called Orion who had a belt and some other one, long long ago, called that arrangement of stars after him?'

'Well, that was just a story they used before . . .'

'Before what?'

'Before Galileo invented the telescope, I imagine.'

He was quite proud of that. The Galileo reference and the rather superior 'I imagine'. His mind was slowing its tumble-drying and getting back to proper thinking business. But the heather beneath him still felt comfortable and the smell of pollen and purple and pods of all kinds was heady and delicious.

'But there was a story there before the telescope.'

'Well, they had to find some way of explaining things.'

'And the story was the easiest.'

'I suppose.'

'So when you look at those stars you think of the story.'

'But the story isn't necessary any longer.'

'It just hangs about, like a name no one has any use for.'

'I suppose.'

'So when you look at the night sky you're looking at a million, maybe a gazillion stories that people have forgotten?'

'Maybe.'

He was getting tired of the night sky, and the talk about it. He knew she was going somewhere, he knew she was going to win whatever the argument was, and he was almost on the point of forgetting what the argument was.

'So you're looking at a universe of lost stories. But there's no telescope to define them. There's no kind of astronomy to sort them out. They're wandering in their dark space, wondering why no one remembers them. All of the characters, the heroes and the villains, the lost princesses and the evil stepmothers and the changelings and the Rapunzels and the Rumpelstiltskins . . .'

'Stop,' he said. 'Please, you're confusing me.'

'I know,' she said, smiling. 'And my goodness, look—'

She leaned her face over his so he could feel her breath on his. And her breath smelt of heather.

'They're wrapping up the carnival.'

He turned, and saw that they were. The amazing sight of the takedown, almost in miniature, so high they were above it. The tent billowed downwards, like a deflating skirt. The roustabouts, the talls and the squats, were breaking up frames, folding lean-to shutters, crawling over the rollercoaster like ants, consuming it, so they took it to pieces as they moved. And Burleigh's Amazing Hall of Mirrors was becoming a dance of reflecting beams, as each piece of mirror was moved, catching the lights of the streetlamps above. The lorries began belching their exhaust pipes, shifting forwards and backwards, churning up the dried grass so the whole miniature spectacle became gradually dimmed by a pall of smoke.

'Would they leave without us?' he wondered aloud. And for an entrancing moment he relished that prospect. He could have happily spent the evening in that heather.

'Do you want to find out?'

She was already standing, brushing the tiny leaves from her gabardine coat.

He did, actually. He would have loved to find out. He would have loved to have arrived at the acres of crushed grass with just the odour of petrol fumes left, as evidence of the carnival and circus, long gone. He would have turned to her and said, 'We're walking home now.'

But he knew, as he saw the tiny spangled pumps she wore and the fishnet tights and the glitter of the body-hugging thing above them, that she wouldn't survive without it. She would wither and die, or maybe be condemned to wander in her own private darkness, the black hole of forgetting, like that Orion, whoever he was. She was a carnie, and had to make it back there. He knew this, but he didn't know how or why.

But whatever she was, she was his friend, he felt, descending from the gentle slope of dark hillside back towards the promenade and the rapidly diminishing carnival. It was amazing, he thought, how it telescoped into itself, as if its mode of expanding in the first place had its diminishment already built into it, programmed, so to speak. Huge structures folded, like three-dimensional geometric puzzles, into cuboids, anhedral octagonal blocks and strange geodesic pyramids that could be carried, manhandled by several roustabouts, the talls balancing the tangled structures with their elongated arms while the squats bore the weight on their broad shoulders. Pushed then, with much groaning and grab-a-hold-there-would-yous, up the retracted back panels of the waiting trailers. One massive heave after another, the cuboids, the anhedral and the octagonal and the geodesic pyramids were rolled into the gaping maw of the interior, snugly fitting together into a mysterious complicity as if volume and space were collapsing in on each other, no longer at odds, as if the hard-edged was becoming round and the angled, curved.

Could she be more than his friend? he wondered. He felt that strange attraction that he recognised but had never really known, and remembered walks along the wooden bridge with its massive barnacle-encrusted staves, vanishing into the dark water, the girl Georgie from the last but one bungalow at the cul-de-sac's end, her hand clutching his, as if the very pressure of her fingers on his palm signalled the beginning of a new adventure. He let Mona walk ahead of him then on the night-time promenade and saw the strength of her calves under the gabardine coat, the ancient litheness of her gait, and knew that no, that kind of adventure would never be theirs. So what was the attraction then, he wondered, what was this whorling in the pit of his stomach? He would discover in time, he hoped.

Would he make the grade, Mona wondered, or would he be thrown into that all-too-human panic by the knowledge, when it came? Had she snatched him from his loving mother – and Mona couldn't imagine her otherwise, couldn't imagine Dany giving rise to anything but love – only to be wrong-footed, forever waiting for the changeling to emerge? She thought of Walter then, the stillborn one that had followed Jude for two sad decades or more, appalled by his own body as it insisted on ageing. Walter the unfortunate.

She walked ahead of Dany, and felt his glance from behind. Did he have the thing, the sult, the shine? It was odd, she knew, to have Burleigh's Hall of Mirrors deliver them one last specimen, many years after its decommissioning. Burleigh's aims may have been true, but his design was far from perfect. It had delivered too many mutant variations; the talls and the squats turned out to be acceptable as roustabouts, but she shuddered, now, thinking of the variations in between. His banishment had been a long and painful episode, one of the many carnie memories that had to be banished in turn. But every dog has its day, she supposed, and it's a long road that has no turning, and out of every parched desert a flower can bloom. And he had the elegance, not so much of a flower as of the thin, almost too-delicate stem that bears it. It was a delicacy that could turn into strength, that could grow with surprising sinew, she felt this already, but would he, no matter how strong his development, have it in him? That might be for others to decide. Because she was already compromised, she knew, in her feelings; her hard carnie edge had been softened by his presence and the promise of his possibilities. So she waited while he caught up behind her, took his hand and as they stepped down from the promenade's edge to the flattened field beneath it and made their way towards the massed vehicles that were already, so to speak, uncircling their wagons. The billowing exhaust pipes could well have been the flaring nostrils of mythical horses, dragons, magical beasts of burden preparing to drag their mysterious load. He deserves better than a lion truck, she thought, and ran across the crushed grass, leapt up a set of aluminium steps, pulled open the side-door of a trailer, just as its tractor redoubled its exhausting roar. 'In here, Dany,' she said, and as the caravan began its trundling departure he ran to catch up with her outstretched hand, past the illustrated panels of the wonders that the trailers enclosed, a giant caterpillar that bore screaming minions on its hollowed spine, a screaming, distended mouth that promised entry to a ghost-train tunnel and an elegant, gilded horse with its mane blown back in a stiffened, golden whirl.

His hand reached hers and gripped and he felt all gravitational reality suddenly vanish. She pulled him up and inside and once more had the sense that he definitely had it in him.

Inside, they swayed for a moment in the darkness. Mona pulled shut the aluminium door, and in the ensuing gloom all he could distinguish was a small pipe glowing, like a shifting firefly. There was a smell in the air, like bitter almonds.

'Put it out,' whispered Mona, 'I've got the boy with me.'

'And welcome he is too,' a female voice murmured. He could hear a knocking as the pipe was extinguished, and he got the sense of a foot quenching the ensuing embers. The smell of something like burnt almonds was soon overpowered by the acrid flare of a match and a slowly yellowing oil lamp. He could see then, several hammocks gently swaying in the caravan-like space of the interior. Virginie lay in one, her long hair dangling backwards from the curve of the netted rope. The one he would come to know as Paganina swayed in the other, her bronze legs crossing the dark space between them. Her toes seemed to be caressing Virginie's crown, but when the lamp grew brighter, he saw they were pulling out strands of the brown hair, knotting them into delicate braids with a fluidity that astounded him. The toes he had known to date were never as dexterous. But he was tired now, and longed for a bed, and when Mona gestured him towards another hanging tangle of rope, he realised that it was a hammock and that this hammock was his. So he gripped the knotted rope at the top with both hands and twisted his body upwards, so it fitted inside. And he was amazed at how comfortable a hammock could prove itself to be. So what with the smell of burnt almonds and of the burning oil lamp and the soft murmur of voices below him and the gentle swaying of the convoy as it gathered speed, he was soon asleep.

19

DANY SLEPT THE SLEEP of angels, swaying backwards and forwards in the hammock with the movement of the convoy as it made its way through the mysterious night. The ache for the old home had gone and a strange new sense of belonging had replaced it. The gentle outbreaths of Paganina and Mona filled the air around him. They did nothing so vulgar as snore. They were wrapped in their own sleep, a spicy sleep with its dreams of millennia and aeons.

So when the convoy stopped and the boy staggered out to meet the pale dawn, he was well and truly rested. His dreams lost themselves in the memory of sleep, a sleep that was full, to which the new world outside presented a refreshing contrast.

He saw the convoy of vehicles around him making their odd figures of eight, separating one from the other, gouging their back wheels into the deep, oak-coloured earth. There was no grass here. There were just endless open fields of brown earth, nothing to break the horizon but large conical chimneys in the distance, and huge stacks of turf, at odd intervals, between them.

The carnival was already reassembling itself in this wasteland of manufactured bog. He was getting used to the process: the assemblage of the very large from the impossibly small.

He threw himself into the business, as if he had found his perfect space, his holiday from life. He was a runaway now, and he had run to here. To this strange field of dried earth, the cabins circling round it, in search of the perfect indentation, the soft bowl beneath the low hillock where those stanchions can be set, where the sideshow can unfold itself. And the roustabouts in their torn dungarees rousted about, guiding the mechanical wagons belching smoke and oil, their leather belts swinging with wrenches, clamps and vices, drills, pliers, sockets, ratchets, claw, tack and squirrel hammers, all of the tools necessary to reassemble this caravan of the unexpected that will expand, melodeon-like, into pleasure domes and ghost trains and whirligigs of manufactured terror.

And by mid-morning, with the sweat pouring off his naked torso and the hot sun turning his shoulders red, it was almost fully constructed. The small maze of haphazard stalls, the giant maw of the ghost train, the pennant of the big top looming above them, and the neon sign of Burleigh's Amazing Hall of Mirrors glittering uselessly in the early-afternoon sun. But above them all loomed those conical chimneys, far off, sending their volcanoes of industrial smoke into the blue sky above. His only question was, who would attend? Where would the punters come from, the families, to wander the stalls, buy their tickets to the multiple carnival delights, pay for the sticks of sugary candyfloss? There seemed to be no houses in this wasteland around them, not to talk of villages and towns. But then, to his further amazement, he saw figures were already trickling in. Rough-faced youths and children, boys mostly, dressed in tattered jeans and T-shirts, with scraps of torn cloth tied round their heads. Nut brown, all of them, as if they had emerged from the dried turf beneath their feet.

'Bogmen,' one of the squats muttered to him, proffering a half-smoked cigarette that Dany felt loath to accept. But accept it he did, as, again, it seemed to be expected of him. He inhaled and did his best not to cough, handed the butt back as soon as it seemed appropriate.

'Bogmen,' he repeated and tried to hide the fact that it was a question.

'They work the turf fields, sleep in the tents beyond the smokestacks. They have little enough to spend their money on.'

The flat turf desert hid its own inhabitants, it seemed. And Dany, now that his part in the assemblage seemed finished – it was difficult, if nigh impossible, he was realising, to know the beginning and end of certain tasks here – took an empty seat on the Big Wheel to get some better idea of the landscape all around him. And he was amazed to see, once it had taken him to the apex of its circle, that what he had thought to be empty bogland was in fact alive with lines of bent, labouring figures. All stripped to the waist, burnt brown by the punishing sun, feet awkwardly moving through the fields of already cut turf, assembling it into tidy stacks. Further off, huge rectangular vehicles moved, with long mechanical blades cutting whatever turf remained on the topsoil. They cleaved through the brown earth like a knife through butter, chopping it into rectangular sods, which would be assembled, he assumed, by the lines of bent bogmen into regulation stacks. Which would be ferried to the smokestacks beyond and burnt, to pollute the heavens and keep the earth below electrified. And for the first time he got the sense of what would become his abiding intuition. That the world outside the carnival was harsh, cruel, a saga of endurance from which the carnival alone provided some respite. He heard a huge, industrial horn blow; his chair began to curve below its apex. He could see the crowds below were thickening now, into what could well become a flood of visitors.

A riot, almost, as it turned out. They came from the empty, denuded fields, from whatever factories huddled beneath those smokestacks, with the brown stains of peat still on their hands and the smoke of industrial grime on their faces. Hair tied back with scraps of tattered cloth, queueing up to be thrilled by vertigo, appalled by gravity, terrified by darkness as the Big Wheel spun them upwards, the rollercoaster hurtled them downwards and the ghost train accepted them into its dark, unknowable maw. And to be tickled, after the sun went down, by the aimless tumbling of clowns, entranced by the sight of Paganina, balancing on a circus pony, her naked toes clutching its manicured mane, while the other leg arched upwards to bow the violin she held under her tilted chin; awed by the spectacle of Mona, ascending with too much ease on the rope he once more pulled. Peals of laughter, he found, were liberating, like a door opened to a fresh wind. But the inhaled breaths and the gasps of wonder were indicative of transports to quite a different realm. She seemed gravitationless again as she spun on his rope, sailed from trapeze to trapeze with no protective net beneath her. And she was gravitationless, he realised now, barely human, and had to remind herself to catch the arms of leotarded youth, swinging upside down on the trapeze bar, on the other side of the vertiginous top.

The laughter, the gasps of shock and awe, the gazes of rapture and enchantment, seemed more innocent out here, in this boggy wasteland, as if the wonder of quite another universe was being brought to their backwater. And as Dany watched them file out into the night, he heard phrases that could have been uttered more than a century before.

'Mighty.'

'A wonder.'

'A feckin' marvel.'

They made their way through the darkening stalls, with their freckled faces, their windswept hair, the girls with their kerchiefs tied at the back in a style that he found wonderfully, almost erotically foreign, and they gazed at him as if he was part of this thing they had paid for and been privileged to witness, but that would be forever foreign to them, this mighty, this marvel, this wonder, and he began to wonder himself – was he a carnie now?

He had dreamed of running away from home, when the tension in the household grew so fetid that he could hardly breathe. He had begun to think of this mood as he would of the weather and longed for a forecast that would warn him of it. But he had had no such mood barometer available to him and so only recognised the chill when it was already there. With it came the urge to run, to escape, to cross fields he had never seen before, touched with early-morning frost, to walk down a railway track that pointed to some far-off infinity. But he had always known that when the real weather began to work on him, when the night came down and the rain fell or the cold wind whipped up, he would find it impossible not to return. The thought of his mother's face, sad with its inexpressible anxiety, would have been too much. So he had never tried. He had listened to his father's tales of preserves and condiments yet to be invented and endured the huge silences between them. He had buried himself in his games: Dungeons and Dragons, Dwarf Fortress, Assassin's Creed.

And now here he was, in a carnival that no gamer could have dreamed. He listened to the retreating laughter from the brown fields beyond and the possibility of returning was just a dim flicker, barely moving inside of him. Whoever that boy had been, walking out with his parents from the infinite reflections of the mirror-maze, he was a perfect solution to what one could have called the Huckleberry urge. To escape, on a raft of hopes and dreams, on a river of the unknown. And even if he had allowed himself to be overtaken by that crippling sense of loss that he knew he had to keep at bay, he had no way back.

He was leaning against the metal scaffolding that bore the weight of the helter-skelter. He could hear a thin, scraping sound, like the chirp of grasshoppers. And it wasn't a chirp, he remembered from his days in school; it was a rustling, of their elongated legs against the armature of their bodies. He wandered inside then, following the sound, into the armature of the great beast above him. There was rust everywhere inside, on the old metal struts and scaffolding, the bolts and screws that held the groaning thing above together, with its lost screams of terror and its faded hurtling gasps. But there was more than rust; there were strange wafer-thin mushroomy growths, like the scabs that grow on an open wound. And one of the small, broad-shouldered roustabouts was scraping them off, with infinite care, into an ancient, cracked earthen vessel that should have belonged to a museum if it belonged anywhere.

'Do you collect them?' Dany barely raised his voice, afraid his breath might upset the delicate process.

'My job, my duty, my pleasure,' said the tiny one.

'Why?'

'Now that would be telling,' he replied. His voice was surprisingly deep for one of such tiny stature. It was as if the sound of a trumpet had erupted from a penny whistle.

'For cooking?' Dany hazarded.

'Now come on. Would you ever sink your teeth into this?'

And he held up something that looked like a flattened toadstool, squashed and mangled, that had been passed through the bowels of an extinct creature.

'Although,' the little one mused. And Dany figured then

that the less he said, the more chance he had of hearing.

'Although?' he echoed. Echoes were good, he had learned. These carnival folk had secrets to hide, but couldn't help talking. So direct questions got you nowhere, but good things come to all those who wait. 'There are other modes of consumption.'

He had a scalpel, shaped like a thin, curved Arabian dagger, with which he scraped the growth, whatever it was.

'Mildew,' he said, and handed Dany the implement, pulling another one from his roustabout belt.

'You can help if you want.'

So Dany began to scrape.

'Scraping away,' the little one half-whistled and half-muttered, between browning teeth. 'But don't lose a scratch of it.'

'A scratch?'

'A shiver. An atom. And you might need one of these.'

He held up another small, earthen vessel. Dany took it in his hands. It had a mouth like a tiny open trumpet, and a decoration of years – generations, it seemed – of miniature cracks.

'Mildew?' Dany asked. Again, the repetitive question seemed like the best mode of enquiry into this mystery, whatever it was.

'It has a different quality,' the roustabout continued, 'from the helter-skelter. Rough; some would say nutty. The ghost train, now, renders dollops of hard grain. The best mildew of all comes from the circus bleachers.'

'I work in the circus.'

'You do, bedad. Then you'll know what I mean.'

Dany nodded, as if he knew what he meant. But of course, he had no idea.

'The thinnest, the most refined. Which is why those circus folk can get above themselves betimes.'

'Aha.'

'But if it's quantity you're after, and quantity, let's face it, is what we carnies need, go for the rougher stuff.'

'Of course.'

'The squeals of fright, terror, the oh-my-God-I'm-falling feeling brings out the mildew in all of them. The ghost train now, that's a factory for the stuff. You would disagree, I'm sure.'

And Dany wasn't sure if agreement or disagreement would reveal more of this mystery to him, so he took the option of nodding in a non-committal kind of way. 'Refinement is all very well, but there are times when bulk is called for.'

They scraped for a while in companionable silence, and Dany's mind began its tumble-dryer movement again. Mildew. Fright. Terror.

'And there we go,' the roustabout said, with another toothy whistle. 'The helter-skelter can consider itself done.'

He ambled out then, and didn't have to bend as low as Dany, underneath the rusting struts. There was a harvest moon shining over the empty carnival. Where was Mona, Dany wondered, Virginie, Paginina, all of the artistes? But none of them seemed to be about. Moonlit emptiness. And then he heard it. More of that tiny scraping, as if from a field of crickets. He could see bowed shapes in the underneath of every carnival ride and structure, the same tiny bowls held aloft, the same curving scalpels doing their job.

'Nightwork,' the roustabout muttered, as if Dany shared the same knowledge as he. 'Much more delicate than daywork. But by no means unnecessary.'

By no means unnecessary. Dany considered repeating that, but it seemed too much of a mouthful.

'Why don't we try the big top?'

'Why not?' Dany asked again, and followed him past the shuttered stalls to what he imagined would be the empty sawdust floor.

'Laughter,' the roustabout murmured, as if he had to keep his voice low, 'delight and – what do you call it? wonder – give rise to the thin, refined mildew. Closest, some would have it, to the original spice.'

And Dany remembered the phrase 'the Land of Spices', and had the wisdom to keep his mouth shut.

'The wafery stuff, for the more refined amongst us, of which,' and he lifted the fallen flap of the circus tent here, gesturing Dany inside, 'I believe you might be one?'

Inside then, in the silent tent. The great pole, soaring up towards the darkened top. But not so silent after all, Dany realised then, since the same cicada-like scraping emanated from beneath every bleacher.

'Let me show you,' the roustabout whispered, and led him round the sawdust floor to where the bleachers raised themselves in serried rows. And beneath every wooden seat there hung wafer-thin strips of the same mildew. Of the same substance, indubitably, as the growth beneath the helter-skelter. But as the roustabout had intimated, so much more refined.

'Quite the harvest,' the roustabout muttered. 'And let us now join the circus scrape.'

The circus scrape turned out to be much more arduous. The long, thin strips of mildew had the substance and fragility of a communion wafer, but a wafer that had been shredded and drawn into something that had the lack of substance of a spider's web. Though there was a definite point of clinging at the top, a tiny bead of moisture that kept the diaphanous structure in place. And the trick, as he observed from the other roustabouts working beneath the bleachers, was to pass the scalpel delicately along the wood, above which child or bogman had sat, and cause, by a process almost as delicate as osmosis, the beads of moisture to cling instead to the curved scalpel, and to delicately drip the resultant harvest into the tiny vessel. Although drip was the wrong word in this context, since the mildew was moistureless; indeed it wafted in whatever breeze there was inside the big top, a wafting that made the harvesting all the more difficult. But Dany mastered the process, keeping a weather eye on the other harvesting roustabouts, the squats bent beneath the low bleachers and the talls stretching up their seemingly expandable arms to reach the highest. In fact, Dany realised, between the tall roustabouts and the squat roustabouts there should have been multiple other classifications, since some of these roustabouts were so small as to do their scraping under the bleachers nearest the sawdust, without any necessity of a hunched or bent back; in fact, standing upright, with the curved scalpel in their tiny, reaching hands. And some of them again were so tall as to stand stretched beneath the very highest bleachers, as if the very act of stretching and of scraping had provided the necessary elongation of their roustabout form. Mysterious, he thought, and felt his mind tumble-drying again, but he had to stop himself trying to work the mystery out, since the mildew scraping needed all of his concentration.

His tiny bowl was soon full. Could it fit more, if he squashed the harvested mildew down? He had barely formed this thought when his trumpet-voiced roustabout companion answered it for him.

'Of course it could.'

But Dany found his finger could barely fit in the conical, earthenware mouth.

'And no need for squashing either. Just give the little bleeder a shake.'

So Dany shook. And the gossamer-like substance he had harvested fell gradually to the bottom, as if to the bottom of a very deep well. He sighed then with exhaustion, as he put his scalpel to work once more on the fronds of mildew hanging from the bleachers above his crouched head.

'What's that sigh about?'

'What sigh?' said Dany, irritated now, since even his private emotions seemed to be shared by this harvesting companion.

'I heard a sigh. Did anyone else hear a sigh?'

And scraping was suspended for a moment in that strange, beneath-the-bleachers amphitheatre. Every one of them, tall and squat, elongated and miniature, had heard a sigh.

'A wheeze.'

'More like a moan.'

'Sighing's not on. One thing about the harvest, it won't stand the sigh. The moan.'

The roustabouts in general seemed to concur.

'The groan.'

'The whine.'

'The sough of despond.'

'And other forms of complaint more pernicious—'

'Deleterious—'

'More capricious—'

'Meretricious—'

'And if not done with capernosity and function, is it worth doing at all?'

The question remained unanswered. And Dany, as he wisely decided against any riposte, remembered the word for such a question. A rhetorical question. They enjoyed their multiple-syllable words, these roustabouts, and might have relished that one. But he kept it to himself, for another day, or another harvesting night. He sensed, somewhere inside himself, that there might be many of them to come. So he continued with his methodical scraping of the hanging stuff that they called mildew, into the tiny receptacle which, it seemed to him now, might possibly never be filled.

But it was filled, eventually. And as he wandered through the canvas entrance, into the hesitant roseate glimmers of another day, he felt an almost mechanical tiredness overtaking his limbs. He dropped his earthenware jar and his curved scalpel into one of the many wheelbarrows that were ringed in a semicircle on the brown, heavily trodden earth and made his way back to his sleeping quarters. He could hear a roustabout harvest song echoing through the sleeping carnival, as they too made their way to their roustabout hammocks.

'Your hay is mowed
Your harvest reaped
Your barrows full
Your trailers heaped
The mildew's jarred
The spice is hard
And the rousties gone to sleep.'

He would do well to learn it, he imagined, as he opened the trailer door, crept silently between the two hammocked figures, gripped the web of his own ropy bed and pulled himself up.

20

MONA, OF COURSE, HEARD him enter. She heard the rustle of his hammock, the soft wheeze as sleep took him over and the odour of harvested mildew filled the cabin. She knew that smell and she wished him well with it.

The spice, the gum, the glue, the sap, the resin, the mildew, whatever the correct word for it, and there was, in the end, no proper word for it. There were things before there were words for them; there was emotion before the mildew; there was the void before there were things to fill it; there was the gasp before the void and the gasp filled it. The gasp was the breath and the breath was the mildew and the mildew was the spice and the spice just was.

She would one day have to tell him all she knew. But then, as she lay there in her unrocking hammock, what did she know? The mildew was, she knew or thought she knew, the only remnant of the breath that made them. Why it congealed in those wafer-thin, undulating fungal layers of stuff, as if one had spun a mushroom or a toadstool in those drums that spun the candyfloss, she could never tell. Perhaps carnies knew once, but the race itself has been spun so many ways – mingled with the snatched and the changed, not to talk about the cousin and mongrel carnies from other parts – that if they knew, they had long ago forgotten. So, like most of the rules and rituals that governed their lives, it was left unexplained and all that was left was the habit, the need to harvest it wherever it gathered, and it gathered in the strangest places. Beneath the bleachers and the circus stalls, underneath the rollercoaster, in the floors of the ghost-train cars and like a fine-spun spider's web around the pole that kept the big top afloat. They all knew that laughter, terror, shock and fear and awe and joy – emotion, in a word, human emotion – left the mildew as its residue, which is why, in effect, the carnival existed. But how to explain its presence under the table on which Dorothea read her fortunes, clinging, like a diaphanous web of furred parchment, to the dragon claws of the table legs? And how to explain Virginie, who would wake some mornings covered in it? Was it because Virginie dreamed sometimes, with such astonishing intensity, of the Land of Spices? The only remnants of those dreams would be the webbish accretions of the mildew that clung to her naked body, wrapping her like a cocoon to the hammock beneath her? She would ring the small bell that hung from the rope above her and Mona would gather her ancient bowl and brush and harvest that precious gossamer of mildew while the coffee boiled. And having gathered each atom of the sacred crop, they would sometimes spice their coffee with a few filched strands of it, which undulated in the brown liquid before they finally disappeared.

Maybe Virginie should tell him, instruct him in the carnie mysteries, since Virginie knew more. But then they were changelings, both of them. Mona's inductor – her mother, in effect – was an original and could have enlightened her before the Fatigue took hold. And she herself had that carnie idiom of talking in evasions, diversions, stories that entranced and enchanted, but the enchantment took over and the point, if point there was, was never arrived at, let alone explained. Why they had to hide their essential natures, why so much had to be forgotten, erased, hidden in webs of obscurity, why clarity was a vice, never a virtue, why things were as they were. To know nothing, to her, seemed to be the sweetest thing. And carnies, on their best days, seemed to relish knowing nothing. On their worst, they knew some great reality had to be hidden, some truth that itched them like a scab they knew they should not scratch, lest the wound beneath revealed itself. As if to live, it was necessary to forget. But all of that they did, and here was the rub, was a form of remembering.

Ursula, the only mother Mona remembered, her carnie original, who always seemed younger than her, with a never-ending spring in her step, woke up one day tired. The Fatigue, she answered, when Mona questioned what was wrong, and if anything was to be explained to her it should have been that. But no, the Fatigue, like most carnie things, just was. And if there was one memory Mona wished she could erase, it was the memory of her stepping off that cliff into the churning seas below. The body that fell was as young as it always had been, but the body that plunged through the water and was tossed back up, only minutes later, was that of an ancient, wizened crone. As if age had been kept in abeyance and would only take its tribute when the Fatigue took hold.

She had gone, Mona knew, to the Land of Spices. That place that carnies sometimes dreamed of, always whispered of as a place of return, when the Fatigue took over, a homecoming, which didn't make sense, since none of them, even the originals, could ever claim to have been there. Even Jude, Jude who could well be the last original, with no memory of anything other than a carnie life; Jude only knew of it as a rumour, the ghost of someone else's memory, familiar to her only from occasional dreams, or from whatever tinctures of the mildew she allowed herself. And Jude remembered as far back as the first scattering, long before the Hunger, when the Adzed Heads came over the Eastern Sea with their hollow-headed cloaks and their curved staffs. They chanted false religion, as the carnie lore went, sat on stones facing east, with their cries of amen. So be it. And so it was, as the old world turned grey with their chanting and the new, disenchanted world took over. So the Fatigue claimed, not one, not several, but whole clans of carnies and they took the leap that legend had it would bring them back to where they had once belonged, their Land of Spices. It was a communal Fatigue that Jude described and Mona could only imagine the terror, having seen just one take the leap. Whole swathes of her kind, with their perfect bodies, walked to the edge of that huge, curved cliff and didn't hesitate at the sight of the churning western waters so far beneath.

One by one they stepped off the cliff and consigned themselves to the waves. They knew what awaited them once they had pierced the water; the sudden splash, the rush of foam, the explosion of brine up the sinuses and then life would hit them, make a kind of return, with all of its delayed anger intact. The years, which had been waiting, like those coiled dimensions string theorists go on about, exploded inside them in a pure rush of interrupted time, compacted into microseconds, and old age withered them before their downward plummet had been interrupted by the brine. And Jude, on the cliffs above, who had neither the courage nor the inclination to take the leap, suddenly knew that carnie life was what she would learn to call, many centuries later, an oxymoron; it was life suspended, with all of those inchoate longings held in check. She saw body after body bob up in the uncaring foam; ancient, twisted, convulsed by more years than any human had to ever live through. And she hoped against hope that their carnie selves had made it to the promised Land of Spices.

But of that Land of Spices, even she had no memory. It was one of those rumours, heard about so often, told of in tales round a rath or a fireside and of late round a carnival bonfire, that one felt one knew, one felt one should know, one never thought or dreamed of questioning. In her dreams she seemed to know it, and she couldn't deny her dreams. Nor could she deny the mildew that all their carnival delights and terrors gave rise to in humans. They left it behind them, quite blissfully unaware of their leavings, like snails leaving a gossamer trail. They didn't need it, carnies did. And if carnies harvested it, carnies gathered it, carnies hoarded it in their ancient carnie jars and left in tribute at the sacred places on the sacred equinoxes, surely there must be a land that was worthy of all of this spice? Jude was the oldest, and perhaps her memory was faulty. And how could the others, the half- and quarter-blood ones who over generations attained pure carnie characteristics, the changelings, the snatched and the thatched; how could they deny a homeland which they were told was theirs but which none of them had ever directly experienced? But what none of them could deny was the effect of it, the heady odour, the rush and the transport back to somewhere which should have been, must have been, and must still be. When they imbibed, inhaled, tasted on their carnie tongues on the ritual occasions allowed (and on those odd times they indulged in an illicit tincture), they could glimpse the hazy outline of their lost paradise. The mildew did things to them, the purified spice did more, so the Land of Spices, by that strange logic, surely had to be?

Mona breathed deeply then, into the odour of mildew the boy had brought with him and felt herself falling back, once more, into a delicious, familiar dream. She must explain things to him, she thought, as the warp of sleep took her over. She remembered Walter, the wannabe

21

SCHOOL WAS COMING UP. The long summer was approaching an end. But the weather was still hot; Eileen relished her walks along the wooden bridge, down from the sprawling suburb and the grid of bungalows beside the football pitch. Andy's friends were returning too, from whatever summer pleasure grounds their families had dragged them to. She had a strange shock of recognition when she encountered a group of them on the corner of Bayview Avenue. They had grown, their shoulders were hunched, their faces leaner and browner. It was reassuring, in a way, to think that whatever changes the onset of adolescence had wrought in him, he was not alone. They were all of them growing up.

The girls, too. The differences in the girls were, if anything, more severe, more pronounced, more flamboyantly displayed. Some returning with tans that seemed to boast of hours spent on beaches in hotter climes, though they could well have been bought, Eileen surmised, over the counter. An almost orange glow came from their faces, their exposed midriffs, their long legs and their painted toenails, peeking out from that fashionable oxymoron, sandalled high heels. She remembered transformations from her own schooldays. Luxuriant hair cut into punkish spikes, ripped jeans and safety pins and piercings. But they at least had the virtue of ersatz rebellion: the Clash, the

Ramones, Iggy Pop and 'I Wanna Be Your Dog'. It had to be better than this Barbie-doll aesthetic.

She passed Carmen then, by the chip shop adjacent to the bridge, and saw, with grim satisfaction and a hint of regret, the transformation in her. The same fake tan, Oompa Loompa orange. With one significant difference. Carmen was smoking.

'Hello, Mrs Rackard. Is Andy about?'

Carmen had the grace to attempt a desultory concealment of the cigarette behind her spandex tube of a dress.

'You've been away, Carmen?' Eileen asked. She had liked Carmen in her prepubescent childhood, and hoped she would still like her, under the force of this current transformation. But, she thought, and felt a little guilty at the supposition, Carmen and Andy had always been close, like brother and sister, in a way, and Carmen might provide some map to the changes evident in her son.

'Gorey,' she said, 'then two weeks in Majorca.'

'Lucky you,' said Eileen. 'And Andy's around. I'm sure you'll bump into him. He'll be glad you're all back.'

'Tell him I was—' but her next words were lost in a flurry of wind from the sea and the squawk of a seagull, foraging after a discarded bag of chips. Eileen presumed the words were 'asking for him', or something like them, and smiled, nodding her farewell, not before she noticed Carmen's high-heeled sandal, propping itself against the red-bricked wall behind her, the better to display, Eileen supposed, that long expanse of suntanned thigh to the passing world. So it goes, Eileen thought, as she crossed the Clontarf Road towards the bridge; it's as if some strange creature had taken root inside them. Some second self, all muscular silences and hunched shoulders, and in the case of the girls, exposed navels and enhanced cleavages. Or something in the water, she mused, after discarding her clothes in the cement shelter, taking a few languorous strokes through the bay, towards the horizon line and the Pigeon House towers. She wondered what it would be like, in her lazy, water-dreaming way, to keep swimming, to leave all of her concerns, her almost mute son and her inattentive husband to themselves in that bungalow bound by the oppressive privet hedge, like a figure in a movie; that's what they would do, keep swimming and leave it all behind. They would find her clothes, her summer skirt and her flat heels and construct a mystery around it, to do with adultery and emptied bank accounts, sallow strangers she may have been meeting in city-centre cafés. And all the time the simplest of solutions would be staring them in the face, but never occur to any of them, least of all to her shellshocked, caring husband Jim, whose only relief from his ever-present grief would now be his carpentry table in the back garage and condiment samples. That she had just kept swimming, all the way to Wales. How long would it take to reach Wales, she wondered, and at what random stretch of beach would she finally walk ashore, the water cleaving from her frozen flesh like one of those models in bodywash commercials? Something beginning with Llan, she thought, Llandudno, Llangollen, pronounced with a 'C', for some reason, like Clan. Then she turned and was hit by a wave of panic, realising how far out she was. She took a deep breath to calm herself, and thought, slow down, Eileen, less of the dramatics, and if that hyperventilating panic takes over, just float for a while. And she saw them then, two figures on the cement walkway that led to the long spit of sand that was Bull Island. He was walking, hands in his pockets, shoulders bent forwards as if avoiding a question she had just asked. And she held one of his hands, buried in his own pocket, the slut. The girl's legs looked even longer from her watery vantage point; there was a bank of grey clouds building up behind the hill of Howth which lent a dramatic backdrop to their silhouetted figures. Eileen was calmer now, and began the long swim back. She saw their figures vanish as they headed towards the dunes. One breaststroke after another, she thought, and if you get out of breath again, just tread water. As if some strange creature had taken root inside them, she thought again. But how would it take root? And she imagined then a conger eel, sliding between her own thighs, taking root inside her. A small one, like a grass snake, before it had developed those loathsome teeth and those greyish gills. She had heard it could happen; all sorts of odd things take residence under the skin, the fingernails, the hair, the nostrils, the ears, the mouth. Any orifice could act as a conduit, offering a host to the invader. And the word invader made her mind wander again, from conger eels and grass snakes to Viking sails on the horizon; they were the first invaders, before the English, weren't they, or were there others before them? The Tuatha de Danaan, the Firbolgs, lost in the grey mists of time. Fairview Park, Jim had told her, was where the Battle of Clontarf happened, Sitric the Viking cleaving Brian Boru with his broadsword. When he was kneeling, at prayers, she remembered. And there were other swimmers puffing around her now; she was closer to the shore and the panic was gone. She began a traversing stroke then, in close reach of the shore. She would loll here for a time, in the water that wasn't quite warm, but that had lost the cold bite after the long summer. Was loll the right word? she wondered. One didn't loll in the water, one gambolled. Or one cleaved through it, like that muscular creature that passed her, with a steady, mechanical stroke, broad shoulders and a blue swimcap, heading back towards the concrete steps. He steadied himself at the lowest step underwater and rose then, himself like a Viking, broad, sculpted shoulders and a narrow, hour-glass waist. Men have smaller hips, she reminded herself, and continued her lolling or gambolling movement, enjoying the spectacle, as he headed back towards the dark shadow the sun threw in the men's cement shelter. So close to the women's, yet so far away. He pulled his trunks off, in one fluid, busy movement, and she saw the flash of nakedness before he drew the towel round him. A bronzed body, with two white buns for bum cheeks. And she couldn't help comparing the spectacle with her husband Jim. The long white underwear he favoured, and the braces, since he couldn't stand any pressure across his stomach. His tummy, as he called it. She had to widen the girth of each of his trousers, and wondered would this widening have to go on, as his girth continued its bloom. It probably would, she concluded. It would expand into the shape of a pear or one of those lemons that made his lemon curd and his entire wardrobe would have to expand with it.

home, any home, a carnival home being obviously preferable to the cold halls of Clifton College, from whence he had fled. He became a fixture of kinds and Jude, being kind, became a sort of mother to him. So to call him one of the snatched would be to Jude a disservice, since, if anything, he had attached himself – like a limpet, like a mollusc, like a tick that burrows under the skin and feeds on what it can find there – generally blood – to Jude, to the carnival, and the carnie thing. And being of a bookish bent, this Walter began to catalogue everything he found there. The cataloguing process began, oddly enough, with Jude's navel. Or, to be more precise, with Jude's lack of one. How he discovered this lack remained unexplained and, carnies being reticent types, reluctant to enquire into embarrassing matters, never really asked. Did he see her naked at her toilette, her still-lithe body that needed the same care and nurturing as a young nineteen-year-old, and notice the flat, taut, unbuttoned expanse of her stomach? Or did Jude allow his boyish fingers to play across the same surface? Did he take a peek at night, as Jude's chemise fell free in her hammock, with Jude herself in the arms of Morpheus, or, more likely, wrapped in the embrace of mildew? However it happened, he found that Jude lacked what most people had: a belly button, a navel, any evidence of attachment to one who would have given birth to her. And so his enquiries began. With the first fact, so to speak. Jude, one of the last of the originals (possibly, he was to hazard later, the last) of the Ur carnies, the unsnatched, the unchanged. She was born, apparently, of nothing. And the question began to plague him. What was that nothing? If there was no womb, no amniotic fluid, what was there? A primeval slime, a cluster of gas, even, and as his enquiries progressed, he began to think this was closer to the truth, a carnie Garden of

Eden? Jude turned out to be the last one to answer such questions. But so began his enquiries into carnie nature and reality. And while this enterprise was to remain unfinished, he had a clear sense of it himself before it all went sideways. It was to take the shape of a treatise, a summa, if you will, which he himself considered calling, rather pretentiously, but given his minor-public-school background, not surprisingly, *De Rerum Carnivalis*. He struggled mightily over several years with this tome, hindered by the intractable fact that carnies themselves were the most unreliable of narrators. So he began with one pivotal supposition, obvious, unoriginal, but impossible to deny: that carnies knew little of themselves. In fact, the more they knew of themselves, the more they had to unknow. Thus carnie dialogue, which he called, variously, cant, Shelta, argot, klang, was constituted almost entirely of elisions, evasions, obscuranticisms, hints that assumed they were understood but were designed to be impenetrable, whole cornucopias of allegory and fable that never came to a conclusion or a point. For them, understanding was a form of occlusion. Now these were heady concepts for a young boy, but at least he had a grounding in classics, and Walter saw himself as a chronicler of kinds, almost medieval, of this strange breed he had happened among. His chronicle would create sense where now there was nonsense. It would be a carnie bible, a grand, heraldic, genealogical saga, among other things. It would, and this would eventually lead to his undoing, let in the light. And carnies, as he saw it, badly needed 'light'. Anytime they approached clarity, they breathed on the mirror of sense and made it nonsense once more.

Which led to Walter's second supposition: carnies needed to know little of themselves. There was an interiority to carnie existence that would be an enigma to humans. For them, knowledge and experience could never be separate. Moment by moment, they knew. Not for them the emotional event, the reflection on it, and the getting of wisdom, be it in the long maturation of subsequent thought, or the blinding, sudden, clarifying 'epiphany'. Their very being, their experience of the world, was epiphany, and for them thought, language, metaphor, culture, was an escape from that fact. They saw something clearly, too clearly, by the mere fact of their existence. And this clarity was only made bearable by the evasions, the digressions, the fables they created to occlude it.

Now these are hardly the reflections of a runaway from the junior form of a minor public school. No, they are the thoughts of a mature, unbearably lonely chronicler, unmoored from his natural habitat, attached and obsessed by a brood that never quite welcomed him into its bosom. Walter followed the carnival in all of its peregrinations between two world wars, and found himself beset by an issue that never affected them: ageing. Which led to his third, and some would say, most critical supposition: carnies experienced time in a radically different way. In fact, one could argue they hardly experienced time at all. For them time was a mangled circle, a balloon twisted into a donkey shape, a series of interconnecting doughnuts to be prodded, licked, tasted, but never consumed.

Now Walter's treatise, being unfinished and unpublished, only ever existed in scrawls on school copybooks; half-developed theories, various attempts at thesis without any antithesis and nary a hint of synthesis. But his scribbled queries and annotated insights provide invaluable hints as to the broader realities that Dany found himself confronted with. And Dany, given the sad outcome of the Walter saga, should consider himself lucky. The questions he asked were internal, acceptant and without any hint of intrusion. When answers were offered, he accepted them; when the demands of natural logic were contradicted, he allowed the tumble-dryer in his mind begin its job. Contradictions, in a word, didn't bother him too much and he was already halfway to being a carnie, one of the changed, a condition and a consummation that was denied to the unfortunate Walter. Or Walter the Unfortunate, as he perhaps should be known. For while carnies don't mind a question, an enquiry, the odd probe into what we could call their psyche, what they cannot stand is the persistent niggle. The vain and foolhardy, and, not to put too fine a point on it, impossible urge to 'let in the light'. Carnies lived in light. And so as the years passed, as the caravan moved, from Scunthorpe to Liverpool to Blackpool, to Hull on the Humber, over the North Sea to Rotterdam, through the countless capitals of the remains of the Austro-Hungarian and Ottoman Empires, back to the waste ground in the shadow of the huge derricks on the River Clyde, from Stranraer to Belfast and the shadow of a whole new set of derricks, Walter found himself gradually excluded. And with his exclusion came premature ageing, in a grotesque contrast to the agelessness of what he had come to regard as his subjects. Thus it was a stooped, grey-haired thirty-two-year-old who crossed the cobbled train tracks outside the gates of Harland and Wolff and was blown to bits by the Luftwaffe raid of 6 April 1941. The carnival felt the ground shake, saw the sky ablaze and buried its head for the evening. It travelled west the next day, towards Coleraine and Londonderry. It only noticed Walter's absence on its journey south, several weeks later. It presumed he had found some avenue of enquiry more forthcoming than carnies. The shipyard builders, maybe, in Harland and Wolff. Then it forgot about Walter. He

23

EILEEN COULDN'T HAVE BEEN sure how long she spent in that shelter after her mid-morning swim. She had sunbathed for a while, making a cushion for her head from her towel, letting the sun do the job the towel should have done. She had then draped the towel over her bare shoulders and shared a flask of coffee, offered to her by one of the old-timers in the men's section.

'You immersed the corpus,' he said, the kind of statement that didn't need a reply.

'Nothing like it,' he added and she saw the Viking, now clothed in one of those Velcro bicycle suits, fixing a helmet, awkwardly, to his cropped head. Oh dear, she thought. How disenchanting. And she realised, with a whimsical, inner smile, that her husband Jim would never be seen dead in leisurewear. Small mercies.

It must have been a while, though. A good half an hour, at least, maybe even an hour. Long enough for that dreadful thing to happen, whatever it was, on the dunes behind. Anyway, after her thanks to the old-timer for the coffee, after peeling off her swimsuit underneath her towel, after dressing and drying her hair into what she hoped was a fetching tangle, she finally emerged from the shelter to see the figure of a girl staggering from the sandy dunes on to the cement pathway, one heel on her sandal broken, her body covered in patches of damp sand, and what seemed to be a personal cloud of midges swirling round her head.

For a moment Eileen thought she was wearing a veil, or a hijab, one of those Muslim headscarves. But then she recognised Carmen, who was swatting the air desperately with her hands, hands that had visible streaks of blood on them, as if to ward off an attack of bees, or hornets.

'Carmen!' she called, and saw her turn, eyes wide with a strange kind of horror.

'No,' Carmen was saying, 'Oh God—'

Carmen staggered then, and almost tripped over one of the cement blocks designed to stop the cars. Eileen reached out and gripped her elbow to steady her.

'His fucking mother – get away from me—'

And that's when Eileen heard it. The buzzing, or the pulsing, like the intermittent drone of cicadas in a horror movie. But they weren't cicadas, they were midges, or some kind of flying ants, and Carmen was flailing with her bloodied hands at her own barely visible cloud. She ran then, tripping on her broken heels, towards the bridge beyond, crashing into a cyclist on the way. It was the velcroed swimmer with the hourglass waist. Eileen turned from the splayed bike and the clacking heels to see the silhouetted figure of her Andy, walking from the dunes.

There were many rumours, afterwards, about what had happened. About a clinch, an adolescent embrace on the dunes, that turned into 'something else'. But what this something else might have been changed in the telling, as in one of those courtroom dramas, where the victim herself is the least reliable of narrators, where the trauma suffered leads to exaggerated fantasies that create other traumas in turn. It didn't help that as the legends blossomed, the infestation of flying ants began.

'What's wrong with Carmen?' Eileen had asked, when her son finally reached her, only to be shocked into silence by his terse reply.

'How would I know?'

'Something happened, Andy. You have to tell me—'

'Nothing happened, Mother. She just doesn't like me – did she ever?'

Was that a question? Eileen wondered. Surely he would have known, would have remembered. She took his arm, as they crossed the wooden bridge, and remembered passing them both on the same walkway as children. There was a dusting of sand all over his shirt. She brushed it off. She saw a flutter then, from the folds of the cotton, and realised it wasn't sand. It was tiny, winged creatures, like ants. She felt them brush against her face, and rubbed her face, her hair; she felt an itching in her scalp and shook her head, looked up and saw a cloud of them around her, like fine, Saharan sand, blown in the summer wind, but it wasn't sand, it was an infestation of those winged things, filling the air, all glittering in the late-morning sun. She felt afraid, suddenly, the hyperventilating surge of panic she had felt out in the water, and wanted to cling to his arm for comfort, but then she realised she felt afraid of that too. She took a deep breath and realised she was inhaling them, and almost gagged on the dark sleepers of the walkway, beneath her feet.

And as the rumours circulated in the small grid of bungalowed streets adjacent to the football pitch, the clouds of flying ants circulated as well. There were reports on the news, something about Mediterranean winds and alates, females that create a sexual attraction, bringing the males in swarms, creating clouds that block the sun and moon. For they swarmed at night too and after them came flocks of seagulls, gorging on the swarms of flying ants.

Carmen avoided her glance in the subsequent days. Brushing her face to clear it of the clouds of tiny predators, mouthing a cigarette, turning to the chip-shop window to manage a light, out of the persistent breeze. Andy stayed locked in his room, watching the piles of dead creatures build against his windowpane like blown sand. And Eileen, on the few occasions she ventured outside, felt shunned. Something had happened on the dunes. No one would tell her what it was. Neighbours would cross the street ahead of her, as if she herself had brought this strange infestation with her. And one evening when she entered his bedroom and saw him standing by the open window, enveloped in a dark cloud of minuscule flying creatures, she knew that, somehow, he had.

What had happened on the dunes, as Carmen confided to Georgie, Georgie who had once been Andy's friend before all the mad stuff began, was that a simple snog or shift became something different, something other, something way beyond what the American TV shows called first, second or third base, what the local boys called a wear, a feel, a ride.

Carmen lay beside him first of all in the long grass and offered up her lips for a kiss. She has learned things on her summer holidays that she wants to teach him. How to kiss with her mouth open, how to tangle her legs around his, how to press her hips into his and get things moving. She learned this from a Protestant boy in Kilrush who walked her down by a different set of dunes. The boy had a packet of condoms, but she never let him get that far. And she had just begun her instruction here in the Dollymount dunes when she felt something stroking the stocking of her leg. She had been careful about those socks, rolled them down behind her knees, just so, and when she felt fingers rumpling the edge of one of them and creasing the skin behind she smiled to herself and whispered, 'Where did you learn that?' He answered, 'Nowhere in particular,' and she thought to herself, saucy, saucy as the stroke of the fingers continued upward, underneath the flap of the kilted skirt she was wearing, and she thought, oh dear oh dear, no Protestant boy ever got that far, and she tries to remember a song her father used to sing about Protestant boys and an old orange flute and she felt another touch then, around her blouse on the right side, probing beneath the summer bra she was wearing for the nipple, and another on the left side, and he was all hands suddenly; she wondered how many hands a boy could have to find a way to nuzzle closer and saw when she opened her eyes, that they were not hands but creatures, creatures she didn't have a name for, furred creatures, with ears like probing brown-haired fingers, and she pulled her face away from his then, so rapidly she almost bit his tongue, and she saw a larger one between her outstretched knees, staring at her, the same colour as the sedge grass behind it, its brown furred ears erect, as if surprised by suddenness. And she remembered the name then, hare, a hare, this was the father of hares and the tiny furred family were burrowing all around her. As if she was the earth, she thought, to be probed, tunnelled, penetrated. 'Get me out of here, Andy,' she murmured and that was when she heard the buzzing. Of tiny things like ants, obscuring the hares in a wave of wings and she pushed him off and stood and the hares leapt – that was the only word for it, leapt – like a surprised phalanx of furred spears, and they ran, obscured by the clouds of flying ants. And she knew then something was wrong, very wrong, but she couldn't put her finger on what.

24

WALTER'S CODEX. OR AS Mona knew it, Walter's collection of dog-eared copybooks. Where were they now, Mona wondered, when another boy might have need of them? And how odd that one so obsessed with histories and genealogies, Edens lost and found, should have let them vanish into thin air. Had they been vaporised with him, in those bombs they were told fell on the Harland and Wolff shipyards? Probably. And she remembered him then, intoning some kind of nursery rhyme, as he scribbled.

> Of man's first disobedience and the fruit
> Of that forbidden tree whose mortal taste
> Brought death into the world and all our woe . . .

An odd kind of doggerel that didn't even properly rhyme. But she had no knowledge of Walter before the carnival took him, sitting at his oak and iron desk, turning the pages of *Paradise Lost* with his cane-rapped fingers. And she had no sense of the crucial insight he gleaned from those pages.

There was an Eden from which carnies fell. A mirror of the biblical one, and as with mirrors, the question once more arises, what was the real and what was the reflected? And Walter the Unfortunate would have it that we cannot be sure.

Was it a paradise as we would understand it? Walter demurs. He knows there was trouble in paradise, there was a flight, but was it a flight from or towards? And here we have to allow Walter another crucial insight: it was both.

Everything was doubled in this carnie hermeneutic. The flight was from and towards, it was a flight and a fall, it was a fall and an airborne exodus; the feathered wings that bore them were burnt in turn, by the flight, the fall, the scattering; the air that welcomed them singed them and changed them for ever.

He describes little of this paradise, for which we must be grateful, as prelapsarian descriptions can border on the tedious. There simply was a place, a state, a paradise. He tries out a string of names, Avalon, Hy-Brasil, Tír na nÓg, but settles on the one that carnies favoured, the Land of Spices. And here Walter allows himself some relief from Miltonic bombast, into the quieter measures of George Herbert:

> Softness, and peace, and joy, and love, and bliss,
> Exalted manna, gladness of the best,
> Heaven in ordinary, man well dressed,
> The milky way, the bird of paradise,
> Church bells beyond the stars heard, the soul's blood,
> The land of spices; something understood.

. . .'something understood'. It should have been enough for him, but of course it wasn't. It might have been enough for carnies, but not for Walter. He will elaborate, annotate, elucidate. How the spice was the essence of the mildew, how the carnies fed on it. How the Mildewmen consumed the unrefined mildew from the furred roots of the caverns they inhabited, how consumption became the order of their paradise, how the Land of Spices became the Land of Few Remaining Spices, how the Dewmen emerged from their loamy places with their hoary mouths and their mouldering teeth and asked for more, and more was not forthcoming and battle commenced in the Land of Spices. And on a day without any sun and moon, without any light at all but the glow of decaying mildew, the carnies as a genus, as a race, a species, fled.

It began as a flight, but became a fall.

The fall. Walter describes the fall. He grows rhapsodic, as if the very idea of descent releases something in him. It was like the waft of autumn leaves, the slow collapse of the deciduous cover on the sycamore trees around the cricket and football pitches of the public school he ran from. Like the delicious downward drift of those pink cherry blossoms on the front avenue he could see through the library window, hoping against hope that his parents would soon drive down it. But the cherry blossoms fell silently, never in autumn, in the late spring, a diaphanous downward undulation that carpeted the dull, mud-coloured grass of the front lawns in a blaze of pink. Pink, like the rose-coloured Bentley that always promised to arrive, bearing his mother in the rear; pink, like the kisses she planted on the occasional letters she remembered to write. The fall was magical and brief, and left the dark etchings of the cherry-tree branches isolated against the April sky. And the carpet of pink told a story that he could never bear to think of ending, because the story was about life, about how beautiful things could be and how fragile was the life of those beautiful things. So the carnies, he imagined, fell to earth in the way of those cherry blossoms.

But before the fall there was the flight, with a whizz-bang fury of propulsive escape, with a noise, a thunderclap, a sonic boom that shattered their universe and the arrows of the Dewmen that pursued each one of them created its own terrifying roar. These projectiles were hooked and spiked and taloned, and forged of the metallurgy of the Land of Spices, every lamppost, every crom rath, every gold- or silver-mirrored surface, every vein of ore, all of those hunched and blasted statues so beloved of the mildewed ones having been melted in the boiling pot of their dewless fury for that very purpose. But the carnies outflew them; singed almost to nothing by their speed of flight, they crossed the dimensional barrier and floated to earth, like beautiful burnt blossoms, almost like faeries, indeed, their singed wings outspread, guiding their fall, the last feathers of which were burnt to nothingness by the time their feet touched the surface they would come to call home. And the arrows that followed them melted as they met the atmosphere and fell to earth as molten drops, so for a moment, if anyone had cared to view it, it would have seemed the heavens were weeping tears of melted gold. And this residue from the Land of Spices touched the turfy earth and sizzled its way downwards, to make its home among the ancient fallen oaks, the dead bog-dwellers with their leathery skin and inert limbs and the slithering things that fed on them.

So the carnie flight was from, and towards. From the paradise that was no longer theirs, towards the cold world of sin and death, where they had to survive as wingless ones. Where they searched for the mildew spice and found none. Until one day a carnie made a child laugh (unintentionally, Walter adds, since carnies up to then didn't know they were funny) and that carnie found a tiny furred residue on the branch the child had leant upon. More a gossamer than a residue, an echoing web left by the child's ringing peal of laughter. This carnie smelt the mildew and knew that it was good. The carnie wove a tale then, of joy and wonder, and more children gathered, and with each outpouring of wonder and joy the mildew grew and so the circus was born and then the carnival and the carnies made it their lot to trade in emotions, of wonder, laughter, terror, joy, and to harvest their payment in spice. They left their denuded paradise to Mildewmen, whom they hoped against hope could never take the journey they did. But what if they somehow managed? Then the carnies put their faith in their gravitational freedom, knowing that they were creatures of the air; Mildewmen, on the other hand, being creatures of roots and bark and everything that grows upon them. And so superstition was born. The magpie, the owl, the moonless night, the milk soured, the egg gone rotten, the cowless calf, the number thirteen all became emblems (metaphors, Walter adds, sagely) of that carnie fear: that the Mildewmen would somehow manage that flight to their new-found home. And so the carnies paid the unseen race of Mildewmen a ritual tribute, a kind of talismanic tithe. They gathered the excess spices in ancient jars and at intervals, decided by the movement of the sun and moon, they left the Mildewmen their spicy luckpenny. Spring, summer, autumn, winter, all of the equinoxes included, on circular mounds, drumlins, whitethorn copses and forests of ash and elder. Was this tribute ever collected? Ever consumed? Carnies never asked that question. Because, and here we encounter another of Walter's insights, this very tribute was a tacit acknowledgement of their deepest fear: that something of the Dewman was already here.

That it was goes without saying. Those golden arrows, melting in the sun's rays, fell to earth. The burning tears of the mildewed ones.

And yet the carnies thrived, condemned to travel the earth, to keep their origins secret, to pay their mildewy

as the explosion of flying ants, and they had both decided to consult the child psychiatrist that helped the young McEntee down the road, when his adolescent moods had developed into a condition called bipolar, which was once termed depressive, or manic, or both, and affected close to 10 per cent of growing teenage boys. Although, as the reassuring voice on the phone said, when Eileen had rung to make the appointment, there is so much happening in youths of that age, so many hormones coming to bursting point, so many physical and mental changes, that a touch of what parents perceive as 'moodiness' is only to be expected. As Jim was, naturally, busy, it fell to Eileen to accompany Andy to the old Georgian building by the Five Lamps, and Eileen sat there examining the features of this drabbest of rooms, trying to occupy her mind with anything other than the absence that sat beside her.

He was rubbing one hand off another, the nails scouring small white streaks along the skin, and she had the awful sense that if he pushed the nails in a slight bit harder, those streaks would turn red. So she looked at the carpet, which had a pattern of interconnecting circles, brown upon green. Was it brown, she wondered, or had it once been black, the severity of the circular whorl smudged brown by feet? Then she had no more to think about this, and in a fit of panic wondered what else she could think about, what else would take her mind from the boy beside her, and she looked at the wallpaper. It was equally unpromising, but had a strange set of repetitive illustrations, a fading shepherdess with a staff that curled at the top and spread across the wall to the unlit fireplace, above which a framed diploma hung, that read 'Gerard Grenell' beneath the copperplate logo of a therapeutic institute. And as she couldn't read the name of the institute, so ornate was the print, she set her mind to trying to remember the name of the shepherdess.

And when she couldn't remember that, she tried to remember the term for the staff that rose above her bonneted head. A crook, she remembered, a shepherdess's crook. And then the inner door opened, and the name suddenly, and uselessly, came to her.

Bo Peep was the shepherdess's name, of course. Little Bo Peep.

A man was walking towards her, through the open door. He had a kind face and corkscrew red hair that rose unbidden above his crown, no matter how carefully it was combed. And as he introduced himself, Eileen wondered did he know what a crook was for.

But she knew that was the last question she should ask him. There was only one question she was here for, and it was to do with her son beside her, who, to her shock and surprise, was already standing, shaking hands with the kindly Dr Grenell, or was he even a doctor, she couldn't be sure. Until he was gracious enough to shake her hand too and ask the question 'Mrs Rackard?' Well, it wasn't a question really, but it was phrased like one, and Eileen nodded as her right hand was angled up and down by his and tried to smile when he said Dr Grenell and would have even curtseyed like Bo Peep on the wallpaper, she was that anxious.

He brought them inside, to a smaller office with more plaques on the plain wallpaper of the wall, and here Eileen noticed it had two doors. One door to lead patients out, she assumed, and another, through which all three of them had come, to lead people in. Did men in white coats ever manage the transition between the two, she wondered, and then said to herself, you have to stop, Eileen, being so dramatic.

Because her son, oddly enough, had perked up in front of the therapist. And Eileen, who could think of him more clearly now that her thoughts were mediated through another, wondered was that because he was at the age where he needed role models of men, and not of women. Was that why his eyes crinkled with something like pleasure when he saw the smudged ink-blot drawings the therapist held up, answering rapidly in a stream of word association that surprised even her?

Until suddenly he stopped dead.

'Is there a problem?' the corkscrew-haired therapist asked. And Eileen thought to herself, he really ought to have it cut before it grew like a plover's crest above those luxuriant eyebrows. 'I find it hard to concentrate,' Andy was saying, smiling at the therapist in a way that seemed to imply: if I hadn't got a friend before, I have one now.

'And why is that?' the therapist asked, equally brightly.

'Too many people,' the boy said, and they both exchanged a glance and Eileen thought, well thank God someone can make eye-contact.

'Well,' the therapist said, smiled at Eileen a little too brightly and asked her softly, 'Will you give us some time alone together?'

So Eileen found herself back in the waiting room, alone now, looking at the Bo Peep wallpaper, wondering what on earth a crook was and however did she lose her sheep?

to a purpose. He had no guidelines for the unmoored environment he found himself in; he was using the only references he had. Milton, Lucretius, a touch of Virgil, the odd Shelley quote. And from them he drew another crucial insight. For if the carnie fall was a mirror of kinds to the biblical one, what was Burleigh but the carnival's Mulciber? Mulciber, who had 'found out the massie ore' and built the halls of Pandemonium? Architect, thief of precious metals, confounder of the very large with the very small? And Burleigh's Amazing Hall of Mirrors was to become the carnies' Pandemonium, the great confuser, the creator of two from one and of infinity from both of them.

Was it always a quality of mirrors that they separated children from their reflections, sent one home, the reality robbed of all of its substance, and sent the other, the substance robbed of all of its reality, off on a carnival journey? No, of course not. Mirrors did what mirrors did. They reflected, acted as a conduit for vanity of all kinds, captured an image, but relinquished it willingly; in fact, relinquished it inevitably, the moment the observer departed. But Burleigh, as Walter came to discover, was a born tinkerer.

Burleigh had begun his critical experiments with mirrors after viewing the first public screenings of the Lumière brothers in the Salon Indien du Grand Café in Paris. The caravan had set up its tents on the rattier end of the Bois de Boulogne, among the ice-skating pimps and their prostitutes, and Burleigh had taken the afternoon off and was amazed to see projected, on the flickering wall of the Grand Café, a series of living images. Men and women leaving a brightly lit factory entrance. Walking from what seemed to be a moored canal barge. Exiting a train, which magically began to move, and to almost overwhelm viewers with its mass. And what stunned him was not what stunned everyone else – the apparent and shocking reality of the image. No, it was the simple fact that the image had been separated from its reality. There had been an exit, in a factory in Lyons, the year before. And here, before him, was the same exit. There had been a pier, somewhere, anywhere, jutting out over crashing waves. A succession of figures, diving in, swimming back out. And here now, before him, was the same event. And what, he wondered, in his half-demented way, if the same trick could be replicated with his Hall of Mirrors?

He was a tiresome type, this Burleigh, half-carnie, half-oddjob man, but wholly and unfortunately himself. A lumbering, slope-shouldered tinkerer, in his grey shopman's coat, with odd, greasy coils of battery copper spilling out of his pockets. But he had one particular talent, amongst his oddities. He was a genius with mirrors. Their arrangements, their distortions, their repeated curves and multiple reflections, back, if he arranged them correctly, as far as infinity itself. And with his Hall of Mirrors, which was doing a tolerable business on the unkempt fields of the Bois, he had set himself one simple task. To distort reality in as many ways as he could. To enlarge it, squash it, multiply it, flatten it, thin it and fatten it; to make the beautiful ugly and the ugly beautiful, in other words, to give the reflected as much life of its own as was optically possible. But, he wondered as he wandered into the cold December air and saw the freezing globules of breath emitted by the Parisian crowds, what if he could separate them entirely? What if he could, either through the construction of the mirrored surface itself, or the arrangement of mirrors and their mutual reflections, give the reflection life? An impossible task, you might say, a paradox, but Burleigh revelled in impossibility and paradox.

And so began his exhausting, tiresome and ultimately fruitless reconstruction of his Hall of Mirrors to find that particular arrangement of angles, that magic placement of mirror on to mirror that would allow reflection separate from reality. That he failed goes without saying. And when the magic possibilities of rearrangement had been exhausted, he extended his experiments into the shapes of the mirrored surface themselves, concave, convex, conical, parabolic. And when these in turn yielded no fruit, he concentrated his efforts on the silver-backed surfaces of the same mirrors. He scraped and resilvered, experimented with tin and mercury, sputtering aluminium, other alloys and spraying techniques. He wasn't helped through his years of experiment by the development of the cinematograph, from crude images of an oncoming train to the first one-reelers, to the riotous ballets and horse operas that became known as Westerns. If they could perfect their mechanical processes, why couldn't he? Thus it was a disappointed and melancholy Burleigh that wandered down a shadowy laneway in old Rotterdam, before the bombs flattened it and long before the music festivals made it unbearable. The carnies were assembling on adjacent waste ground and Burleigh's Amazing Hall of Mirrors was now the least of their attractions. So Burleigh did what Burleigh always did when bored: he wandered. And he turned a corner, on to a cobbled dockside with a mooring rope as wide as his torso that bound a ship to the dock as big as any street he had ever been in, and stopped outside an old antique shop with an object made of a certain metal in the window.

Burleigh had by now tired of chemical processes. The thought of nitrates and silver and aluminium coatings made him almost physically ill. But in the window of this antique store there was a small, gnome-like statue that would look to the untrained eye to be made of copper or bronze. It had a patina of dust over it, with barely a sheen to its metal surface. But the tortured face that glared back at him through the glass window had a scrape on its metal nose, and in the indentations of that scrape, Burleigh recognised the gleam of gold.

He thought of alchemy, the philosopher's stone, the transmutation of base metal into something infinitely more precious. He looked down at his fingers, stained by the oxides of baser metals, and must have shrugged, and said to himself, why not?

He walked in and heard the tiny bell above the entrance door make its petulant announcement. The tinkle echoed through the empty interior, past rows of abandoned statuary, bronze nymphs holding bulbless bowls to the ceiling in frozen, supplicant arms, the whole array of them covered in many months of undisturbed dust. It reached the ears of a bent figure in a mottled shop coat, not unlike Burleigh's own, who seemed to register it not at all, and only gave the merest hint of the recognition of another's presence when Burleigh had reached the desk over which this figure was bent. Two ink-stained fingers brushed a lock of hair from a pair of wired-framed spectacles and an asthmatic voice sounded out, as if to accompany the dying echo of the bell.

'*Kan ik u helpen?*' this voice asked, and as this was Holland and as Burleigh had not a word of Dutch, a ponderous mime followed.

Now Burleigh lacked almost entirely the mimetic graces of the other carnies. He had the roustabouts' strength, but without their compact stature, and whatever carnie elegance may have once enhanced his frame had been lost in that crab-like stoop he had come to adopt, bent over his bubbling pots, his quietly hissing batteries, his infinitely expanding coils of hooped copper wire. So he was a bad mimic and a worse linguist, but he tried and somehow managed, through a succession of jabbing fingers and monosyllabic grunts that he hoped were beyond language, a kind of Esperanto of need and desire, finally to communicate what he wanted. So the antique-shop assistant finally raised his elongated head until the flat discs of his wire-framed glasses came into Burleigh's field of vision and he saw himself reflected there, above two pale whitish eyes.

'*Ah, de aardmannetje!*'

Burleigh nodded furiously, in an affirmation which the assistant took to be another mute question, and elaborated.

'*De geest, de elf, de hobgoblin!*'

'Indeed,' muttered Burleigh, 'the hobgoblin.'

Hobgoblin my arse, he thought. It looked more to him like one of those pudgy Cupids that adorned Valentine cards; in fact could well have been a Cupid, were it not for the deformed shape, the hunched shoulders, the outstretched and muscled arm clutching what he now recognised as a bow with a blunt arrow tip, quite fearsomely spiked. But all he cared about was its constituent metal. So he lumbered behind the shop assistant through the various dust-covered caryatids and held out two trembling carnie hands into which, after much sliding of glass panels, displacement of the displays behind them, a small hunched figure made of some precious metal was placed.

Burleigh was so surprised, initially, by its weight that he almost dropped it on the foot that stood directly below his clutching hands. And it would have hurt, he knew that somehow; the prodding arrow might have pierced his boot, causing a pain that would have been sudden, sharp and probably lingering. Because there was a lingering quality to this creature, this thing, shoulders bent like an old crow's wings, behind a head that hunched forward as if to hide from the watching world all of its secrets. All its effort seemed bent on the bow, from the arms to the downturned mouth, to the eyes, crinkled and ancient. A small cap adorned with feathers or wings sat above the immobile hair and the whole thing was clad in a robe that seemed windblown, despite its dusty, metallic folds. And Burleigh perhaps should have asked more questions, but all he could think about was, is it gold or is it not, so that froze any further enquiry as he brought the creature to his lips and bit into the arrowhead. And a taste then flooded his mouth, metallurgic, ancient and amber; he saw a liverish, lapping river for some reason, crowded with boats like sampans, and a full gibbous moon reflected in the waters, and he shivered, closed his eyes, saw steppes, vanishing into the distant distillation of a setting sun. He opened them again and saw the marks his teeth had left in the tiny spikes of the arrowhead, and saw, beneath the dust, the unmistakable gleam of gold.

So Burleigh haggled, Burleigh extended his repertoire of mimetic gestures and eventually Burleigh bought, not knowing what he had bought, caring only for that gleam of gold. He walked down the Rotterdam dockfront, past battleship after battleship, the already massive trawlers dwarfed by their immensity. A war was coming, but Burleigh didn't care; all he thought about was this weighty, golden burden between his roustabout hands.

(And Walter here went into Miltonic overdrive, pondering the origin of this mysterious *aardmannetje*, *geest*, hobgoblin. Was it Thammuz? Belial? Azazel? Or Mammon himself, who

> dig'd out ribs of gold. Let none admire
> That riches grow in Hell; that soyle may best
> Deserve the precious bane.

He was close, Walter, but would have got no cigar. Paganina would have won it, had she ever been given a glimpse of this thing, this *geest*, this *aardmannetje*. Paganina, who had known those Hyperborean steppes, had fired arrows not unlike that one, would have recognised Abaris and his golden arrowhead, given to him by her soul sister in those fanciful legends, the chaste huntress Artemis. But even Paganina would not have known that precious metal's source: the golden tears of the mildewed ones.

The carnival thrived, those few months in the Rotterdam waste ground, under the shadows of the giant derricks, which tracked their dark shapes around the helter-skelter, the infinity of stalls, the circus tent, like a series of giant sundials. Something was ticking, the whole world knew; armies were massing, ships were stacking, sailors were gathering with nothing to assuage the anxiety of waiting but carnival, and so the carnival thrived.

All but Burleigh's Hall of Mirrors, which managed only desultory returns. And Walter found a function for himself at last, to the immense relief of the carnies at large, who had grown tired of his incessant enquiries. He managed the entrance till, while Burleigh busied himself in the hall's fathomless depths. For the Hall of Mirrors was like that, Walter found, a dimensionless space, with ever more tiny corners to get lost in:

Thus incorporeal Spirits to smallest forms
Reduc'd their shapes immense and were at large,
Though without number still amidst the Hall
Of that infernal court.

Walter saw Burleigh enter each morning with his hammers and his measuring tapes, his lens grinders and his planes of glass. Walter managed the drunken sailors who wandered through with their afternoon doxies on their arms, talking in their incomprehensible Friesian or Dutch. He could hear a distant tinkling, behind the squeals of mock delight and pretended horror as the ladies saw themselves elongated to the lengths of ninepins or squashed into gigantic sixpences. The distant tinkling was Mulciber, the fallen architect, building a Pandemonium that would only come to fruition many years later after the war to end all wars had spent itself and surprise surprise another war began; it was Burleigh, hammering the gnomic shape he had no name for into infinitely thin, infinitely febrile and infinitely sad sheets of gold. He had sliced the *aardmannetje* into sections and set to hammering them down, the winged hat first of all, then the silver hair beneath it, the crown, the face, the nose, the clutching hands, the bow, the arrowhead . . .

Walter would live long enough to see what he termed 'that Pandemonium' built. But before he would experience its full transformative power, he would be transformed himself by a 250-kilogram Luftwaffe bomb on the tracks of a motorised railway on quite a different dockside. *Sic*, as Walter himself might well have put it, *transit gloria mundi.*

27

THE FUNCTION OF A crook, Eileen surmised, was to act as a kind of sheepdog in the hand. When Bo Peep's beloved flock found themselves tangled in briars, or wandered too closely to a cliff's edge, she could reach out her crook and hook it around their tiny collars and gently ease them to safety. But then she began to wonder, and all the while wishing she could think of something else, do sheep have collars? Perhaps in fairy tales, with little bells attached, but in real life? Collars that dogs and cats wear, which could be hooked by that rather unlikely staff, with not so much a hook at its apex, but with something more like the decorative end of a curtain rail. And now that she began to think of it, still wishing that she could stop, that Bo Peep crook couldn't hook anything, even a compliant sheep with a convenient collar. It curled outwards towards the tip, and if it was made for anything, it was most definitely not made for hooking. And, besides, did Bo Peep give even a thought to catching or hooking her errant flock? No, she let them alone and they came home, wagging their tails—

And this point her truly maddening conjectures were brought to a welcome halt by the door opening and the benign face of Dr Grenell entering her vision once more. His hair was unchanged, as of course it would be, that kind of corkscrew hair defied any brush, but it was unruly more than unattractive, now that she came to think of it. And she thought for a mad moment of asking him to clarify the issue of Bo Peep and her shepherdess's crook, but stopped herself just in time. Because he was inviting her inside now, so 'they could all have a chat'.

Eileen rose to her feet and stumbled, realising her leg had fallen asleep with the waiting. Dr Grenell caught her by the elbow, raised those capacious eyebrows of his and smiled with reassurance. 'My leg,' she said. 'A little numb.' And she stamped her left foot off the floor to make the blood flow. 'We did rather throw things about,' he said, in that chocolatey voice of his.

'Things?' Eileen asked, as he helped her towards the office.

'The issues you mentioned on the phone. Not so much issues, really, as the normal concerns of a transitioning adolescent—'

'Transitioning?' Eileen asked. It was a word she had heard before, on the radio talk shows, but she was inside his office now, and he was closing the door and Andy was standing by the window, still digging the nails of one hand into the skin of the other.

'What I want to do,' the doctor began, and he had lowered his voice, so it had the quality of cocoa more than chocolate, a tone that was definitely designed to soothe, 'is to prescribe a short course of medication that would help with all of these feelings of anxiety . . .'

He had that habit, this doctor, of inviting you to finish his sentences for him. So Eileen, dutifully, complied and felt a brief flash of optimism, at last.

'Medication?' she asked softly, as if this consultation room demanded its own hush. And then, she felt obliged to ask, 'You feel he needs that, doctor?'

'Oh, it's not for him,' the doctor said, already pulling a pad from one of the drawers in his desk. 'It's for you.'

'For me?'

He formed his lips into a gentle, meant-to-be-reassuring smile. And Eileen saw at that moment her son turn towards her from the window, with a version of that smile on his lips.

'Look, the boy is on a normal, healthy, but inevitably turbulent journey to adolescence. And there's no stigma in that. Nor in admitting to the stress of it all.'

Just what had transpired in that room, Eileen wondered. And she wished then she could go back to her cogitations on Bo Peep's crook.

'Yes,' Eileen heard herself saying, 'it has been quite stressful of late—'

'Children can prove themselves remarkably resourceful. But the wear and tear on the parents' nerves often leaves a hidden cost. And these rather delusional conclusions about your son are a decided worry.'

'Should I be worried, doctor?'

'For him? No. For yourself, maybe . . . just a little . . .'

He scribbled on the notepad and tore off a page. He smiled then, with a nauseating presumption of understanding.

'He was not responsible, Eileen – can I call you Eileen?'

At which, she nodded.

'And I can't believe I'm saying this—' He drew a deep breath, and exhaled in a bemused smile. 'He could not have been responsible for an infestation of flying ants.'

'Of course not.'

'So you admit it? I'm glad. It was reported on the news. One of those Saharan winds. From Somerset to here. But the fact that you thought he was—'

'I thought he was?'

Eileen felt defenceless. She couldn't bring her eyes to the window, where she knew without seeing that Andy was smiling too.

'Didn't you?'

'I have to admit – I did, for a little while—'

'So as a family, you need to take a deep breath, and calm down. And these might help.'

She reached out and took the prescription. She never asked what the medication was. 'Three times a day, with water. Always after meals.'

As he led them both back to the waiting room, Eileen wondered in a panic had she imagined the Bo Peep wall-paper as well. So she was strangely relieved to see the bonneted head, with its crook angled beside it, repeated endlessly over the walls.

28

'CURIOSITY,' JUDE SAID.

'Killed the cat,' Mona replied.

'Still,' Jude murmured. 'The cat is a necessity, betimes.'

'What are you saying?' This from Mona, who was resting her pert head on the circus guy-rope. She could see Dany on the sawdust floor inside the canvas flap, exercising the Arabian. It was that hot, restful hour before whatever crowds would come. He barely stroked the horse with the whip. A backwards flick, and it reared on its heels.

'He's asked me,' Jude said. Her mouth barely moved. 'How the mirror did its thing.'

'A bit like Walter.'

'Poor Walter. Did curiosity kill him?'

'It made him old before his time.'

And the truth was, it exhausted him. The attempt to rationalise the fundamentally irrational. To trace the untraceable. For the carnival, by the time Walter experienced it, was such a mélange of changelings and Ur carnies, that if a proper genealogical study had been made (and no such study was ever likely to be made, because carnies would have scarpered long before such a study got close to beginning; Walter's codex is the closest one comes to one) it would have been well-nigh impossible to distinguish between the original and the ersatz, between the one true inherited link to the Land of Spices and the interlopers, the wannabe carnies (of which Walter himself was one) and the changelings. Walter was writing before the discovery of DNA – and here the question arises: did carnies have such a thing as DNA? But any such study would have told the same mongrel tale. Denied all of the benefits of reproduction – and most carnies felt this infertility to be a blessing, the ultimate distinguishing factor between themselves and the outside world – they replenished their ranks by abductions of various kinds. A process, as Walter observes, like most carnie realities, obscured, mythicised, dramatised in the most charming of allegorical tales, but which he himself defines as the 'changeling process'. Now the snatching of a child may have had a logic, may have even constituted a virtue in a world where children were many, and mostly unwanted. But in the middle years of the twentieth century, when the images of missing children were posted in newspapers and on street lampposts (this was long before the rash of 'Have You Seen This Child?' legends on plastic milk cartons) and created what in the eighteenth century would have been known as a 'universal hue and cry', abduction was no longer an option. So the carnie ranks went through a gradual depletion as the inevitable Fatigue thinned their numbers.

Burleigh's efforts with his Hall of Mirrors, therefore, would have led to a solution of kinds. To wit, a steady stream of changelings ('reflectives') who could be observed, monitored (or to use the repellent current usage: 'groomed'), while their reflected others happily returned to the human fold. And those that were found fitting could be inducted into the mysteries of the spice. But, as always with Burleigh, there were problems. Native ingenuity is one thing; mechanical, not to say optical, perfection, quite another. And Burleigh's first efforts with what came to be known as the Rotterdam gold led to the most extraordinary aberrations. The moment of separation of the reflection from its bearer proved arbitrary, to say the least. And the first unfortunate reflective came out long and thin, a pitifully stretched version of the original that had viewed himself, surprise surprise, in the elongated mirror. Still, he was welcomed by the carnies, given various inappropriate nicknames ('Stretchy', 'Indiarubber') and put to work with the roustabouts. His long, thin fingers proved invaluable in the tightening of barely reachable nuts, bolts and sprockets that would otherwise have gathered dust and rust in the inaccessible scaffolding beneath the carousel and the helter-skelter. They could now be oiled by Indy with his stretchable, pneumatically agile arms. And so, eventually and happily, he became one of them.

More thins emerged through that carnival season, before the carnies had to call a halt. And Burleigh pleaded his case, begged to be let go back to what he called 'the drawing board'.

But the next reflectives came out with a shape even more alarming. Short, squashed versions of their originals (like the Munchkins in *The Wizard of Oz*, a film the carnies first viewed in the autumn of that fateful year, 1939). A positive bevy of them emerged from the mirror-maze on successive hot July days. Their voices were squished, as if they breathed laughing gas instead of air, and they proved addicted to the most charmless practical jokes – most of which involved belching and farts of stupendous reach. The carnival had to call another halt to Burleigh's efforts (and Walter writes, in a scribbled footnote, that this latest mishap led to the first whisperings about his banishment).

But the squats, as they came to be called, proved as useful as the thins. With unnaturally broad shoulders, stupendous muscle mass and a centre of gravity lower than most, they could lift many times their own body weight and took their place with the thins amongst the roustabouts. But by that time, sadly, Burleigh's banishment was almost complete.

Rotterdam began it and Rotterdam ended it. Jude, always a light sleeper, was woken by a loud, sad foghorn from the North Sea. She crawled from her hammock, clenched her pipe between her teeth and took a walk around the sleeping caravans. There was an intermittent moon shining, turbulent clouds scudding over it, and she could see the dim shapes of a new generation of battleships on the night horizon. Even without her crystal ball, she could envision the carnage they would soon create, for Jude had lived long enough on this human shore to know there was never a weapon designed that hadn't been used. And was it that sense of endless futility that led her to the half-open door of the mirror-maze and to venture inside? Carnies rarely looked in mirrors, hated to view themselves, since they feared they would catch a glimpse of the years they had lived. They reserved that pleasure for humans. Burleigh had laboured alone in his reflective workshop; carnies had seen the questionable results and been happy to leave him to it. But some premonition of the imminent end of things led Jude inside. And she saw herself, in the barely perceptible darkness, a long, thin, emaciated ancient thing, with more years etched on the face than anyone, human or carnie, could count. Jude recognised herself, with a shudder of the Fatigue that she barely managed to keep at bay. She took the deepest of breaths and continued wandering through the Hall of Mirrors, into the gathering darkness, and saw the same image squashed, like a Neanderthal toadstool, the same ancient version of her repeated, then, an infinite number of times. All of this amused her, saddened her, filled her with an ennui that grew inescapable, and for some reason Jude kept going. And there, in the bowels of Burleigh's Amazing Hall of Mirrors, she finally glimpsed something that chilled her to the bone. The mirror-image of all carnie selves, as if the Land of Spices had never been abandoned, an image that had the elusive quality of hoar frost, of fungus on an ancient wound, of hanging tendrils of curdled whey: the Dewman.

Had Burleigh purchased more than he bargained for when he haggled his way to possession of that *aardmannetje* in that antique store on the Rotterdam docks? Had Burleigh himself some demonic design when he beat it meticulously into ever thinner sheaves of gold? Had forces beyond his ken – and Burleigh's ken was as stiff and quasi-scientific as all of his optical efforts: he had little of the true carnie insight or talent for evasion – led him through that pinging door? No clarity was reached on any of these questions during the proceedings for Burleigh's subsequent banishment. And, to be fair, the thought of carnie judicial proceedings is a contradiction in kind. As Walter records, it was more of a bear-baiting than a court, a carnie pillorying, a babel of blame and accusation, which had two recorded results. Burleigh was to be banished and his Hall of Mirrors was to be shuttered and scraped. Scraped of its Rotterdam gold, and the job of scraping fell to the roustabout children of the mirror, the squats and the thins. So they re-entered their womb of mirrors and scraped them back to clear glass, replaced the Rotterdam gold once more with dependable silver. Why not destroyed? Walter asks, and adds an asterisk, and explains in a footnote: 'Carnies were hoarders. They would happily bleed rather than let anything go.'

Burleigh's long banishment began. And the new-minted Hall of Mirrors took its place among the other carnival sideshows in the shadow of Edinburgh Castle, in the spring of 1940. But the scraping and the silvering left much to be desired. Among the swathes of mirrored silver there remained some tentative threads of gold, a kind of palimpsest of the original intention and design. And Andy's emergence from the mirror-maze, many generations later, would have been the culmination of all of Burleigh's ingenuity, had he only been there to witness it. A perfect reflective, a true child of the mirror, of the Rotterdam gold, identical in every possible way to its source, all of his features intact and each of his limbs in accordance with what should have been. In fact, Burleigh's ingenuity, as we shall later learn, had surpassed even his hopes for it. Because in Andy's case, the difference between reflector and reflected was reversed. And the Rotterdam gold had finally and impeccably worked its magic.

awake, had she been bothered to observe one passing village, flickering under the night-time clouds, might have been able to peel back the encrustation of new-built suburbs and industrial parks and see again what once was there: a church perched over an ancient bridge, under which flowed a river of memory. Beyond it a rath, with a jagged, broken comb of whitethorn.

But Jude slept, with the bitter whiff of burnt mildew about her, gently rocking in her hammock. Dany slept in the hammock beside her, Mona in the hammock above. Maybe some common thread in their dreams propelled the convoy forwards, gave it a direction that they couldn't have, in their waking hours, defined. Whatever the case, by daybreak it was crawling through an ancient limestone landscape each carnie would have known, whether they had seen it before or not. Cracked ridges of stone, where there should have been grass. Fields of undulating rock, amongst which occasional flowers, unaccountably, bloomed. The white wash of the Atlantic beyond, spent after a night of futile thundering. The caravan moved through these ancient roads, and seemed at once too weighty, too wide and too colourful for them. There was only one possible destination. Downwards, on a gentle curve towards a town square that glittered in the distance. Other villages showed themselves, perched on the Atlantic shore, through the morning mist. But this one, with the yucca trees and the odd Edwardian wooden verandas attached to the grey façades of the hotel fronts, was the one the caravan chose. It soughed through the mist of the morning square, passed a barking dog, and turned by a castellated façade of old cement block. It had once been a cinema, then a dance hall and was lately a petrol station, with two disused and rusting pumps listing towards each other in the gravel forecourt. The caravan raised a quiet tornado of dust around them as it headed towards the acreage of dead field behind.

There was the usual roustabouting, unpacking, uncleaving, unwinding, distending, unfurling, telescopic poles untelescoped, widgets driven into long-forgotten ground, pistons pneumatically raised, stanchions greasily unstanched, old generators belched and whipped into motorised life; there were many clangs and kerrangs of chains and hawsers and metal shutters unshuttering and by breakfast time it was done, magically or not. A school-going child would have seen the pennant of the big top fluttering above the fuchsia hedges on the old Ennistymon road.

Dany stretched back on a set of metal stairs that led up to the dodgem cars. A film of unodorous sweat covered his muscled torso. He wore an unbuttoned denim shirt and a roustabout's belt, with an array of implements hanging from it that he wouldn't have been able to name three months before. But he wouldn't have been able to function without them now. Monniker pulled himself lithely, upwards and downwards, upwards and down from a lip of metal jutting from the dodgem-car floor. Every muscle had its own distinct shape, its own particular ripple on his ancient, adolescent body. Monniker never tired. In fact, Dany rarely tired either these days. And that muscled carapace that could be called the true carnie form was beginning to clad his own boyish limbs.

'Where are we?' Dany asked.

'Lisdoon,' Monniker replied with one of his exhaled breaths.

'You know it?' Dany asked.

'Too well,' Monniker was inhaling this time. He pulled himself up and down, up and down like a mechanical toy.

'What happened to the big world out there?' Monniker

continued. 'We used to travel all over. Been stuck in the old country for how long now?'

'Who decides?' Dany asked. He would love to have known, though he didn't expect an answer.

'Let us just say, it is decided,' Monniker answered, on an exhale this time. Then he hung from one arm while he brought the other palm close to his face.

'Powder it for me, will you?'

He gripped an open tin with his feet, and brought it to the level of Dany's face. Dany took the tin and sprinkled a small cloud of whitened dust over his calloused palm.

'Thank you,' Monniker said and resumed his pull-ups.

Dany decided to walk then and was almost surprised that he could. He half expected, if not an invisible force-field to prevent his exit, at the very least an enquiry as to where he was going. But none came. It would be midday, he supposed, before the first punters trickled in, so a stroll to the world outside must have been, if not expected, at least unremarkable. So he strolled, past the pinioned guy-ropes of the circus tent into the riot of nettles in the fields beyond. There were a few masticating cows there, and he followed the path their hooves and their dried cow-pats had left among the dock leaves and the nettled grass. He could see the triangle of a church spire peeking above the grey slate roofs of the town beyond. It awakened a strange sense like memory inside him, though a memory of what, he couldn't fathom. He had never been to this town – Lisdoon, Monniker had called it – so he couldn't have remembered it. But he had been alive with strange instincts lately that he couldn't really comprehend. He passed from the fields to a broken-down gate and a small, decrepit alley of half-ruined cottages that led to a sloping square. The wooden verandas, almost like lean-tos, against the grey cement of the hotel fronts.

Posters, faded by the weather, tied to the wooden lamp-posts. None of them for the carnival, which never had to advertise itself, he realised now. For some kind of match-making festival. He crossed the empty square, ascended a series of wooden steps and glimpsed a large empty bar inside, with stools and chairs upturned on tables, a young girl in a white blouse and a dark skirt sweeping the floor.

'You up for the weekend?' the young girl asked and Dany nodded. He was indeed up for the weekend. Maybe more than the weekend.

'A bit young for it, aren't you?'

Dany smiled briefly and said nothing. But he stayed, leaning against the wooden doorframe. There was something pleasing about watching her, the rhythmic movement of her plastic brush.

'No more than myself. Old drunken farmers, looking for a squeeze. Have they never heard of the internet?'

And the mention of the internet caused a slight pang in Dany. He remembered playing Dungeons and Dragons under the inattentive eye of his sleepy father. He stared at the pendulum-like movement of her brush, sweeping over the boards of the floor. But that sight brought another pang. He remembered his mother sweeping the cement patio by the kitchen door. Her pink slippers.

'So what brings you here?' the girl asked. She glanced at him slyly, under the bobbing swish of her hair. He registered a pair of blue, flashing eyes.

'The carnival,' he said.

'You're going to the carnival?'

'No,' Dany said. And he felt a sudden rush of shyness, for some reason. He was an outsider now, to her everyday world. 'I came with it.'

'A carnie?' she asked, and stopped her brushing.

'Yes, I'm a carnie,' Dany replied. And it felt odd, saying it, as if he had never until that moment known quite what he was.

'Look at you there, all I'm a carnie and leaning against the door with the sun behind you.'

'What do you mean?'

'You think it makes you special? All special and mysterious?'

'No, I don't think anything, really—'

'Have pity on us poor souls who have to sweep floors and clean up the vomit of drunken bachelors.'

If she was joking, she was very good at hiding it. But she smiled then, as if to let him know that she was.

'My auntie told me the carnival came through here once. But I'd be too young to remember it.'

She set aside the brush then and walked closer to him. He was overwhelmed by the smell, of shampoo and soap and the faintest tang of sour milk. A human smell. It was all he could do not to reach out and touch her.

'Do y'need tickets to get in?'

He shook his head. 'No tickets.'

'But you have to pay for the rides.'

'A bob or two.'

'A bob or two? What century are you in?'

And he wondered, what century was he in?

She smiled again, and he saw the gleam of silver braces. Her teeth were protruding slightly underneath her full red lips. She reminded him of every girl he had ever known, before what he realised were now his carnie days. Georgia, Carmen. They had braces, too.

'Would you do a girl a favour? Give her a free ride? Or two?'

'Maybe.'

'Only maybe? What kind of carnie are you?'

'Maybe, definitely.'

'Definitely maybe?'

She raised her palm. 'Come on, gimme five.'

She meant him to raise his. Of course. He remembered. And he did it.

'OK, carnie.'

They touched hands. Her fingers lingered on his, ever so briefly. Then slipped away.

miracle, fathered. He needed a body now, to reclaim them, and any body would do.

So Vladic, the homeless, was truly unfortunate. He hadn't always been Vladic the homeless, he had once been Vladic 'The Dozer' and had journeyed here from Łódź in Poland to find work and send money back to feed his growing family. And for a time he did work, in tiny villages the names of which meant nothing to him – Dunboyne, Tara, Mornington, Loughshinny, Naul. These villages were spreading into whole suburbs and he had bulldozed old pastures for more suburban developments than he could count. He was not unappreciative of the landscape he was obliterating, the hordes of memories and customs, good bad or indifferent, that he was cladding in what he was learning to call, from his Irish colleagues, 'two up, two downs'. But if he did know, as he flattened another grassy knoll, that this was the mound from which the whole townland once watched Termonfeckin destroy Loughshinny in a hurling match, he could not have truly allowed himself to care. He was here to do a job, a job that put food on the table in the small apartment where his family waited, in the shadow of the abandoned carpet plant, back in Łódź. One day, however – and although he could never understand the source of his misfortune, he could pinpoint the day – he found his huge, mechanical beast facing a mound that no other 'dozer' would touch. On the mound was a small, wizened tree, with a few scraps of faded cloth tied to its leafless branches. And Vladic, more concerned with his ongoing paycheck than with talk of holy wells and whitethorns, fairy raths and ringforts, shifted his gear stick downwards and drove the toothed maw towards the pitiable tree. He crushed it in one sweep, buried its branches with their thorns, their scraps of faded cloth, their scapulars, their miraculous medals, their scribbled prayers and wishes, in a chaotic mess of roots, earth and stone. Two more reversals, two more shifts of the gear stick forwards, and the job was done.

But from that day forward, nothing was the same. The development, called 'Windy Arbour' (and it was windy there, there was little protection from the great north-easterly gusts that swept down from Dundalk), ran out of funds.

Vladic found himself 'let go' and joined the rest of the recessionary crews queuing for benefit outside the dole offices in the customs house on the Drogheda Quays. His wife, Matilda, took a gainfully employed lover in Łódź, and Vladic's trips home to see his unhappily estranged children took on the quality of a mournful pilgrimage. He took to buying cheap Russian vodka in the Mornington Spar, could barely keep up with his rent, and so Vladic the bricklayer slowly morphed into Vladic the homeless. He found himself a cheap mouth-organ, which he would play outside the churches on the Drogheda Quays, but the only tunes he knew were faltering versions of 'Nie Chodź Marysiu' and the Polish national anthem. Vladic took to sleeping in the groundkeeper's hut off the Baltae Golfcourse and, when his sleeping quarters were discovered, to making his bed in the bunker of the eighteenth hole. And that was all right while the weather held, but when September came and the north-easterly began to blow again, he stumbled down the marshes, with only a cheap bottle of Slivovitz for warmth, and made his way into what the locals called the Taw Wood and curled himself into the mossy mound beneath the middle oaks and drank himself into a drunken slumber.

So he slept through the buzzing of tiny winged creatures that emerged from somewhere in the undergrowth beneath him and the accretion of the lichen-like old man's beard that gradually covered his unwashed jeans and his vomit-stained denim shirt. His battered hat acquired the same substance, almost like a fungus, which seemed to emanate from the moss beneath his broad, Slavic head. He was finally woken to a fury of those buzzing wings by what he thought was an animal crawling over him. A rat, a small bird, a vole. He drew a sleepy hand up to swat it away. But the hand moved as if through an invisible glue, wrapped in that clinging beard of grey lichen. He gestured more violently then, and something twisted round the hand, gripped it, and dragged it back down. He awoke fully at last, and through eyes blurred by a mist of flying things saw his left hand literally crawling with tiny roots that squirmed from the undergrowth, encasing it in furred handcuffs. He put his right hand to service, but a surge of ivy, erupting from the bed of moss, caught that in turn. Both hands were pulled back, he was spread-eagled on that delicious moss, with its foam of surging lichen, twisted on the rack of the mound beneath it, and the shape of a wizened tree arose before him. He knew it, somehow, in the dim recess of his shattered brain. It was born of the earth, had risen out of moss, and scraps of the same moss clung to it like faded pieces of cloth. He knew them too. Then a thorned arm reached down, and he was gutted from sternum to the red-smudged flesh of his throat, around his Adam's apple.

There was blood, of course. Much blood. But the whitethorn tree had flesh now, to bury itself in. And the Dewman had a body, to dress itself in. The process took some time. Something that was not entering something that was. That had been. And Vladic the homeless was no longer there to witness it.

31

THE CROWDS BEGAN TO trickle in around midday. Bachelor farmers mostly, hungover, dressed in last night's sweat-stained shirts, some in twos and threes, some with female partners already on their arm. There were squeals on the rollercoaster, buried shouts of terror from the ghost train, peals of innocent laughter from Burleigh's Amazing Hall of Mirrors. Oh my God, look at the cut of you. Dany watched, winched, collected coins and twirled his rope in the big top with a strange sense of abstraction, of listlessness, even. He watched Mona twirl, fly and soar with a feeling inside him he didn't recognise. The rope in his hands seemed disconnected from her for once. He was waiting for something and he didn't know what. And walking back then, past the carousel, silent, because all the children had long gone, he saw her. Sitting on a carousel horse with a golden wooden mane, idly rocking it backwards and forwards, her brown chunky-heeled shoes barely reaching the trodden grass.

'You promised me a ride, carnie.'

'But you seem a bit old for that one,' he said.

'So what do you recommend?'

'The rollercoaster?'

'I could never stand heights.'

'The ghost train, then?'

'Oooh, scary stuff, Mr Carnie. Can I hang on to your arm?'

And it suddenly struck Dany that it was the oddest thing. He had assembled that ghost train more times than he could remember. Taken it apart the same. But he had never been inside it. In fact, he had given hardly a thought to any of the carnival rides, apart from the mesmerising business of their construction and reconstruction. What did that mean? And again came the same strange sense, of waiting for something. Had he been waiting for her?

He lifted her down then, from the carousel horse, and was surprised to find her weight like that of a diminutive doll. How long had it been since he had touched someone? And not just someone: a girl in tight jeans and a cut-off T-shirt that said SOCK IT TO ME over her bouncing breasts. He placed her on the grass then, carefully, as if any untoward movement of his would cause her to shatter and break.

'What strong hands you have, carnie.'

'Have I?'

'Not the right answer.'

'What is the right answer?'

'All the better to—'

And she stopped, and smiled at him, exposing her silver-braced teeth.

'To what?'

'Don't ask me. You're the wolf. I'm the granny or – or whatshername – Little Red Riding Hood.'

'All the better to feel—?'

'Altogether too wolfish now—'

'—yours?' He phrased it like a question. And took her freckled hand in his own.

'Oh, how sweet. Even nice.'

And she drew her hand from his then, and slipped it through the crook of his arm. He could feel the push of her breast against his elbow.

'Come on then, carnie. Show me this ghost train. And tell me your name, I can't keep saying carnie.'

'Dany.'

'Can I call you Dan? And since you didn't ask mine, call me Maggie.'

And he walked then, thinking of too many things, towards the wide-open mouth with the graveyard teeth that was the entrance of the ghost train.

There was a creaking of old machinery, the groaning of a rusted chain, and she sat in the small wooden car unnaturally close to him, her face pinched and smiling until it was consumed by darkness. Then there was a swoop downwards through plastic ivy, a succession of graves that opened their skeletons to the moonlight, ghouls that materialised from above and below, and hands, gripping his neck, his throat, his chest, his waist, that he gradually realised were hers. There was a kiss then and the taste of her saliva in his mouth and her tongue on his, the taste of sharp metal of her braces that he didn't like at all. Then they were illuminated by neon light and the ride was done and there were three youths watching him from the end of the tracks.

'Found yourself a carnie?'

One of them lit a cigarette, a large freckled face under a shock of red hair.

'Scuttin' off on us?'

'He just took me for a ride—'

'Took my sister for a ride, did you?'

'She asked me to—'

'Is that true, Maggie, you asked him?'

'What if I did?'

'Well now. I wonder—'

He walked forwards, large Doc Marten boots on the well-trodden grass. And Dany saw the blow long before it came. He reached one hand out, caught the large, reddened wrist in his smaller hand. He bent it then, on instinct, and saw the red-haired one crumple suddenly to the ground in a strange kind of agony.

'Let me go, you carnie fucker—'

He sensed another fist swinging towards him, ducked his head to one side and caught it with his left hand. There were two now, squirming in the shadows by the ghost-train tracks. A third aimed a head-butt towards him, and Dany met it with his upturning forehead. A loud crack, a gush of red from a broken nose.

The girl behind him screamed, 'Jesus, there's no need for this!'

And Dany realised there wasn't. He released both hands. He saw the bleeding one rise, one hand held to his streaming nose.

'What the fuck was that?'

Dany didn't know what it was. He stood there, lithe, electric, confused, as he sensed her leaving the protection of his shadow to help her brothers.

'Didn't I tell you never to mess with carnies?'

'You started it.'

'Will I finish it now?'

The freckled one rose then, and swung again. Dany saw this one coming but let it arrive. A fist of knuckles to the face bobbed his head back. It hurt, but it wasn't pain as he remembered it. The other two came forwards, emboldened, and the rain of blows began. He let himself suffer them, like a pneumatic rag doll, thrown back and forwards between them. He rose in a strange arc with the final blow, and then let himself lie crumpled in the grass. He felt the kicks come then, while the girl exhausted herself with screams of protest. And then it was over almost as quickly as it began. He heard phlegm coughed from a mouth above him and a gobeen of spittle hit his cheek. He heard their feet retreating, the tears of the girl, confused whimpers now with the word 'carnie' scattered between them. And then there was silence.

He lifted his head, slowly, wiped the spittle from his face. And he saw a figure move from the shadow underneath the scaffolding and he recognised Mona.

'Are you learning?' Mona whispered.

'I must be,' Dany answered. He got to his feet, felt all of his limbs intact; the pain of the beating fluttered round his body like an electric charge.

'We don't cross over.'

'No?'

'We can do things, but we don't advertise it.'

'I see.'

'I heard the rumpus, I saw you catch the first one and the second. I wondered what the outcome would be. Then you settled back and took it. Wisdom, I thought.'

'I could have killed them. Now why was that?'

'But you didn't, and that's the point.'

She took a handkerchief with an ancient fringe of lace from her pocket, and dipped it in a tiny jar and wiped his face with it. The feeling of relief was delicious.

'That's good.'

'It's mildew. Heals all ills. Now come here with me.'

She took his hand then, the way the girl had, and led him through the scaffold to a small mound, a perch really, on the broken grass beneath it. It smelt of engine oil and heather and crushed buttercups. Tinny music drifted from above, from the triangular metal tannoys on carnival poles.

'We can't do what they do,' she said, lying her girlish cheek on the heathery mound. 'But we don't talk about it. The way they endlessly talk about breeding, making money, whatever that thing is they call work, retirement and, at the end of it all, "giving up the ghost".'

She plucked two pieces of succulent grass from among the heather and offered Dany one. They both chewed there, for a while, as Mona cogitated.

'Though that phrase never made any sense to me since the ghost wasn't being given up, was it? The ghost was what they were becoming.'

She turned to him and prodded his blade of grass with hers. She spoke through a half-closed mouth.

'You still with me?'

'I suppose.'

'Good. Because it's tempting to envy them. The way time hits them, the way they grow and change and, most of all, their breeding habits. But are they for us, Dany?'

'No,' he gave the expected answer. 'They're not for us.'

'Not for us all the stuff they sing about, with their sighs and their kisses and their lipstick and their tears and their lover man oh where can you be, I've been around the world and I–I–I can't find my baby—'

And oddly enough, it was playing now from the tannoy speakers, the rich tobaccoey Barry White voice, 'I don't know how, don't know where she can be.'

'And sometimes I see them underneath the scaffolding fumbling with buttons and zips, curled underneath the flap of the circus tent, and I think here we go again, the same old round with its honey child and its baby loves and the night I met you baby I needed you so. I could wish I was that thing and maybe I wish because I was that thing once, but it's the great seducer, that feeling, the one you have to watch out for, even more than the Fatigue—'

And here she turned to him.

'And you know what the Fatigue is, Dany?'

Fatigue, he knew. But the Fatigue? He shook his head. It was the first he'd heard of it. 'Your hands,' she said to him. 'Show me your hands.'

He held them out to hers. As if she expected what the sweeping girl expected, a high-five. But no, she examined them with her fingers in the neon light that came from the carnival beyond.

'It's what I noticed, the first time I saw you in Burleigh's mirror. You have what Jude has, the hands of an original. Now how can that be, Dany?'

He felt proud for a moment, to have something beyond her own attributes. But of course he answered dutifully, 'I don't know, Mona.'

Mona. The sound on his tongue was old, enticing, full of promised knowledge.

'Is that the first time you've used my name? Called me Mona?'

'Mona.'

'I had no want for a captured one, for a changeling. No desire whatsoever. But when I saw those hands, I knew they were special. I had to touch them. Whether you were to come out tall or squat, another roustabout, no matter. And out you came, perfect in form. I almost whispered, "Burleigh, all is forgiven."'

Dany looked at his hands. They were ordinary hands, as far as he could work out. Then he held them up against hers, to check.

'High-five.'

She held hers up, the way Maggie had.

'Jude read them, when you were sleeping. And I could tell she knew something, though she was loath to share it.'

And Mona closed her fingers round his.

'Come with me, Dany.'

'Where?'

'The circus, where else.'

She took his hand and walked, and led him through the emptying stalls, the way the other girl had. But there was more, here. Her steps became longer, lighter. She led him through to the covered flap of the circus-tent entrance. She unclasped it and gestured him inside.

There was a huge pool of darkness and the diminishing central pole, heading towards the circular gap above, through which silvered clouds could be seen.

'You know you don't need a rope, Dany, to take me up?'

'I always suspected.'

'Like this.'

She held two palms out and rose, softly, gently, into the gloom above, where she gripped the swing of the redundant trapeze.

'Come and join me.'

He gripped the rope then, and began to climb.

'I said join me.'

She reached one hand downwards, towards him, and he dared to take it. He felt himself weightless for a moment, swinging below her.

'Now reach for that.'

She swung him in a gentle arc, towards the trapeze across the gloom, and then let go.

And he was weightless, tracing a parabola away from her. He reached out, caught the opposite trapeze, and allowed his momentum to swing him back and forth.

'Now, back, to me.'

He angled his legs, making his weight double his momentum, and at the moment of letting go wondered, if weight can swing me, why doesn't weight drag me down? but he sailed, as if carrying on an invisible melody, back towards her hands.

'Now, you want to high-five?'

She wrapped her fingers round his and soared, dragging him upwards as if gravity had been reversed. She wound her knees around his, guided him past the diminishing pole, through the circular hole above it towards the silver clouds outside.

'We need to journey, you and me.'

'Journey to where?'

'Over the limestone fields. To the cliffs.'

It was strange, to journey with her and see her released from what he knew never held her down anyway. Gravity, weight, mass, all of those terms he had learned in school, which seemed almost inaccessible to him now. He followed, of course, gravitationless himself. It felt not so much a flight as a continuous fall that just never pitched itself downwards. They moved past the gradually quenching lights of the carnival, over the town, where the festive crowd were spilling from pubs, over the limestone fields that seemed to have a luminance all of their own, to the cliffs beyond. They came to rest on the edge of one, and he could see the Atlantic waters, pitching and roiling far below.

'Will you show me what you're made of, Dany?'

Her face was tilted towards him and a cloud shifted above them and the silver ghost of moonlight crossed it.

'How would I do that?'

'Hold me.'

So he held her waist. He felt substance there, under her tiny cinched jacket, a strength that matched his own.

'I'm holding you.'

'Hold me for good.'

And she pitched herself forwards then, off the cliff edge, down the cliff-face towards the dark waters below them.

Dany held, tight. He saw the foamed surface hurtling towards them and still he held. They hit the waves and, in something like a long, slow exhale, kept plummeting downwards. But he felt the contours of her waist contract then, into something thin, skeletal, hardly there. He saw her hair, grey and then white through the foaming bubbles that moved above them on their descent. Her face became a wizened map of tiny lines, until the skin became parchment thin, so the bones showed through. She was ageing as they plummeted downwards. As if the fatigue of years had come, with a vengeance, to take all of its toll. There was seaweed around them then, tendrils of it from the ocean's floor, entangling his ankles. He kicked himself upwards and kept his hands gripped fast to her skeletal waist. He saw the surface again, impossibly far off; the broken moon forming and re-forming with the water's movement. There was something like body returning to her cinched waist. There was flesh on her watery face again, the lines were diminishing, youth was returning as the slivers of moon-silver came back into view. And he broke the surface again, was tossed amongst the roiling foam, with Mona, as young as he had known her, still in his arms.

'It makes no sense,' she whispered, or murmured, or sputtered, 'I should have never come back.'

'Glad you did.'

'The Fatigue, now, you've seen it. We carry all of our years inside of us. But you, you pulled me back.'

'Was that some kind of test?'

He felt angry for the first time in all of this strange evening. To have been played with like that. He felt exhausted, as if the crashing waves could achieve what she did not.

'Those hands, my boy love, lovely one, come straight from the Land of Spices. You were born a carnie. And there was never a need to be snatched.'

She drew him back up then, like two dripping fish drawn from above by an invisible line. He saw the water cleave off his boots in successive drips to the disappearing sea. He saw puffins and gannets, perched on their spotted niches in the cliffs.

'Can you explain it?'

'I wouldn't try. Might spoil it. We are carnies, after all.'

32

FOURTEEN DEAD BIRDS FELL out of the sky and landed at the outer circle of twisted oaks. They were jackdaws, surprised from their perches in the upper branches. And as the shadow of something moving within made its way towards the soft light outside, there was a rustle, as of falling leaves. But they weren't leaves falling, they were more dead birds. The tiny, woodland kind, sparrows, robins, tits, and a woodpecker, its tawny feathers stiff with rigor mortis before it hit the roots above the loamy earth. The leaves came afterwards, with the huge wind he brought with him. He was his own tempest, this Captain Mildew, and he stripped clean whatever bits of nature he happened across. So the wind, which normally happened upon trees from the outside, happened from the inside. It propelled from inside the circle, the little wood, the copse of oak, every leaf that had fallen and was yet to fall, and after this flock of oak leaves came the flock of dead and dying birds.

There was a boy with an improvised fishing rod hanging over the marshy waters and as these leaves whipped by him, the boy turned to see a quite ordinary man emerge, one hand clutching his tattered hat to his head. Then the wind died round him, and he let his hand fall and walked on, the hat perched at an odd angle. There was greasy hair hanging beneath it. His eyes caught the boy's eyes and something in them made the boy turn away, back to the marshy water, where the weight of a dying fish had bent the tip of his rod.

The boy pulled the fish in, didn't reel, since he had no reel; the rod was just a piece of bamboo with some catgut tied to the top. But he pulled the fish in, a small carp of some kind, and tore the hook from its mouth and laid it out on the flattened grass beside him. He was amazed to see a worm slowly sliding from its dead mouth. Three dead birds fell then, in quick succession, on the flattened grass beside the dead worm, the dead fish. The boy turned then and saw what he somehow knew was a dead man, walking with a shambling gait, from the border of the Taw Wood towards the Nanny River.

Captain Mildew (or *an fear drúcht*, *spiorad spiosra*, the Dewman) was getting used to walking. He had lived in an immaterial zone for so long and was just getting used to the body he had filched. Filleted might be a more appropriate word (after being grossly mildewed and powdered), for the tramp had been truly gutted, from the crotch to the sternum, and if it were not for the ancient stains of sweat around his denim shirt and his tattered trousers, the drying blood resultant would have been immediately obvious to anyone passing. To the young boy who had seen him emerge and now stared in perplexed horror from his perch above the salt-water pool. To the widow Maguire, taking her morning constitutional along the path made of abandoned railway sleepers through the marshes. She saw him emerge over a low dune, like a walking scarecrow, boots shambling through the unfamiliar sea grass and sand with what seemed to be his own personal rain cloud behind him. But of course it wasn't a raincloud, it was a vaporous swarm of flying ants with a fluttering penumbra of dying birds. Larks, meadow pipits, greenfinches, gulls of various kinds and the ever-present jackdaws and crows.

They fell dead from the sky as he passed beneath them, as if dead from a lightning bolt.

He would have made an excellent scarecrow. As it was, he merely puzzled the widow Maguire as she ploughed down the sleeper path regardless, her arms flailing in the manner her heart-specialist advised. She would make it to the mouth of the Boyne, round the Maiden's Tower and back again, and neither an errant tramp, nor the golfers driving towards the eighteenth hole, nor the couples flagrantly embracing in the long grasses, were going to stop her. So she gave him a quizzical glance and registered neither the dying birds around the path he took nor the apron of blood from his collar to his crotch. She was bent on her constitutional, no matter what.

He made his way southwards, parallel to the line of sleepers and through the golfcourse, towards the sandy road. The fury of birds around him died after a while, as if he had emptied the skies immediately above him. And all the golfers saw was a vagrant like any other, an anonymous tramp, crossing their line of vision, seemingly deaf to their cries of 'Fore!'

33

DANY SPENT THE REST of that night in the Hall of Mirrors. Whether he needed to process whatever he had learned, or to return to the mirrored womb from which, apparently, he had been in some way born, he wanted to lay his head somewhere other than the hammock, next to Mona's. So he placed his head on the scuffed mirrored floor, gazed up at the sky above him, where he saw his own reflected face and realised how much time had passed. Not that much, really, but the face that gazed back down at him looked somewhat older than the boy that gazed up. Four weeks, six weeks, eight? And the boy below was a different creature now. How different, he wondered, and was it a difference he could ever eliminate, so as to make the journey back to what he once was? He tossed and turned that night, remembering the cherry tree in the hedged garden that turned magically pink each spring. He remembered raking the fallen cherry leaves into the burlap sack his mother held open. He remembered the hair falling round her face. He remembered his father's quote, as he sat behind, under a sun umbrella, on a canvas chair, his schoolboy copy of *A Shropshire Lad* open before him:

Loveliest of trees, the cherry now,
Is hung with bloom along the bough
And stands along the woodland ride
Wearing white for Eastertide.

Why white, he wondered, why not pink, as he shifted his head backwards and forwards on the glassy floor and gradually fell asleep.

He awoke to a reflected dawn, bounced from the entrance through a series of mirrors to appear like pink cherry blossom in the mirror he faced. He watched that blossom grow and seemingly wither into pale, whey-coloured clouds. Everything will change now, he realised, except for him until, apparently, the Fatigue took him over. And he wondered, was he feeling that fatigue already in the strange lassitude that flooded his limbs, when he noticed another reflection. Tucked between two mirrors, another reflection, lost somewhere in the avenues of reflections all around him, was what seemed to be the well-thumbed edge of a school copybook. He stood then, walked through hall after mirrored hall, until he finally found the reality. It was in a tiny gap beneath a low sloping mirror that angled towards the most inaccessible part of the floor. He edged the copybook out, then saw another, and again, one more. He edged them all out, with infinite care, between the mottled slats of glass and examined the copperplate handwriting of what, many years ago, had been a schoolboy not too far from his age. And he began to read then, page by unstructured page, the Walter Codex.

He read of Burleigh, the carnival's fallen angel; Burleigh, whose Hall of Mirrors had somehow spawned him.

He spent the whole day there, crouched in the depths of the mirror-maze, reading. He heard the carnival wake up outside, the sounds of another day beginning. He saw figures then, like shadows on Plato's cave, warped, enlarged, distended, multiplied many times. He heard the laughter of reflected bachelors, the giggles of their bach-elorettes; he saw them clutch and tickle and initiate waltz moves, hand on hand, heel and toe, to the tinny distant music from the carnival tannoys. He registered some of them kissing, their faces enlarged by pleasure or hope or desire, but most of all by the mirrors that distorted them briefly before they went on their ways. Their ways, he knew, might lead to romance, children, birth and death. But those ways were not for him. He read until the sun was setting, making another, more lurid explosion of blossom in the sloping mirror above him.

And by the time darkness took over he was done. He knew more, now, of carnie ways than anyone in the darkening carnival outside. He had read the addendum to Walter's codex. Walter's prediction, scribbled on to those schoolboy notebooks, drawn from the fractured legends of half-remembered carnie lore. That a Captain Mildew would one day find a way to traverse those dimensions, travelled aeons ago, on burnt carnie wings. That before he usurped some poor human's form, he would engender two sons, each a mirror of the other. And Dany wondered, as he wandered back out of those mirrors, into the darkness, whether he himself was one of them. He felt barely human; all carnie with a tincture of something else that, however much it might thrill and terrify, would be very dangerous to know.

Money was never a problem. He had long ago perfected the three-card-trick stunt, his only issue being the expertise with which he could manipulate the hidden Jack of Diamonds. So he fleeced even the most adept of ordinary conmen and often had to run, with his portable table, his three cards and his pockets jingling with coins.

After Rotterdam he had joined a gypsy troupe and travelled with them to Vienna. They had plied their trade along the pavements and cafés, with the whiff of poodle dogshit in their noses and the echoes of Strauss waltzes in their ears, until they came to realise that the banknotes thrown at them, in ever-increasing dimensions, were worth nothing but their weight. And when they saw the stormtroopers march down the Ringstrasse, they realised that any entertainment they could provide would be dwarfed by the staggering fantasy in front of them. They moved south, and found the borders blocked, and tried to lose themselves in the crush of would-be exiles: Jews, gypsies, suspect politicals. They used their sacks of Viennese currency to buy a place on a Roma barge, which moved at a canal-horse's pace, up the Danube, through the remnants of what once was the Austro-Hungarian Empire. But even rivers have borders, they discovered, and fast-moving, steel-bottomed barges that police them. They were stopped by a flotilla of these, emblazoned with the swastika that Burleigh now saw everywhere and had known before in its old, Zoroastrian incarnation. And Burleigh, with his carnie's second sight, knew their time had come. He hid himself beneath the canvas matting that covered the engine room. He elbowed his way through the crawlspace beneath it, through the intoxication of the diesel fumes, and slipped over the side, into the cold, foul Danube waters. And as he sank beneath the surface, into that half-world of rusting hulks of blasted vessels, old bicycle frames and abandoned tractor tyres, he wondered should he grow himself a pair of gills, and wait out the coming apocalypse.

But the water was cold and as his lungs came close to bursting, he surfaced, far from the sordid little drama in the oily waters downstream. He saw the distant shapes of stormtroopers on the barge, the hands dolefully raised, the fleeting shapes of figures diving to the side and a quick succession of flashes. The sound of the gunfire came some moments later as the current was strong, already bearing him away.

Burleigh made it to Berlin and spent the subsequent years of the Reich in the Babelsberg Studio, his expertise with mirrors proving invaluable to the Reichsfilmkammer. He could multiply a platoon into a division for the studio cameras. He could fabricate a mountain backdrop behind whatever Aryan starlet needed it, snow-capped peaks and misted alpine vistas echoed to infinity, with their yodelling contralto or soprano voices. But nothing could quench the ache he felt inside for his lost carnival.

And he felt it now, outside Funland in O'Connell Street, the streetlights glittering off the spire that rose in front of him, and the neon flashing from the emporium behind. There had once been a pillar there, but he didn't care. The ache still remained, over all of those years, but had changed, subtly, like a grand old wine into something bitter, tart and vinegary. The ache was now the ache of hatred, of an old wound that finally knew what it all along should have been. His exclusion was final, he knew, final and for ever, and he was waiting for whatever final reckoning the Dewman would bring.

He had been waiting for this Captain Mildew too many years now, it seemed. And he had, like a slouching John the Baptist, done his bit to pave the way. He had made his contribution, he had played his part, done the Captain no small service. He could remember the belching fumes of the Bombardier bus, the low privet hedge, the sad cherry tree on the lawn in front of the bungalow door. The housewife who answered, an unlikely vessel for the Captain's progeny, but pretty, nonetheless. He had gone through the motions of his routine, mirrored scarves and bracelets, objects of distinct value, oriental in provenance; taken in the ornamental details of the living room as he did so. The smiling photographs, the brochure on the mantelpiece, fertility clinic, called something like Auberne. Audabe? Auberge. So even before he removed that spurious ball of crystal from his battered cardboard case, she was already softened putty in his hands. Madame is missing, has a longing for, there is a wood Madame knows from her childhood days. The loss of carnie company was so acute inside him, he could bear it no longer. The thought of a child, outlandishly born, no need for snatching; the thought of a recompense, a reward, a reacquaintance with the lost Land of Spices almost made his soft hands shake. And what if it was the warped mirror of the true carnie shape, the only Captain Mildew; any company was better than none. So he had left that small bungalow, taken the bus back along the glittering seascape, past that bridge with its staves vanishing into the mirroring water, his only concern being how long he would have to wait.

Years, as it turned out. There was a buzzing round his face, tiny flies, ants, mosquitoes, but what were mosquitoes doing on this windswept Dublin street? He brushed them away and noticed the passers-by swatting, as if at invisible veils around their faces. And the strange thing was, with all of his carnie's insight and prescience, he still had no idea what to expect. A lumbering beast, making its way down the tawdry street? A thing, made of roots, moss, of that strange hoary fungus that passes for mildew? A monster that would clear this street finally of humanity? Then he heard the sound, the inhale, exhale, of a badly played mouth-organ. Two or three notes, with a hint of ancient melody. He turned and saw the tramp squatting by the spire, the battered cap on the pavement, in front of his open-soled boots. Then the voice, and when he heard it, he knew the Dewman had already mastered the miracle of Dublin speech.

'Any odds, mister?'

35

THE BUS WAS THE same. The once-white panels dulled by years of exhaust fumes, the melodeon doors opening with an exhausted hiss. It was already moving as they made their way up the circular stairwell and Burleigh noted how his companion had to grip the rusted rail to steady himself. Bodies are strange things, he thought to himself, prisons of a kind that must take some getting used to. The main difference was the absence of tobacco smoke. He seemed to remember choking in it, on that journey he had taken a decade or so ago. Small blessings, he thought, and watched the streets pass by through the breath-fogged window. Then, gradually, a sense of the sea overcame him. He didn't need to see it through the dark anterior windows, but he knew it was there.

There was little need for speech between them. He could see the calloused, bricklayer's hands gripping the seat in front of him, the dried bloodstains on the denim shirtfront that he knew would have to go. The body was ill-chosen, Burleigh knew that already without having to ask, but beggars can't be choosers after all. And which of us is happy with our physical shape? Burleigh, alone among carnies, had spent decades unable to avoid the sight of his. That dreadful posture, sloped shoulders, slouching around his Hall of Mirrors as he worked on his optical improvements. He came to hate it in time, wished he never had to see it, but mirrors were his expertise, his destiny, and now, it finally seemed, his salvation. So maybe it would have been worth it after all. Maybe those years of effort, those unbearable years of exile, would prove to be – what? he wondered, as he stole a glance at his travelling companion. The face was buried in a grubby collar, as if loath to be seen, the hat sloped over the forehead, occluding the eyes, which maybe was a good thing, Burleigh pondered, given the mode of transport they had adopted. No one should see those eyes unless they had to, and if they had, some game was up.

'I quite fancy,' Burleigh heard, somewhere deep inside him, and knew the Captain was addressing him, 'the cut of that one.'

There was a youth up in front, his shapely head framed by gigantic earphones, his muscular tattooed arms stretched across the metal frame of the top of the seat.

But Burleigh heard again and saw the mouth move this time, 'There is someone else waiting. And every son needs a father, after all.'

And that's when Burleigh knew there would be more blood spilt. And in the dim recesses of what we must call his soul, he remembered the housewife bent over the reflecting ball, and hoped that whatever blood was spilt, it would not be hers.

The bus juddered to a halt then, at its final stop. They both rose, as if with one instinct. And Captain Mildew, *an fear drúcht*, the Dewman descended the stairs with considerably more agility than he ascended them. As Burleigh followed him, past the driver who, just as he did all those years before, kept the engine running, he realised he had neglected to pay either of their fares.

36

THE BUS IDLED FOR a time, releasing a cloud of exhaust, as if to provide a misted backdrop for a melodrama. The two principals walked from it, through the creaking gate and past the cherry tree in the front garden. They paused by the front door and seemed to reflect for a moment before the more lumbersome of them moved to the small half-gate to the left of it, past the garage. One hand reached over, a latch clicked back and they both walked through and out of sight. Then the bus drew off on the last run of its shift, leaving an even denser cloud of exhaust, which took its time to disperse in the still night air.

There was a long interval of silence. Then the sound of a circular saw, one of the small table-top kinds, used for home carpentry. A symphony of extended, agonising screams then, which gradually changed to a diminuendo of whimpers and groans and eventually reverted to silence once more.

And the last wisps of exhaust fumes dispersed then, as if exhausted themselves.

37

DANY WAS DEEP IN carnie dreams. But these dreams were not of carnivals. They were of a small privet hedge that led past a manicured garden lawn towards a half-gate, which a calloused hand reached behind to release a latch. He recognised the gate, the hedge, the house, but not the hand. The house was a bungalow and was now sliding past his vision, towards a scuffed back door he knew only too well. The same calloused hand tried the door handle, then reached down to a well-trodden mat, which it lifted aside to reveal a key. Now why his mother left the key under that mat, which was the first place any intruder would look for it, was a thought that had hardly time to divert Dany's dream, since the same hand was inserting the key in the lock and turning. The door slid open, scraping over another mat, a sound he recognised, and that, had he been awake, would have brought his whole childhood back, and the kitchen itself came into view. A simple kitchen, its furniture a little tawdry, its decorations perhaps kitsch, with its red-lozenged tablecloth and its framed view of Amalfi on the wall, but a beloved kitchen, nonetheless. But this dream had no place for nostalgia or fondness, and was now plodding its way through an even smaller dining room into a hallway, where the streetlight gleamed on the brown carpet, through a half-open door where the sound of adolescent breathing came from, urgent, occupied in a drama of some intensity, and Dany found himself looking with sudden and unexpected emotion at himself. His Bose QuietComfort headphones were silhouetted by the screen in front of him and his hands were tweaking the game console.

38

ANDY WAS PLAYING ASSASSIN'S Creed, swooping over the turrets of Renaissance Florence, unleashing a fearsome array of sharpened weapons at his cowled pursuers. A spiked bolero round the neck of one, a crossbow bolt through the heart of another. Shaven-headed prison guards, their muscled torsos wrapped in chainmail, did fearsome things to prisoners in prison cells, unseen, but not unheard. Andy had the option of releasing the tortured ones or continuing his flight, and he had just chosen the latter, when he pressed the starred Stop button. The cries of pain still echoed in his headphones. He removed the headphones, gently, and the cries continued. Although they were not cries now, more like a drawn-out sob, a dying whimper. And he recognised his father's voice.

The door was open behind him. A sliver of streetlight shone on the hallway carpet. He heard another sound then, the high-pitched whine of a carpentry saw. It, too, was dying, like a long-extended breath.

He stood up. He walked from the hallway to the dining room and through to the kitchen, where a man sat, his shoulders sloping over the red and white tablecloth.

'He's in the garage,' this man said.

'Who?' Andy asked.

'Your father,' the man replied. 'But I wouldn't go in there just yet.'

'Why not?' Andy asked.

'Some things,' the man said, 'are best left alone.'

Andy waited a while and when he tired of waiting made his way through the back door to the garden outside.

The garage door was open. As was the small wooden gate that led to the front lawn. Whatever the thing was that should not be seen must be in here, Andy thought as he pushed it open further and saw, with the help of streetlight that came through the windows of the double-doors, the detritus on the cement floor.

It was underneath his father's carpentry table. And whatever that detritus was, it had been carved and gouged and sliced on the table above. There were pools of stuff that could have been part of his father's condiment samples. But Andy knew blood when he saw it. This stuff was blood, not jam.

Blood, and screeds of flesh and something like bone, stuck to the circular saw in the gap in the table's centre, through which more blood dripped on to the detritus below it. There was one body there, in the remains of a denim shirt, which seemed scooped out from the inside, and the remains of another, which seemed to be those insides scooped out, but which Andy knew couldn't really be. It was as if someone had gutted an animal, used the hacksaw and the small array of chisels and the circular saw to remove the insides of something, because the outer core was all that was needed, all that was desired.

'Your father,' the man had said.

And he had the strange sense then, somewhere in the unfathomable depths of himself, that he was being watched. Whoever was watching was part of him: family, friend and blood. He had felt alone for so long, he realised then, unmoored like one lone starling, beating its way through unfamiliar skies; even the least desirable of us has to be wanted, he thought, or he felt, and he knew in his heart of hearts that he was as undesirable as this mess that had been left on the garage floor.

He turned and saw a figure in the garden outside, dark against the shrouded apple trees, wearing his father's suit. This figure also wore his father's hands, his father's expression round the mouth; in fact, this figure was like his father in every respect except for the eyes, which let Andy know in no uncertain terms that this figure was wearing his father, like a suit.

'Call me Father,' this father-figure said.

'I will,' said Andy. 'Gladly.'

And Andy felt like the starling reaching its old familiar telephone wire, and wondered why he had used that word, 'gladly'. It was an old-fashioned word but it sounded the way he felt. And he felt glad.

'I should bury all this,' he said, 'somewhere.'

'Where?' the one who was now his father asked. And the boy registered another fact: that he didn't question the need for burial. The mess on the cement floor was unsightly, dead, and had once been human.

'Under the cherry tree,' Andy said.

'Fine,' his father-figure said. 'Even, if I may say so, perfect.'

The speech was rusty as yet, the boy noticed. This process of becoming human must be like entering a new country, learning an entirely new set of rules. But he felt a thrill of anticipation when the father-figure took the old shovel, threw open the double-doors of the garage, headed for the soft ground around the cherry-tree roots and began immediately to dig.

This figure dug furiously, with an extraordinary and repetitive strength. It demolished crabbed roots and resistant shards of stone, cut right through an old bicycle wheel buried in the earth, and within minutes a gaping grave had been opened, with the cherry tree sagging pitifully above it.

'That tree,' the boy said, 'was planted the year I was born.'

'Not you,' the father-figure said. 'You were born much, much later. In fact, given certain considerations, under some jurisdictions, in the opinion of certain parties, you have yet to be born.'

And the boy felt another thrill, hearing these odd, legal archaisms. And he wondered what being born would entail.

Why should she feel relief, even pleasure, at the very real troubles of others? So after the PTA meeting she had driven across the familiar bridge that she had walked over so many times, always in daylight. She swung left, past the cement bathing shelters, and parked in the hardened sand amongst the darkened dunes. She saw the movement of shadows among the distant humps of sand grass, and remembered the reputation of these dunes, as a lovers' hideout. And she wondered once more what could have occurred between Carmen and Andy on that afternoon of the flying ants. Something that could not be named. Whatever it was it belonged to the shadows, a shadow somehow deeper than all of the shadows about her. She turned her attention to the sea then, to calm her teeming brain. A crescent moon sat in an expanding halo of clouds and was reflected in the quiet September waters. Was it September already? she wondered, and she realised her thoughts were rambling again, turning and turning in some echo chamber of the mind, when she heard the rap of knuckles against the passenger window. There was a man there, in a leather jacket, and he was fumbling with the buttons of his trousers. Eileen reached for the keys, pushed the car into gear, too quickly, far too quickly, she realised, since the car began to buck and shudder like a horse suddenly confined to a box. She found first gear then and the car roared towards the shoreline, leaving her unknown Casanova in a veritable cloud of risen sand. She heard a howl as she drove, and could see through the rear-view mirror him hopping on one foot, and she had to allow herself a smile at the thought that she had somehow driven over the other. Serves him right, the weirdo, she thought. She turned right then, when the indented sand nearest the shoreline began to rattle the car once more, and headed back for the wooden bridge, and home.

Her sense of guilt returned, though, when the empty bus stop came into view. Had she broken his foot? she wondered. Pervert or not, he hardly deserved that. And was guilt to become her constant companion now, guilt at her relief that the sons of others were faring no better than her own, guilt at the loss of the son she had been so close to, guilt at all of the secrets she had kept from her dear husband, and she was turning through the cement pillars into her driveway, when she saw them both, Jim for some reason with a shovel in his hands and Andy, stamping a rough circle of exposed earth around the cherry tree.

Jim began to walk, in an odd series of uncoordinated movements, across the lawn, to the hard cement of the driveway itself. She heard the loud scrape of the shovel, as it moved from the surface of the lawn to the surface of the drive. Andy did what he had been always doing lately, just stood by the cherry tree and stared. Her eyes flashed from her son to her husband, whose face flared like a ghoul in the headlights, and another came behind him, from the small half-gate by the garage that led to the back garden. Something about the sloped shoulders, the down-angled head, brought a memory flooding back. A cardboard case, out of which came a ball of silvered glass. As the one that was her husband staggered towards her, she knew nothing would ever be the same again. She knew, in fact, as she pushed the gear handle down, that things had not been the same for quite some time now. He took one ghoulish step more and she drove the car forwards, caught him somewhere between the knees and midriff, and sent him spinning back towards the garage doors. She put the car into reverse then, and saw Andy, blocking her exit. She spun the wheel, and felt the sickening crunch as the back bumper hit the cherry tree. She saw Andy stretch his arms out towards his father, who, although it seemed not

40

DANY WOKE WITH A long slow gasp of something like terror. He held his left hand up against the webbed curve of his hammock. He had dreamed of an explosion of pain there, as if his thumb had been severed. It throbbed now, where the joint met the hand, with sudden, sharp pangs of pure-white agony. Then the pain gradually dispersed with the memory of the dream.

But Dany was awake. Wide awake. He could hear the gentle snoring of Mona above him, Jude to his right. He gripped the webbed net with his unpained hand and slid himself, deftly and silently, from the hammock. He felt sleep had abandoned him. He padded quietly on bare feet to the door and pushed it open. The carnival sat under a bank of low September clouds with the faintest outline of a moon behind them. The crowds had long gone and the only sound was a gentle, familiar scraping from the frame that held the dodgem cars.

Dany walked then, easing the door closed behind him, knowing sleep was hardly an option now. He followed the sound and saw three squat roustabouts, bums to the hard ground, feet spread-eagled, while they judiciously scraped the scaffolding above them of its filigree-like tendrils.

'Slim pickings,' said the nearest.

'But,' said Dany, 'every little helps.'

He knew the conversational mode by now.

'Ah now,' said the roustie, 'who are you tellin'?'

Who else but you, Dany thought but didn't vocalise.

'Though with the holiday coming, we should be drownin' in the stuff.'

He heard a soft creaking then, the sound a metal pole makes in a rusted socket, and at first thought it was coming from the empty carousel.

'There's a townie girl,' the roustie said, 'been asking for you.'

And Dany thought oh no, or oh yes, and his mind began to turn with that slow, tumble-drying motion once more.

'Trouble and strife,' the roustie said.

'Meaning what?' Dany asked.

'Oh, I said nothing,' the roustie muttered, and returned to his diligent scraping. 'A shut mouth catches no flies.'

And there were flies about, Dany noticed now, tiny airborne ant-like creatures, catching what was left of the moonlight in their transparent wings. They brushed off his face, like barely visible hands, as he left the harvesting of the dodgem cars and headed for the empty carousel, and that sound of rusted creaking.

The carousel was silent, the horses gleaming with the colours of lost party balloons. Not a whisper of movement. But the rusted broken whine continued and Dany followed it round the curve of the carousel to where a series of white swans hung beneath triangular poles, the metallic wings concealing a children's seat inside. Silent empty swings, and only one of them was moving.

There was a girl's leg crooking down from the metal wing, with green leather shoes and a block-like heel. Above her the suspension pole shifted in its metal socket. Dany recognised the shoe, and remembered the sweeping brush that moved around it, and the shoe seemed to recognise him, because it began to swing, lazily, as he approached and a brown head of hair lifted from the sleeping swan and he heard the same voice saying, 'Been looking for you, carnie.'

'Are your brothers about?' he asked, and he didn't know why, but he felt the same darting pain suddenly in his thumb.

'I should say I'm sorry, shouldn't I? They've only one sister; they can be a bit protective. But you—'

And her leg stretched out here, so the green leather toe of her shoe stroked the back of his hand.

'—you showed them what was what.'

'I wish I hadn't.'

'I'm sure,' she said. 'And I'm still wondering how you did that. Little slip of a thing like you.'

'Don't ask,' he said.

'Why not?' And she stretched one hand out as if waiting for his to grasp it, which of course he did.

'What use is a dead metal swan,' she asked, 'if it doesn't fly?'

'It's for children,' he said. 'They can imagine it does.'

'And I was imagining, lying here, thinking of you. I was imagining all sorts of things.'

'I should take you home,' he said. 'The carnival's over.'

'I can see that,' she said. 'Over for the night. So I was lying here, all on my lonesome, wondering about it.'

'Wondering what?'

'It has secrets,' she said. 'You have secrets, carnies have secrets, even this metal swan thing has secrets, and the only way to get me out of here will be to let me in on some of them.'

She released his hand then, and stood up in the creaking swan. She looked at him, six feet below her, and held her small white arms out.

'Catch me, carnie,' she said, and she fell.

He reached out and caught her in one fluid move, and she sank, like a large human feather, into his arms.

'You did that well,' she said, and kissed him.

He could feel braces round her tiny teeth. Her tongue darted over his and he felt a rush of blood and of that hidden sap that seemed to hold his carnie muscles together and, without meaning to, he began to rise.

'Again,' she said, pulling her lips away and meeting his again, and they both rose, over the rusting swans, over the poles that held them, over the wooden frames that held the poles, over the carousel and the idle pennant of the big top until the carnival seemed to huddle below them, with its tiny canvas streets and its strange crushed geometry in the limestone fields that stretched away to the town beyond.

'I knew,' she said, 'you were something else.'

'And I'm taking you home.'

He left her on the town square with her head full of questions by the shuttered hotel where he had met her first. There were, thankfully, no brothers about.

'Can we do that again, tomorrow?' she asked. Although she was already uncertain what it was they had done.

And he said yes, they maybe could, and thought it better to walk his way back.

41

EILEEN'S DRIVING WAS ERRATIC at the best of times, but the sight of the bleeding thumb in her rear-view mirror did lead to some major traffic infractions. She ran a red light at Dollymount Avenue and crossed the double-white line so many times that a traffic policeman flagged her down before the lights at the Bull Wall Bridge. Her attempts to explain the severed digit in the knuckle of her wing-mirror led to suspicions of intoxication by the arresting officer, so she was blowing into a breathalysing condom when she was unfortunately recognised by a limping male in a black leather jacket, making his painful way across the bridge. Accusation followed counter-accusation, an ambulance arrived, a forensic team assembled, and the last to be called was Dr Gerard Grenell, who eventually accompanied her to the public ward of Beaumont Hospital. Her insistence that the severed thumb belonged to one who had somehow infiltrated the body of her beloved son and that her husband was no longer her husband and that, by the by, the broken foot of the limping pervert was a well-deserved punishment for an attempted sexual assault on the dunes of Bull Island didn't help her claims to veracity or sanity. The end result of which was that Eileen was prescribed a new round of medication and, when she protested, forcibly confined to a temporary stretcher, since there were no hospital beds available. She succumbed eventually, swallowed the pills with the regulation glass of water, and soon fell into a fitful sleep, as the late-night drunks began to spill over into the corridor from the emergency ward.

42

THEY WALKED, THE THREE of them. They had no sense of time. They were headed west, they knew, following a carnival they knew, and of all carnivals on the small island there was one that was of particular interest to them. The one parked in the field behind the abandoned petrol station servicing the matchmaking festival of Lisdoonvarna. Andy, after the bloody burial and the chaotic exit of Eileen, had tapped on the computer with his thumbless hand and tracked it down.

So they walked, past the Five Lamps in the early dawn, towards what Burleigh had once known as Kingsbridge Station, now Heuston. They were early for the trains heading west but they didn't mind waiting.

Something about train tracks endeared them to the Captain. Or was it to the corpse he now inhabited, the hapless Jim, who seemed amazed by every new step he took, as if performing tasks that in his own, recently terminated lifetime would have seemed impossible? This incarnation of Jim didn't mind jostling; in fact, he liked pavements to himself, thrust passers-by violently to one side or the other without consideration of age or sex. He had yet to learn the art of the blend, an art carnies had mastered aeons before. So when he crossed Burgh Quay, straight into the path of one of those new green rubbish trucks, he stopped it with an outstretched hand that brought a spider's web of cracks to the windscreen as the truck shuddered to a halt and left the driver wondering if he had hit the brakes rather than the accelerator. But when the Captain reached the grimy Victorian façade of Heuston Station, a veneer of calm descended. The tracks that threaded their way along the Liffey seemed to promise a route to something new and old, something west and quite outside of time. And the empty train, when they boarded it, seemed to have its own peculiar geometry. The sun poured through the right-hand windows and made strange rectangles of the light and shade. And the rectangular swathes of light that hit the floor were themselves moving with a shimmering cloud that looked like dust, but that, to the observant eye, would have revealed itself to be a host of tiny winged creatures, almost smaller than dust themselves.

The train gradually filled, and filled more with every station it passed. Teenagers in ripped jeans and T-shirts with collapsible tents and backpacks, families with buckets and spades at the ready, the odd lost farmer in a pinstriped suit, shiny with age, looking like an implant from another era. Which is how the three of them must have seemed, to anyone who took care to look and examine them closely. But Burleigh saw that none of them did. The Dewman stared at the tracks whirring by, as if they had a hypnotic power all of their own. His ersatz son reached out a hand every now and then as if to catch that ungraspable dust. When he opened his thumbless palm, Burleigh noted it to be covered in tiny wings, the fluttering of which was barely perceptible. It could have been chaff, it could have been harvest dust, from some strange, unearthly harvest reaping. Burleigh reached his own hand out and clutched a handful of what seemed to be air, and opened his palm to view the same fluttering harvest. But he knew, and he had to contain his excitement here, that it was just a harbinger of the reaping to come.

The train took them so far, then a bus took them further, and when the bus turned on its turnaround they had the option of hitch-hiking or Shanks's mare. The possibility that the kindness of strangers would extend to their unlikely and probably visually off-putting trio seemed remote so they walked. There was no discussion about this choice; they just tramped on. The Dewman could have taken to the air had the body he had adopted been more adaptable, but Jim's ample girth, with a body mass index of 32.5, on the cusp of obesity, made that highly unlikely.

Over tarmacadam roads first; then, when the roads departed from their sense of how the crow flies, over small drystone walls on to what were once called boreens and when the boreens curved away beneath the imaginary crow's path, they blundered through hedges on to the limestone fields that stretched towards a landscape of low, stone-capped moon-like hills.

Time was no problem, in the beginning. The Captain, the Dewman, *an fear drúcht* collapsed it, stretched it, condensed it at will. Thus it came to pass that the early-morning train deposited them in the western hinterland when it was still early morning and the bus, renowned for its lack of punctuality, arrived late and departed long before its advertised departure. Once they left the road, the boreen, the drystone walls, time became a problem, compounded. For the Dewman whorled it with him as he walked. So he dragged the ancient landscape – or moonscape, Burleigh would have called it – into a strange kind of motion and caused ancient things to wake with each footfall.

These ancient things were without shape, unlike him. They had found no host as yet. But they were all need, these remnants of old forgotten whispers, and latched on to whatever crossed their paths. A hare found itself transfixed in a sudden mid-dash rigour, jumped on its hind legs, twisted horribly in an airy freeze-frame and came to ground possessed. Its eyes streamed red, its fur bristled with sudden grey and it spun itself around them, Burleigh, Andy, the Dewman, searching for whom it might terrify, if not consume. And the Captain whispered, in a language the hare understood, '*Fan beagan*,' wait a little.

And so as they crossed the limestone floor a host of reawakened repossessed things slithered with them. Stoats, voles, mice, freshwater eels and crabs, and all of the barely visible winged things.

'Wings,' Burleigh rhapsodised, 'miraculous constructions, from the swooping crane to the tiniest midge, they did what no invention could, kept their constituent bodies airborne.'

Could he have done as well? No, he thought, some deity or some demiurge with powers of thought and mechanical construction way beyond his paltry capabilities. So they hummed, they buzzed, they slithered their way forward behind the three lumbering bipeds like a cloud and a carpet all at once.

43

IT WAS A CLEAR day, the Friday of the holiday weekend, and as such, a red-letter day for carnies. The whole caravan had been 'staunched' for four days beforehand without any noticeable flow of punters. But it did its thing, if not happily, at least with a patience born out of five thousand years of practice. And yes, carnies were almost Roman in their reservoirs of endurance. The crowds may have been desultory, the income frugal, the mildew harvest only appropriate for home consumption, but that patient breed knew they had the bank holiday to look forward to. And it was odd, Mona pondered, as the Friday morning trickle threatened to become a flood, how often the mistermed 'bank' holidays fell on the same day as far older, long-forgotten feast days. Swithin, Brigit, Patrick, Lugh, whatever impulse those banks followed, when they deemed a day appropriate to holiday, they followed, like carnies themselves, old forgotten patterns that they didn't care to understand, or examine. Did it matter what they called it, she asked Jude, who herself had a holiday named for her, as she helped her prepare her stall and saw reflected, in one of her many crystal balls, a figure from her own long-forgotten past. She recognised the sloping shoulders, the grey gabardine flapping in the summer heat, and remembered the tedious, never-ending and ultimately self-defeating enquiry into all things carnie. Burleigh? Could it possibly be he?

Under what rush of insanity would he attempt a return? She turned quickly, on instinct, and saw a pair of heels vanish, round a canvas tent.

He would never, she thought, and made her way through the jumble of stalls to the big-top entrance. Inside, in the lazy mid-morning gloom, she saw Monniker exercising a pair of Arabians in a cinched jacket and a pair of riding chaps. There was a discarded gabardine coat lying on the bleachers beside a diamanté-studded caparison. It must have been left by one of last night's punters, she thought, and returned to Jude's tent and her preparations for the coming weekend.

44

THEY HAD ENTERED THE carnival separately. One from the south, one from the east and one from the north. There was a rapid surge through the well-trodden grasses, as if a wind of renewal had suddenly blown them to life. But it was no wind it was the deathly unseen carpet of voles, stoats, mice and freshwater eels, seething through the grassy roots, with the odd crazed bound of a maddened hare cresting the now undulating and awakened wave of green. And any carnie who had seen it might have known some doom was coming, for carnies knew too well what hares brought with them.

But their entry would have been blurred to anyone who saw them, as if they had brought their own lack of focus with them. For accompanying each was a wavering cloud of tiny winged harvesters, each of them more efficient than the most diligent roustabout, needing neither scalpel nor bowl for the reaping that would soon commence. They would soon swell with mildew, grow fat like a blood-consuming tick until their wings could no longer bear the weight of their harvest, and they would flutter to the ground like exhausted grey parrots, to be harvested in turn.

Burleigh's entrance brought, to him, the most conflicting of emotions. He recognised the disused, sagging petrol pump and the field of crushed grass beyond. He had been there before, he couldn't remember how many times.

But any tiny flutter of sentiment was nothing to the rush of ennui that flooded him when he entered the carnival stalls. He had missed it, and he now felt the full force of his missing. With the missing came anger, a kind of fury and more than fury, a full-blooded, overwhelming urge for revenge. They had come for the mildew, he knew, the full harvesting, the reaping that would refine it into spice, and he remembered the sorry classifications the unfortunate Walter had made in his school copybook all of those years ago with his ink-stained fingers. Every emotion the carnies evoked rendered its quotient of mildew. But of all those emotions, terror rendered a crop that was quite off Walter's scale. So in his confused welter of ennui, anger and subdued revenge, almost as confused as the buzzing of wings around his bent head, Burleigh realised the dreadful reckoning was coming. Burleigh thought to savour this moment of anticipation. To relish it. To engorge himself in this cloud of impending. So he moved through the stalls and each stall brought a different memory back. Past his Hall of Mirrors, which he couldn't bear to enter, since the sight of himself might bring him to bursting. Into the mid-morning shadows of the circus tent, down through the bleachers, where he saw Monniker cracking the whip, putting his Arabians through their paces. He saw stains on his gabardine coat, and realised it was drenched in sweat. He slipped it off, and slid out, knowing there would be many more reasons to sweat on this day.

45

MAGGIE HAD PAID FOR a ride on the Ferris wheel. How she had got home last night was a blur to her now, but something magical had happened, some kind of airborne swoon. She remembered the taste of the thin carnie's lips, his tongue searching out the interstices of her teeth braces; she had begun the kiss, she knew, but he had continued it, and somehow transported her to a realm she couldn't quite understand. It was to do with soaring and great height; she had woken with the thrill of anticipation, done her morning clean-up in the hotel bar and changed, from her black skirt and white blouse into this summery dress, with a pair of polka-dotted socks over the same green-leather block-heeled shoes. He had noticed these shoes, she knew, as she wandered through the carnival stalls without any sight of him and decided on the Ferris wheel. She might recognise him from up here, she thought, and the lazy motion of the airborne chair seemed to suit her mood. It bore her up, slowly, with much creaking of joints and ratchets. She saw the carnival stalls descend below her, the cone of the big top to her right, the fluttering pennant of which seemed so close that she could almost touch it. Then there were the limestone fields stretching out beyond the town, the threads of tiny drystone walls delineating them, the thin, misty lines of the ancient cliffs and the white foam of the Atlantic beyond. And then the Ferris wheel jerked.

It shuddered forwards, in a stomach-crunching lurch. Jerked backwards then, with a sound of grinding metal, and an accompaniment of terrified screams. Then shuddered forwards again, and began a sickening whirl.

Maggie's first, absurd and irrelevant thought was for her dress, which the sudden wind sent fluttering round her face. She pulled the dress down then, covering her exposed legs, and wondered was this a new carnie thrill, a speeded-up Ferris wheel, and for a moment did her best to enjoy the accelerated ride. But the screams from all about her caused her to scream in turn, in mock alarm and enjoyment at first, and then, when the sounds of straining metal and whipping wind threatened to drown out the scream, she screamed a scream of pure, unadulterated terror. The protective bar was digging into her ribs, her cheeks were hollowed by the whirling wind and tiny winged ants were filling up her nostrils and her mouth, which she tried to keep closed but which each new gust of terror opened in another scream.

46

THE GHOST TRAIN, MEANWHILE, was on a track to some strange hell. It lumbered, it ground its way into greater horrors than it had ever been designed for. There were ghosts, sure enough, for those unlucky enough to have paid their fares, ghosts of long-dead parents, stillborn infants, dead and rotting pets, but something more, some buzzing, moaning Neanderthal and buried dread, the horror of which could only be measured by the howls that made it to the surface, at the entrance, where the queues stumbled back from the turnstile with another kind of dread, or the exit, where the Dewman and his ersatz son, Andy, waited for the harvest reaping. Tracks, the Dewman loved tracks, and he stared at them now, two grease-covered railway tracks with half-buried sleepers, over which the horrors far inside reached them in a dying kind of moan. A buzzing then, always the buzzing, and the cloud of winged things, bigger now, their quantum-like random movement slowed by the weight of mildew they had gorged. These things that had grown to the size of bluebottles, from fragments hardly greater than dust, fell in a dying curtain around the feet that bore the shoes once worn by Dany's father. Then a grinding of gears, a progressive crunch of metal chain on rusty sprockets, and the first car of the ghost train emerged, the four unfortunates who had proudly paid for the very first tickets huddled unmoving, buried skeleton-like in a cocoon of their own mildewed terror.

Was there a plan? The buzzing creatures round them seemed to think so, but whatever plan they fluttered to was that of an appetite born long long ago, in a forgotten time, with long-forgotten rules. But it was an appetite, no doubt about it, a need for consumption embedded in some unknown DNA. If there was a plan, the Dewman seemed hardly to care; he left his ersatz son to relish the spectacle while he lumbered through the collapsing carnival, in search of his real one.

And the Ferris wheel was by now just a blur of movement. Mildew was whirling from it, like the spray on the Atlantic waves in a winter storm. Or just like, Burleigh thought, viewing it from close to the collapsing helter-skelter, the threads of floss in a candyfloss spinning drum. Soon the sounds of groaning widgets, of metal bolts and braces strained to breaking point, of the buzzing of engorged insects, of the whey-coloured horse's mane of mildew flapping in its own storm, drowned out the screaming of the clientele that, it was frighteningly easy to forget, were still strapped within the flying cars.

There were carnies everywhere, struggling with this new chaos; roustabouts straining to keep the rides intact, carnival tents bursting into spontaneous combustion; they had had to forget to enable their kind to live, and couldn't remember now how to survive this onslaught. Bulgar remembered something, his greased muscles more than his dulled brain, and as he saw the Dewman shambling through, he swung round with a carnival hammer, directed at the mildly curious head. But the Dewman's hand anticipated it, whipped out and broke the wooden stave, and with the hammer's shattered head reduced him to a brawny pulp.

The carnies saw. Some of them ran towards him, in bounds that became greater with each step and ended up in a flight of kinds. They descended from the mildewy air, murderous hands stretched out to grab, scratch and claw, but he swatted them off like what they were to him: flies. And as they tumbled in the flattened grass beneath the combusting carnival stalls, the clouds of engorged bluebottles descended to enact their own dewy punishments. And the carnies ran, this way and that, flew through the smoking air themselves, deluded by the rush of mildew that brought to each of them a private and particular hallucinogenic nightmare.

The roustabouts pulled wrenches from their roustabout pouches, claw hammers from their swinging belts, pipes and bits of bent scaffolding from the collapsing rides and threw themselves upon him, the squats attacking his flailing feet, the thins raining blows down on him from their elongated arms. But the buzzing of flying things confused them, the mildew clouded their eyes, and the small, pear-like shape of the marmalade-salesman form the Dewman had usurped proved stronger than all of their roustie musculature. He left them one by one lying comatose in the flattened grass, and pulled each head free of the buzzing insect cloud, inspected each bloodied face and bellowed: '*Cha cha bhuil se, mo mhach, mo mhicheo?*'

47

DANY HEARD HIM CALLING. He was twirling Mona on the rope, to that point where her beautifully arched body with its angled knees and arms was becoming a blur, when the sounds of screams outside developed into a roar, and he felt as much as heard the words in the pit of his stomach, which seemed to cry out, 'My son, my son.' But he continued with his hauler's task, until the chaos outside became unbearable and the sawdust circle gradually filled with the agonised figures of carnival-goers, each of them encased in a cocoon of mildew, tearing at it with their desperate hands, as if to escape what their terror had given rise to. And the more they panicked, the more the mildew grew. So they were in what could be called a bind. Dany left Mona swinging on the trapeze way above and walked into the bright September air and, when his eyes had adjusted to the glare, a barely describable scene was there to meet them.

The Ferris wheel had become a blur, as if it was a paper windmill blown by a giant child. The rollercoaster was collapsing under the strain of its own movement, the supporting scaffolding flying off like matchsticks, the whole structure only held together by the mildew that the terror of those inside, like a growing mushroom cloud. And Dany knew, with an instinct he could no longer deny or avoid, that some reaping had commenced. He heard the voice once more, *mo mhach*, *mo mhicheo*, booming, as if echoing inside some great interior space, and he saw through the blur of the clouds of dew-engorged insects, a figure, at once strange and familiar, rubbing with a pudgy pair of hands its own slightly myopic eyes.

'*M'athair*,' he said and the father thing turned. He knew, and he didn't know how he knew, that this father thing spoke only dead tongues. He saw the face crease into a thousand smiles. Shapes, or grimaces more likely, since the Dewman had not yet fully mastered the art of smiling. But the smiling figure walked towards him, over the bodies of stunned roustabouts, through the clouds of bluebottle things and reached out a pair of familiar arms.

'*Mab llwyb a pherth.*'

Dany heard the words, dead and old, and a cold wind came with them, bound only for his carnie soul. He felt the arms wrapping round him, the soft hands gripping his shoulder blades; he felt a sudden swoon into a dark place he had never known existed. But it was in him, and he was it. He felt a warp inside him, an ancient, barely knowable warp, and he knew he had to battle this warp, and he knew that the battle had to commence now, or be lost for ever.

48

KILLING HIS FATHER TURNED out to be a gnarly, ritualistic and life-changing business. Oh the battle with the Captain was exhausting, almost endless, painful, battering, ruinous to what remained of the carnival, what rides still remained standing, and eventually sent the Captain back to whatever element he had come from. It was a battle between affection and hatred; a battle of competing affections, competing hatreds. He had loved the affable, greying, paunched body he was destined to find some way to destroy. He hated what lived now inside it (although you couldn't call the Dewman's condition a living one), and hate and love battled so much inside Dany it seemed they were almost the same, shadow and light, night and day, sweet and sour, open and shut, pain and ecstasy, reflective and reflected, all of the opposites, contradictions, antinomies. The sinewy arms that enclosed him in the first embrace; he knew they weren't human, but there was the strange, seductively comforting sense of sinking into something otherworldly that had been waiting for him, for all of us. You think this human shape is your home, your body, your final destination? No, this affection said, there is another thing, another place, another home, another parent, where time will fade and pain will vanish and all of those green squawking birds will cease their chattering. You will be mine, I will be yours, and none of this human stuff need bother us.

So Dany had to fight, he had to fight from the deepest recesses inside him, to resist this call that he knew was him. He felt his father's form judder then, and shift, and saw a form emerge from behind those once-beloved eyes that was not human. This thing changed shape, once, twice, three times, and each time he knew he must hold it, he must smother it, he must bind it with his human arms until he extinguished whatever life was left in it. It was an embrace of kinds, an extinguishing embrace. Did you ever feel when a parent held you that they were squeezing the lifeblood from you, that whatever was yours, uniquely yours, was being smothered and whatever was theirs was designed to replace it? Those were the smothering arms with which Dany embraced his father of fathers, *an fear drúcht*, the Dewman. He held him while his feet kicked them both to the air, while the body he still held lurched sideways and scythed through the windmill of mildew that was the Big Wheel – the screams inside the cocoons of fluttering beard had long ceased – and he still held, while whatever force was left inside the half-living husk crashed them both through the canvas roof of the big top and inside, in the wavering sunlight coming through from above, they sank slowly together downwards, where whatever pulse Captain Mildew had left expired on the sawdust floor.

Dany heard a lazy growl, then, from beneath the bleachers. The old lion padded out, on ancient, furred feet, and nosed around the once-beloved, pear-shaped form of his father. It raised a hind leg and did what it had once done to him. It raised its hind leg and released a stream that was yellow-coloured, ammonia-odoured.

He went searching for himself then. Which sounds like a figure of speech, a metaphor even, but which wasn't. He suspected the other was out there somewhere, imitating him, masquerading as him, even being him. He wandered through the broken shards of carnival rides, down the mangled tracks of the ghost train, past the warped and mildewed cocoons of what had once been lovelorn bachelors and bachelorettes, and was moving down a twisted corridor of mangled scaffolding when he heard the tinkling sound of falling glass.

He turned and saw, through an apse of collapsed ghost-train cars, the entrance to Burleigh's Amazing Hall of Mirrors. The neon sign, which had entranced him so long ago, was swinging on its rusty pinion, small cascades of broken glass falling from it. He bent his head and pushed his way past the mangled cars, and inside.

He saw a squat version of himself approaching. He knew somehow, and he didn't know how he knew, that this was simply another reflection. And he was less entranced this time by his grotesquely misshapen form than by the spider's webs of cracks that covered it. Like the tracings on a lark's egg, he thought, the kind he would find on the dunes when spring came round, that he shouldn't touch, since the bird would smell his fingers and desert the nest, like him. Or like the fontanelle on a newborn baby's skull. He never cared for babies, but he did like that word, fontanelle. He remembered when he had first heard it. Mrs Dignam, two doors down, had given birth. 'At her age, would you believe,' his mother had whispered, as the pram approached, on the pathway outside of the privet hedge. 'You can touch,' Mrs Dignam had proclaimed proudly, 'and feel the fontanelle.'

What he remembered now was the word, and the dribble of tiny veins across the infant skull. The mirrors looked like that, cracked with a delicacy that threatened to collapse at any moment. Whole copses of spider cracks, Taw Woods and forests of them. And as he examined them, he realised the sound he had heard outside might have not been the sound of falling glass after all. Because now he could hear a tiny, cracked, splintering voice, calling for help. He saw a shape then, behind the cracked mirror, a face, with the ancient cadaverous texture of vellum. He remembered the same shape, the same texture, seeing it through an explosion of bubbles as he fell towards the ocean floor. But where there had been the warp of descending brine, here was the warp of distressed glass. And he could see lineaments he recognised, in the skully shape with the papery leather skin, the cracked mouth, like crumpled cigarette paper, pleading, its claw-like fingers attempting to reach, through the cracked mirror, towards him. He held up his hand to meet it, as Mona had done all that time ago. His young, hairless fingers on one side of Burleigh's glass, her centuries-old digits on the other. It was as if an angel had been revealed, ravaged by all of the years it never had to suffer, since the first expulsion of Adam.

'Mona,' he said.

'Ydna,' an ancient voice replied, his name garbled by the leathery tongue into something that must have been before speech.

But still, he recognised it. And he did what she had done, all of that time ago. And when his hands pierced the cracked mirror, he realised that time could now become whatever he wanted it to be. He grasped a pair of ancient hands and pulled a young girl, marginally older than him, out.

They stood there, wordless for a moment, a dumbshow of spider-cracked ghouls observing them.

'*Tusa—*' Mona began.

He knew what she was about to say before she said it.

'*Mo thuaidh agus mo dheas, mo thoir agus thiar—*'

And if he kissed her, it wasn't to shut her up. It wasn't

because he didn't understand that dead tongue. He understood well enough.

'My north and my south, my east and my west—'

It was to prove to himself that her lips were pliable, and that there was nothing mirrored about them.

'I followed you inside,' she said.

'It wasn't me.'

'But whatever I followed is still inside there.'

And he could see another shape move, inside the cracked mirror. It had his own face, his own shape. But it was shifting, as if searching for an exit it might never find. And he himself was not moving.

'Burleigh, too.'

And he could see another shape, behind the broken filigrees of gold. A downturned head, sloped shoulders. It moved, and a host of sloped reflections moved with it.

'Can we leave them there?'

'What do you think?'

She shook her head. And he shook his, in unspoken agreement. He knew they couldn't.

So he glanced at what seemed to be his reflection. It shimmered for a moment, then slithered left. He whipped his head around, and saw it dart down a thousand mirrored surfaces. The slope-shouldered thing darted after.

Fear. Fear bubbled out of them, through the filigree cracks in the glass.

He played a mind-trick then; as the two reflections ran, he imagined a solid mirror in front of them.

He heard a crash, a curse, a howl of agony.

He imagined something else. A descending cuboid of mirrors that vanished into nothingness.

They ran down it and, terrified at their own diminishment, found themselves running back.

She knew he had it in him: the dew, the shine, the sult. She would tell him that later. His mind became mirror and his mirror, mind. He tossed Burleigh's Amazing Hall of Mirrors in his mind's eye, as if it was his own glass kaleidoscope. He sent those reflections spinning down whole doll's-house versions of Burleigh's Pandemonium. Macro became micro and micro macro, until the very idea of size made nonsense of itself. He became an orchestrator of mirrors, a conductor of hidden harmonies from them; he coaxed rills and trills and tiny rippling cascades of something like melody from them; he created whole symphonies of rearrangement, infinities on infinities. He saw the other run down a whole avenue of himself, only to crash into a mutant version. And Burleigh clawed at the glass but couldn't break it; he scratched and beat at his image with his pitiable hands and then retreated from himself into the tiniest corner, where Walter had, all of those years ago, hidden his codex. From that point onwards it was a simple matter. Dany coaxed the Rotterdam gold into motion, into action as it were; all of its molecules bowed their heads and said, yes sir, whatever your bidding is, sir, and Burleigh's immense cathedral of glass began to move. Andy screamed and Burleigh howled as he saw the multiple images of himself approaching, crunching in cascades of splintering glass, to make a cube around him first, then a pentahedron then a dextrahedron then a duodenalhedron and then into not quite a perfect circle, but more like the earth's orbit around the sun, an ellipse, which oddly was the perfect shape for the procedure that followed. Thus they both were confined in their perfect circle of hell, reflected everywhere in the elliptical orb's mirrored surface, shaped like a cry of agony. And in the ravaged carnival, all that remained of it was this giant sphere of Rotterdam gold; not quite spherical, though, more like elliptical. The shape of a giant, golden tear.

As the carnies gazed at it in something like awe (and awe was, after all, an emotion foreign to them up to this particular point. In fact, it could be justifiably stated that it took an awful lot to amaze them), Dany booted the huge golden thing with his foot, and to their further amazement, it began to roll. Because the abandoned field behind the abandoned petrol station was on a gradual slope after all, the kind of slope that is never noticed until a sudden downpour sends water cascading through the tents. Anyway, it began a slight roll downwards which was like waving a red flag to the roustabouts who, talls, squats and thins, as with one mind, put their thick and thin fists to the surface of the rusted gold and continued its roll. And the carnies as a breed needed little encouragement to follow.

So it was that the strange rusted golden ellipse found its way to the town square, carnies and roustabouts pushing, and here the tarmac surface made its passage all the easier. The pubs had long closed and the chip shops with them, but a few mooning bachelors and bachelorettes still sat on the green wooden benches. They were much the worse for wear, but that didn't prevent them from lending what country folk called 'a hand'. So the pushing continued, in the way of those things that gather a momentum of their own, that people engage in not quite knowing why but for the random fun of it. And it was fun, if truth be told, to be pushing this huge thing like an Anish Kapoor sculpture that should have been sitting in a square in Chicago or St Petersburg, but no, it was here, a hard shove up that incline and a little extra and there she goes boys, bouncing down the road, the cars scattering this way and that, for the elliptical thing owned the road now, so she did.

Why they thought of it as a 'her' was a mystery to be solved on another day, perhaps. There was nothing feminine about this huge ellipse, this massive, ever-so-slightly flattened sphere, apart from the fact that it was bound for water. The way ordinary seamen called a vessel, astronauts called a spaceship 'her', this motley crew – carnies, roustabouts, bachelors and bachelorettes – gave the thing sex, and it was female.

And what of Burleigh and Andy, bouncing and rattling around in the mirror of themselves? Well, the less said the better, one supposes. They rolled and their reflections rolled with them. To be constantly circling in a circle of oneself is a kind of hell, but there was another hell coming.

The carnies had pushed, they had toiled mightily, off the tarmac of the old Liscannor Road, crushing the old drystone wall bordering it, on to the rocky fields, and it bounced for a while, needed some encouragement again and they tired for a bit until they saw, as a revelation of kinds, where they were heading. But it wasn't a revelation; there was a feeling of 'of course' about it. Of course, there was only one place this jubilant rolling could end; there was only one home for this giant rusted ellipse, this metal construct like a 2,000-pound bomb, but much more difficult, and in an odd way much more fun, to roll. The thin, wavering edge of cliff with nothing beyond it. The roar of the Atlantic beneath. Of course. Wouldn't it be fun to see it tumble, rock a little bit on the cliff's edge, as if there was no option but to fall, but as if, in a mute, gravitational horror of falling, it did its best to resist taking the final plunge? So they pushed, all hands together now, just this little bit more lads, and demolished the protective fence as if made of matchsticks, and the warning signs placed there by the Board of Works; they pushed, carnies, roustabouts, bachelors and bachelorettes, and a loud cheer went up as it made its final roll.

It hit the water at the gravitational speed of 9.81 metres per second and vanished from sight in a great volcanic plume of spray.

The mirrors began to warp and bend as they plunged downwards. Burleigh saw himself not so much ageing as reverting to a primordial version of himself. Walter had called it Mulciber, all those years ago, 'who was headlong sent with his industrious crew, to build in hell'. The reversion was rapid and the terror unimaginable and Burleigh saw, as the mirrors finally shattered, the reflection of an infinity of Mulcibers and he knew, before the waters foamed and spun him, that seven infinite bad-luck years would be their lot.

For the ocean, Dany realised from above, is the ultimate cleanser. He saw his own body bob to the surface, far far below. He had not so much killed himself, he realised, as cleansed his body for a proper burial.

49

THERE WAS A SMALL graveyard on a soft, descending field of grass, more a fall than a field, since it blended almost imperceptibly into the untamed wilderness of gorse and heather that led to the mound of Howth Head. This graveyard had an oddity about it, in that none of the gravestones were standing. There were no sandstone crosses tilted with age and ivy, no recent black-marble monoliths from the nearby monumental sculptor's. There were even no mute, granite angels, arms crossed, wings chipped, eyes staring blindly at the sarcophagus behind or below. No, there was nothing to interrupt the view of the suburb of Sutton below and the flecked white wilderness of the Irish Sea, other than the souls that wandered through it, searching through the uncut grass for the flattened plinths of their loved ones, or bent in memory, whispering some version of a prayer, at the graves they already knew. Either by the diktat of the municipality or the parish, every grave here was an almost buried plinth, laid flat in the irregularly cut grass. All the accidental poetry of commemoration, beloved wife of, fondly remembered by, life everlasting, face to face, had to be read standing, gazing down, or kneeling, wiping the detritus of whatever season had passed, spring, summer, autumn, winter, from the plinth at the visitant's feet or knees. And that's where he saw her, his mother, standing first, a sad bouquet of flowers in her hand, then kneeling by the new marble slab which read: 'James and Andrew Rackard, dearly beloved of Eileen . . .'

He was as surprised by the sight of his name, chipped by an unknown hand into the black marble, as he was by the sight of her, unseen by him. Andrew. And he wondered what anagram Mona would have made of that. No Dany now, no Ynad; only one rearrangement of the letters leapt out at him: wander. Which seemed, on balance, appropriate to what it was he had become. He would wander, he knew, from his carnie home wherever it settled, for a day, a bank-holiday weekend, a week, but if there ever was to be a return, it would only be to there. Or maybe to here, to watch his mother bend over that plinth in some kind of beloved remembrance. Her grief was, like most of her other emotions, succinct and contained. She laid the sad bouquet directly over his name but he knew from her dry eyes that she felt she had lost him a long time before. Before the Dewman, before the carnival cataclysm, before the death of her half-beloved husband.

But he knew, following on from that knowing, that that very fact meant he would never leave her. There was a robin, flitting between the buried gravestones, from flower to withered flower. He remembered his shapeshifting father, all the trauma of his battle, his fight, his warp-spasm with him, and he performed another warp and found himself inside that robin, in that carnie way, and skittered forwards on tiny, clawed feet. He took a leap then, from a fresh carnation on to her hand that was smoothing whatever leaves had obscured his stone of remembrance.

'Mother,' he whispered.

He saw her surprised eyes, looking down at the feathered interloper on her ring finger. And a tear finally willed itself from her grey eyes. It gathered from a dim mist into clear water and fell and touched his robin's breast.

'Don't cry, Mother.'

He would wander, he knew that, as befitted his new anagram, but could always return to her. In a daydream, one of those sudden fancies that happens on a busy street, she would turn and see an overhanging alleyway in shadow, and for some reason think of him. And he would be there. On the bus journey home, her hand brushing the fog of the breath-misted window, she'd glimpse a figure departing from the light of a streetlamp. And she would think of him. At night, most of all, tossing alone in her bedroom, desperate for sleep, through her half-closed eyes she would glimpse his blurred shadow. And she would find sleep then, and he would be there.

50

THEY REACHED THE LAND of the gentians that autumn. The barest remnants of snow on the peaks, calcified into thin crusts; the unbearably thin high mountain air, their trucks spluttering through the vertiginous passes with barely enough engine oil to reach Xlala, where the throat singing of the monks echoed through the empty valleys. This was a journey towards some kind of renewal, a respite before the rigours of winter, which they would spend in the plains far below them, a few rough fields adjacent to the motorway, the large high fence between them and it, the scuffed Mongolian grassland where the lions could run wild.

Père Barnabas, the order's ancient superior, stood in the bell tower and watched the tiny curls of exhaust wend their way through the twisting road far below him and imagined a parasite inching its path, slowly and inexorably, through an intestine. Oh, they would arrive, whatever mishaps delayed them on the way. Zaroaster would get to work with his greasy toolkit whenever an engine sputtered and died; if a wheel jammed in the apex of a turn, Monniker would be only too happy to exercise his herculean abilities; he could carry the convoy on his back if necessary, truck by crumbling truck. In fact, if the trucks fell apart completely, the entire carousel of carnies would make it to the summit, each in their own specifically magical way. Yes, they would arrive; Barnabas would feed them the ritual bowls tinctured with the ancient mildew that it was the order's duty to preserve and to refine into the true, the essential spice. And the conversations would begin. Confessions, more like it, as each carnie spilled out their soul to him and to whichever other of the elders were willing to lend an ear. A long exhale of allegory, fable, minute and particular invention of the past years' histories, all of it imaginary, none of it true. And this past year's history would involve the tale of a boy who had wandered, whose name sounded suspiciously like Wander, into a mirrored maze and set in motion a train of events that would have apocalyptic consequences. The day, the year, the carnival and all of the infinite possibilities of the mildew were saved by this boy who had, in turn, now as befits his name or an anagram of it, chosen to go on wandering.

Living was not enough for them, these carnies, they had to lie about it. Although they would swear it was truth, on 'their child's life', though Barnabas knew they had none. On their souls, though his suspicion was that they had none either. They had a different organ to the soul, more like a liquid muscle that reflected and shimmered and mirrored the world around in ways of unbelievable complexity, as if some uncaring god had poured this liquid down their throat at conception and smiled at the thought of them living with it forever afterwards. Never forget, he told himself, that however tough these carnies seemed, however well-schooled they were in the lessons of endurance, however spectacular their gymnastic abilities, their tremulous depth of feeling laid them open to emotional agonies he could hardly imagine. So he listened, and he begged the other monks to listen and told them listening was a poor price to pay for the pleasure of watching Mona, airborne and released from all pretence, winging her way round the high alpine peaks. The spectacle of Monniker, climbing the glass-like surface of the Meikaster face, ropeless, clad only in leather drainpipes, his inhuman muscles bulging as his hands struggled to find another grip. Quite apart from the salient fact that the carnies brought with them their yearly tribute of harvested mildew.

So Père Barnabas gripped the ancient rope that was smoothed by generations of hands before his and pulled. The great bell swung on its mount, to the left and the right, three times before the tongue hit the dented surface and its metallic boom echoed through the valleys and the crusted snow-capped peaks. The eerie drone of the monks below paused for a moment, as if stunned by the sudden sound, then redoubled its throat music, creating a choral bed to the continuing boom. On the Meikaster peak, three buzzards took to the air, circling in the thermal winds above them. A chamois deer lost its footing, startled by the sound, and sent gravel tumbling down the slope below. And down in the grassy valley, a herd of gold-coloured musk spread across what was left of the plain.

The pale disc of the autumn sun had almost lost itself behind the distant misted peaks when they finally arrived. The vehicles trundled through the underpass, belching their brown-purple smoke, and arranged themselves in a clumsy half-circle in the abbey forecourt. The carnies got out, one by one, their faces pinched in the sudden cold, their breath billowing outwards from their shivering mouths. Thirty-seven dark-hooded figures moved through the abbey arches, each proffering a steaming bowl of welcome. And the